Across the yard, Lily felt his gaze. She couldn't see him and there was no movement, but she'd known instantly that he was there, watching. Her body told her that Matt Logan was spying on her.

So, she might as well reward him. Carefully she closed the door and walked toward the window in the light of the lamp. After glancing behind her at the closed door where Jim was sleeping and up toward the loft where the children were, she slowly moved between the lamp and the window, knowing the outline of her body would show through the thin fabric.

Just a second. No more. Then she stepped away from the window into the shadows and smiled.

That's what he got for being a Peeping Tom instead of her fiancé. Any other man would charge across the yard and rip open the door. Any other man would put his arms around her and kiss her senseless.

But Matthew Logan wasn't just any other man.

Lily smiled.

She wasn't just any woman either. And she'd just begun to fight.

SHOTGUN GROOM

Sandra Chastain

BANTAM BOOKS

New York   Toronto   London   Sydney   Auckland

SHOTGUN GROOM

A Bantam Book / March 1998

ISBN 0-553-57583-X

Published simultaneously in the United States and Canada

Bantam Books are published by Bantam Books, a division of Bantam
Doubleday Dell Publishing Group, Inc. Its trademark, consisting of the
words "Bantam Books" and the portrayal of a rooster, is Registered in
U.S. Patent and Trademark Office and in other countries. Marca
Registrada. Bantam Books, 1540 Broadway, New York, New York 10036.

PRINTED IN THE UNITED STATES OF AMERICA

WCD 10 9 8 7 6 5 4 3 2 1

My heartfelt thanks to the women writers who've meant so much to me in the last year: Gin, Deb, Donna, Ann, Nancy, Pat, Anne, Shannon, Marion, and the members of GRW who became my memory and my confidence and kept my spirit alive—

And to Meg who came when I needed her and loves chocolate as much as I do—

And to Cassie with the sunshine-coated whip who made me get it right—

SHOTGUN GROOM is for all of you guys. I couldn't have done it without you.

SHOTGUN GROOM

1

Blue Station, Texas—1875

Lily tapped her toe nervously on the shotgun beneath her feet. She felt like a gunfighter in one of those dime novels about the West. The chapter heading would read: "The Showdown Between Lily Towns and Matt Logan Was Set for High Noon."

And the sun was almost overhead.

Chewing nervously on her bottom lip, Lily glanced out the stagecoach window at the endless prairie beyond. The countryside was nothing like home; neither were the people she'd traveled with. Was she making a mistake? Had she spent the past ten years of her life preparing for something that wasn't to be?

No! She wouldn't accept that. Matt's letter was all the reason she needed to come. It was his request that Aunt Dolly send his bride. Lily brushed the dust from her dark green travel dress with the blue-and-white sash and leaned back against the cushions with a sigh.

Until she died, Lily's mother had been the local laundrywoman and had worked for Aunt Dolly for many years.

Lily had been a lanky eight-year-old orphan wise beyond her years when Aunt Dolly took pity on her and gave her a home. The first time Dolly's nephews, Matt Logan and his younger brother, Jim, had come for Sunday dinner, it was Matt who'd tousled her hair, given her a smile, and told her not to worry, that everything would be all right.

A year later, Matt, sixteen and filled with passion and high ideals, had gone off to fight. He'd fought not for the South as his neighbors had, but for the North, leaving his mother, his younger sister, and Jim on their plantation. Three years later he returned to find their farm had been destroyed in a raid by the very army he had joined. His family was dead, except for Jim, who was living in Aunt Dolly's hotel.

Matt had to accept his aunt's offer of shelter and work. But he couldn't take the scorn of the fine people of Memphis who turned their backs on him because he'd fought for the other side, and on his aunt, a southern woman whose Yankee husband had money when nobody else did.

Lily had understood Matt's pain. They shared a common bond. She, too, had been orphaned. But Aunt Dolly had taken Lily in and made her the child Dolly had never had. She would have done that for Matt too, but he was determined to build a future on his own.

On Lily's twelfth birthday, Aunt Dolly asked her what she wanted for her special day. She hadn't wanted anything; she already had her adoptive aunt, Matt, and Jim. That was enough. Aunt Dolly had smiled and said a family celebration would be perfect.

That year Lily Towns had her first grown-up birthday celebration, a dress-up dinner with silly hats and a cake. She remembered it as if it were yesterday. They'd eaten Cook's special fried chicken, corn, and okra. Afterward, Lily had tagged after Matt, joining him in the garden where he was sharing a smoke with Jim.

Lily entered the gazebo silently, certain they'd tell her to go back to the house. Matt saw her first.

"And did you like your birthday?" he asked.

"Oh yes. Fried chicken is my very favorite thing to eat."

Matt nodded absently, as if his mind were somewhere else.

"I like cake," Jim added enthusiastically.

Normally Lily considered the three of them a family, united against the people who said mean things about Aunt Dolly and her orphans. But today, Jim was in her way.

"I like birthday cake, too," she said. "And I think we should have some more. Jim, why don't you go to the house and ask cook to cut three more slices for us."

"Cook won't give us anymore," he argued.

"Yes, she will," Lily insisted. "It's my birthday."

Happily, Jim went off to ask.

As soon as he was out of earshot, Lily turned to Matt and launched into the speech she'd rehearsed for days. "I've been thinking about the future, Matt," she began.

"That's pretty serious for someone who's only twelve."

"It's important. Aunt Dolly says that boys can look after themselves, but a girl needs security. So, she is leaving the hotel to me."

Matt grinned. "Is that so?"

Lily stiffened but continued with her carefully planned explanation. "It is. But you shouldn't worry about your future. I'll need someone to look after things. And after careful consideration, I've decided that it would be best for both of us if we got married . . . not now, of course, but later, when I'm old enough."

Matt burst out laughing. "Us? Get married? Grow up, sprout. If it weren't for the freckles, a strong breeze would carry you off."

Lily was stunned. She'd expected him to thank her for her generosity, not laugh.

Seeing her hurt, Matt smiled gently. "I'm sorry. I didn't mean to hurt your feelings, Lily. That's a very grand gesture on your part." He gave her a brotherly kiss on the forehead. "And I thank you, but it wouldn't be fair."

"Why not? Aren't I pretty enough?"

"That's not it at all. It's because you're still a little girl and you might change your mind. Wait until you're a grown-up lady and let me do the asking," he'd said.

Matt's rejection hurt. She'd come to expect it from the people of Memphis, but not from him. Other than Aunt Dolly, he was the only adult who'd ever been kind to her.

Then Matt added, "In a few years you'll have every man in Memphis courting you. There's time enough for you to pick a husband."

"But I don't want any of them, Matt," she insisted stubbornly. "I'll wait for you, no matter who else asks me."

"I doubt it," was Matt's reply.

Her hurt deepened when Aunt Dolly told her that Matt and Jim had decided to go out west and make a new start. Then the blue-eyed boy she'd already fallen in love with left Tennessee so fast that Lily didn't have a chance to grow up and prove she was perfect for him.

"He didn't even tell me good-bye," Lily had said in disbelief.

"They left too early to wake you," Aunt Dolly said. "Matt told me to tell you to remember what he said."

She'd done what Matt said. That was ten years ago and she'd done a lot of growing and perfecting since then. Not every man in Memphis had come to call, but enough of them had. Jim wrote that he'd taken a wife, but as long as Matt remained unwed, Lily's determination to wait for him had led her to refuse every offer for her hand.

Aunt Dolly's hotel was still in business, but each year newer and more luxurious establishments opened, taking away more of her business. Aunt Dolly was worried that Lily's future was no longer secure.

Then Matt's letter to Aunt Dolly had arrived. He was almost thirty and ready to marry. This time, he was the one issuing the proposal of marriage, and Lily was ready to be his bride.

When the marriage offer came, Aunt Dolly had surprised Lily by agreeing that she should go. She'd even had some sort of legal paper drawn up that made the arrangement binding. But leaving the old woman she'd grown to love had been hard, for Lily knew her adoptive aunt would be alone.

But Dolly had insisted, and so here she was in Texas, ready to marry the man she'd waited for. In spite of the unfulfilled threats of Indians and outlaws, in spite of having to travel alone after leaving her ill companion behind at Fort Smith, the end of her journey was in sight. Lily couldn't wait to see Matt's face when she stepped off the stage at Blue Station.

Lily glanced out the stage window at the position of the sun: directly overhead. If the stage was on time, they ought to be close to town. Nervously, she smoothed the wrinkles from her skirt and adjusted the perky hat with the tip of a peacock's feather attached to its crown.

If her dark green traveling dress and sunshine-frosted sausage curls weren't proof that she was more than matchsticks and freckles, she had other weapons available. She caressed the small handgun Aunt Dolly had insisted she carry in her pocket, and rocked her slippers impatiently on her aunt's shotgun that she'd brought along for protection. Lily never expected to use either, but she was from the South where people had learned how to get what they wanted and carried the wherewithal to guarantee success.

This time Matt Logan would be hers, one way or another.

• • •

"You did what?"

Matt Logan crumpled the unopened telegram he was holding. He didn't try to hide his fury from his brother. He'd been told too many times that his blue eyes gave him away when he was angry, and for the last year it seemed he was angry most of the time.

"I said I asked Aunt Dolly to send a wife, a kind of mail-order bride," the wan-faced recipient of Matt's fury said calmly, not intimidated by his older brother's outburst.

"You sent a telegram? I suppose everybody in Blue Station knows about this."

"I wrote a letter, Matt."

"But Aunt Dolly sent you a telegram in return."

Jim sighed. "Luther Frazier brought it out here, Matt. He promised to keep it quiet. He's a friend. Just think about this for a minute. A wife makes sense. You know it does."

"But, Jim, you're sick. Your heart won't let you walk across the room without stopping to rest. What in hell made you decide to marry again?"

"We're through the drought now. The grass is finally coming back. Our herd is growing and you dug a well. The Double L is going to make it, Matt."

Matt wanted to swear, but he held his tongue. "Exactly. We're just about to see daylight, and you want to take a wife? Damn, Jim! I can't believe my ears."

"All right," Jim conceded. "The truth is, my children need a mother. I thought it would make things easier on you . . . after I'm gone."

Pain flashed in his brother's eyes, and Matt wished he could take back his careless words. Normally he was more careful when discussing Jim's illness, but the idea of another mouth to feed on a cattle ranch only now ready to pull back from the brink of failure was more than he could deal with. Besides, he'd watched Jim's wife have the life sucked out of her by this rough land. He wouldn't do that again.

"I don't want to hear that kind of talk, Jim. When you're better, you *should* take another wife. I'll even help you find one. Hell, it'll be nice to have something besides your scrawny mug to look at around here for a change. But not now."

"You don't understand," Jim began, then broke, looking uncomfortable. "There's more. I haven't been entirely honest with you."

"About what?" Matt asked, forcing himself to ignore Jim's gray skin and his harsh breathing, signs that he was getting upset. "I know you're sicker than you let on. You try to put on a good show for the children, but you don't fool me. If you're worried about who will do your share of the work around the ranch, don't. I've already found a couple of cowboys, and there's always Kitty."

"Kitty is a Comanche, and he's only here occasionally. But it isn't the cattle I'm worried about, Matt," Jim said in a rush. "It's the house, the cooking, the washing. I know I haven't been worth much lately, but who is going to look after you, Will, and Emily when I'm gone?"

"Stop that kind of talk!" Matt said angrily. "Will is almost a man, and Emily . . . well, Emily will go back to Tennessee to Aunt Dolly if something happens before she gets old enough to keep a house."

There was a long silence, filled only with the sound of Jim's raspy breathing.

Matt unfolded the telegram and read it. "Bride arriving Blue Station, May 12. Twelve o'clock noon. It's about time. Congratulations. Aunt Dolly."

"Aunt Dolly wouldn't send someone you wouldn't like," Jim said, trying to justify his decisions. "I'm sure she's chosen a bride who will please you."

"Please me? What in the hell's the difference whether

or not *I* like her? Besides," Matt argued, "Aunt Dolly couldn't possibly understand how primitive the ranch is. I'll bet you weren't honest about that, were you?"

Jim wouldn't meet his eyes. "You're right. And, Matt, I guess there's something else I'd better explain."

Matt could tell even before Jim spoke that he wasn't going to like hearing the rest. He sighed in resignation. "Go on."

"I'm not fooling myself about finding another wife. The truth is . . . the truth is, I didn't tell her the bride was for me."

"Then what—"

"I told her the bride was for you, Matt."

Matt tried desperately to bring some sense to what Jim had just said.

"Say that again, James William Logan," he got out between clenched teeth.

"She's for you, Matt. You know it doesn't make sense to buy a new saddle for a horse that won't be around long enough to be ridden. Besides," Jim said, cutting straight to the truth, "no woman would want an invalid for a husband when a man like you is free to wed."

Matt's blue eyes were almost black with fury. "I don't want a wife, Jim. If I wanted a wife, I'd go into town and get one."

Jim refused to back down. "Where? There are ten men to every woman in this part of Texas."

"There are women at the saloon, and there are Spanish women along the Rio Grande, and Indian women on the reservation."

"There's nothing wrong with those women. I married Maria and she was part Comanche. But I was hoping for someone more socially accepted for Emily, a woman who could teach her to be a lady. Someone like . . . Mama."

Matt swore, his anger ebbing. This wasn't playing fair. Jim knew he'd do anything for his niece. He would have had to do something about her eventually, but he'd delayed making any decision about their future, hoping that Jim might get better.

"The only way a man finds that kind of bride out here, Matt, is to advertise for one through the mail or have someone act in your behalf. At least this way Aunt Dolly has chosen for you."

"There are many who would argue about her choices. She married a Yankee," Matt reminded him wryly.

"A Yankee who took care of her and us."

Matt shook his head. "This is different. What makes you think anybody she'd pick would last a month out here? You know from Maria what happens to women on the frontier. Texas women have to be tough."

Matt mentally counted the cash he could come up with to send the bride home. They'd lost so many cows to the drought and later to the cold, that he'd had to dip into their savings for supplies. He couldn't afford to send the bride as far as Abilene. Let alone back to Tennessee.

"You'd better get yourself cleaned up and go fetch her, Matt. Pick up some beans and potatoes if they have any. While you're gone, I'll make something special for supper."

Matt looked fierce. "I'm not cleaning up and I'm not buying anything and I'm not bringing her here! She'll have to go back on the next stage, Jim."

"The stage only comes through here every four days. If I have to go with you to be sure, then I will. I won't let you make her fair game for every man in the state by putting her up at the hotel. Promise me you'll bring her home," Jim said unperturbed, and closed his eyes.

Matt stared helplessly at his brother. He'd taken on rustlers from Mexico, Apache raiders, and, at one time, the Comanche. But crossing swords with his sick brother was something he couldn't do.

Matt knew he was going to regret it. "I'll bring her. But only until the next stage."

From the time they'd come out west, Jim hadn't been strong. But for the last year his health had deteriorated. Both the doctor in Austin and the one at the fort had said the same thing: His heart was giving out. There was nothing that could be done. It was just a matter of time.

Matt knew that, but damn it to hell, it wasn't fair. When they'd decided to leave Memphis, it had been Jim who picked Texas and cotton. With a loan from Aunt Dolly, they'd spent a backbreaking year building the house and the barn, clearing the land of prairie grass and planting their first crop. The hard work had taken its toll on Jim, but he'd refused to admit that he couldn't keep up. Still they'd managed. But neither had been prepared for the lack of rain. They'd quickly realized the only things that grew easily here were more prairie grass and, in the spring, bluebonnets.

Then Jim met Maria, the daughter of the commanding officer over at the military outpost. They'd fallen in love and married, and they'd been happy. At least Jim had. Maria wasn't the kind of woman ever to be truly content. And she never gave up her wish to go back east where she'd been raised after her mother died.

In the end, even Maria hadn't been strong enough for the harsh demands of ranching. Will and Emily came easy enough, but the third child was stillborn. After that she just seemed to give up. A year ago she died and Jim's health had dramatically declined. For a time, Matt, carrying around his own load of guilt over not sending Jim and his family back east, had thought Jim was simply grieving. But as time passed it became evident that the situation was becoming critical. By then it was too late; Jim wouldn't leave.

Matt hadn't allowed his brother to talk about the future, for they would have had to admit that Jim was dying. Now it was obvious that Jim had given considerable thought to the future and his children, and what would happen to them when he was gone.

But a wife? For him? What in the hell was his brother thinking? The last thing Matt Logan needed was someone else to look after. And no matter what Jim thought, he had no intention of marrying . . . ever. He'd seen what had happened to Jim. He'd built his life around a woman. Then she'd died, making it plain to Matt that this rough country drained the life from the weak—man or woman.

"Please, Matt," Jim said tiredly. "I don't want to die knowing my children won't have anyone to raise them."

"I'll raise them."

"You can't be both mother and father. If you try, the ranch will fail. And it has to survive. I want to leave them something. Don't you see?"

Arguing with Jim was putting him under too much stress. The best that Matt could hope for was that the woman involved would be reasonable. More than that he couldn't hope for until he met Aunt Dolly's choice.

"It's getting on toward eleven o'clock," Jim reminded him.

"What's her name?" Matt said in little more than a growl, running a hand through his dark hair.

"Lillian."

"How do you know that?"

"There was a letter, before. I just didn't tell you."

"Lillian what?" Matt asked.

"Aunt Dolly never said. I'm sure you're going to like her, Matt. Don't you think Lillian is a pretty name?"

Matt didn't trust himself to answer with more than the slam of the door. In the barn, he ignored Will's questioning glance and Emily's chatter as he saddled his horse, then remembered that he was going to fetch a woman and hitched Racer up to the wagon instead.

"Can I go into town with you, Uncle Matt?" Will

asked, putting away the shovel he'd been using to muck out the stall.

"No! Not this time, boy. You take your sister into the house. Make sure your daddy takes a nap. See that Emily doesn't keep him awake."

Matt's unexpected brusqueness caught Will by surprise. No matter how bad things got, Matt was always kind. Rolling down his shirtsleeves, Will stood in the barn and watched his uncle drive away in the wagon without a backward glance. Emily, sitting on an upturned bucket, hugged her rag doll close and started to sniffle. "Are Daddy and Uncle Matt fighting, Will?"

"Daddy and Uncle Matt don't fight, Emmie, they . . . they discuss."

"Cussing is just as bad. Mama used to say that, 'member?"

"Mama was right, Emmie. You should always remember what she said."

"I try, Will, but sometimes I can't 'member what she looks like. I wish she hadn't gone away. I think that Daddy and Uncle Matt need her lots more than heaven does."

"I heard Daddy and Mr. Frazier from the telegraph office talking when he came by last week. I think Uncle Matt is yelling because Daddy is getting another mother for us," Will said, looking solemn.

"Maybe we'd better go and see about Daddy," Emily said in a very grown-up voice.

Will nodded and followed his little sister back to the house, closing the door softly behind them as they tiptoed inside.

"Is he gone?" Jim said, sitting up.

"Yes, sir," Will answered.

"Did he take the wagon?"

"Uncle Matt tooked the wagon," Emily answered, laying her head on her daddy's knee. "But he was mad. He yelled at Will."

"Don't be silly, Emily. Uncle Matt didn't mean it," Will said, studying his father with concern. He was only eight, but he was old enough to see that his father was not getting any better.

"That's right, son. Your uncle was just surprised. But we don't want to get our hopes up. The lady is coming to marry Uncle Matt . . . if he likes her. We'll just have to wait and see."

"He'll like her," Emily said seriously. "I know he will. Mama told me so."

"Mama isn't here, darling," Jim said, stroking his ginger-haired daughter's head with his long thin fingers.

"Oh yes, she is. I see'd her last night by my bed. She was all light and so pretty."

Will scoffed. "I didn't hear nobody talking and I was sleeping right next to you."

"She didn't talk. I just knew. She was so boo-ti-ful. I 'membered her. She didn't move her mouth to talk. She just smiled at me and I knew."

Jim shook his head. Emily had more and more of these dreams. At first he hadn't discouraged her belief that her mother came to talk to her. Now he wondered if he had made a mistake.

For Matt, the day had started out wrong and had gone downhill since. Now he felt like he was stuck in wagon ruts heading straight toward one of those cliffs in Palo Duro Canyon.

Matt knew that their future depended on his ability to supply the army with cattle for both the fort and the reservation. Without continued spring rains to green the range, his cattle could die. But those were things he couldn't change. He'd sunk a well. At least they'd have water for the house and the garden. And there was still the creek that would eventually dry up, and the river beyond his boundaries that wouldn't.

Jim knew he was dying, and Matt could understand his quiet desperation. But misleading a woman who thought she was coming here as a wanted bride was a hurtful act that never should have been committed.

Jim was worried about the children. Matt tried to argue that Emily could be sent back to Memphis where Aunt Dolly would see to her upbringing. Will would do fine; he'd grow up a cattleman like Jim always wanted.

But a bride?

For Matt Logan?

No way in hell.

Matt drove the wagon across the plains, making and discarding plans as the miles fell away. He could only hope that Luther *had* kept the message confidential. The last thing Matt wanted was for the people in Blue Station to know his business, especially not until he'd decided what to do.

It would serve Jim right if he just auctioned this Lillian off to the highest bidder. Women were in short supply in Texas. She'd bring in enough money to repay Aunt Dolly's expenses in sending her. At least this was a weekday, and since there were no cattle drives in the area, there would be few people in town.

With any luck, Matt could whisk the woman away before anyone saw her. Then, on the way back to the ranch he'd explain the situation. He'd figure out how to make it worth her while to go back. A woman from Tennessee wouldn't make it here, and he wouldn't be responsible for bringing her. She'd have to go home on the return stage.

Having decided this, he flicked the reins, forcing his horse to pick up his pace. And by the time Blue Station came into view, the stage had pulled in, and Matt had convinced himself that he could handle the misadventure.

When the only woman on the coach stepped down onto the plank sidewalk at the stage office, he knew he was dead wrong. Her golden hair caught the sun like a flash fire ignited by summer lightning, and he could feel the heat from where he sat. The driver tripped over his own feet in his attempt to assist her, and Luther Frazier was right behind him.

Matt knew immediately that it was too late to whisk her away. This was one time his private business was likely to become public. Drawing Racer to a stop behind a stack of wooden kegs, he sat helplessly watching the woman smile at everyone in sight.

"Welcome to Blue Station," Luther said, his head bobbing like a chicken picking up corn.

"Yes, ma'am," Ambrose Wells, the town's self-appointed mayor, said, suddenly appearing on the platform as if meeting the stage were part of the banker's everyday duties. "I'm the president of the Blue Station Banking Company, Miss . . ."

"Townsend, Miss Lillian Townsend. I'm so very pleased to meet . . . all of you."

Lillian Townsend? Even the name was much too elegant for the Double L. Lillian Townsend ought to be one of those entertainers who traveled around making stage appearances, instead of this elegant vision of sunlight and satin who'd come here to be a Texas bride.

"And what brings you to Blue Station, Miss Townsend?" Wells asked, still holding her hand as if he didn't trust the good fortune that brought such a beauty to town. "Is someone meeting you?"

"Oh yes, I'm being met by my future husband."

The expression on the banker's face froze and he looked at Luther in disbelief. Matt swore silently from his vantage point.

Apparently Luther hadn't shared the information that Matt Logan was getting married, though he had obviously told Wells a new woman was coming on the stage. But Lillian Townsend was about to spread the news.

"Future husband?" Wells questioned, not bothering to conceal his surprise.

"Why, yes. Matt Logan. He and his brother, Jim, have a cattle ranch nearby, I believe."

Christ! Now she'd done it. Matt had always been a very private man, keeping himself away from involvement with the townspeople. He'd claimed that there were no women in Blue Station, but that hadn't been entirely true. There were women, too many women, and their constant matchmaking made his life miserable.

Now this woman was announcing to the world that she'd come to marry one of the Logan brothers. Matt had to stop her quick, before she revealed the foolishness of his brother's actions.

He flicked the reins, moving Racer alongside the platform and climbed down.

"Miss Townsend," he said, his voice a calm facade over the irritation building inside, "get in the wagon. Load up her bags, Luther." He scowled at the stationmaster who quickly tossed her carryall into the back of the wagon.

"I also have two trunks and a hatbox, Mr. Logan," Lily said, trying not to let her voice reflect her unease. "And a shotgun."

She'd been wrong about Matt Logan. The handsome nineteen-year-old was long gone. While she'd been growing up and into a lady, he'd become a man. A big, angry, hold-your-breath-and-run-for-cover man.

A two-days' growth of beard only added to the dangerous look of the rough-dressed, trail-dusty cowboy. He wore slick Levi's that clung to his muscular thighs, scuffed western boots, and a sweat-streaked Stetson that shaded his eyes and concealed all but his piercing gaze.

The welcome she'd expected didn't come. A sliver of river ice couldn't have pierced her any deeper than the coldness of Matt's reception. He wasn't pleased. Whatever he'd expected from a bride, she still wasn't it.

So, he was disappointed in her? Well, it was his turn. She'd been just as disappointed in him ten years ago. With a comforting pat to her derringer, she walked toward the man she'd come all these many miles to wed.

The choice was his. If Matt had changed his mind, she was prepared. Back in Tennessee, folks knew how to stop a man from backing out of a marriage proposal. Lily'd come prepared.

Matthew Logan would be a shotgun groom.

2

Ambrose and Luther stared spellbound at Miss Lillian Townsend, leaving Matt and the stage driver to unload the heavy trunks and carrying cases into the back of the wagon.

Racer snorted as the wagon dipped. The horse might give in to Matt's infrequent demands that he pull a wagon, but carrying two adults and a hundred pounds of luggage was asking too much of the big silver horse. Matt didn't even know how Lillian got the stage to carry everything. He stepped up into the wagon, took another look at the woman, and understood.

"I said, get in the wagon, Lillian."

"Don't mind him, Miss Townsend," Luther said. "Matt's the most unsociable man in Blue Station. We, on the other hand, know how to treat a lady."

The woman seemed not to notice Matt's displeasure. She smiled sweetly and held out her hand to him for assistance.

Matt swore. "Ah, for—"

Both Luther and Ambrose came immediately to Lillian's aid. "Please, allow us."

Matt turned the men aside with a gesture, placed both hands around her waist, and lifted her up. The wagon lurched, throwing her against him.

For a moment they stood, staring at each other, until Racer shifted in his harness. This time Matt took no chances. He shoved Lillian onto the seat, reached for the reins, and sat down, ignoring both Luther and Ambrose.

Matt looked up in time to see Ora Manley, the local busybody, heading toward the wagon. He knew an elegant, beautiful woman in his wagon wouldn't go unnoticed, and that he wouldn't be able to get away from town without someone attempting to stop them. Matt snapped the reins and startled the horse into a trot.

Nodding to Ora, Matt pretended not to hear her calling out to him. "Wait up, Matt Logan!"

He might have to endure the town's speculation, but with any luck he'd have Miss Lillian Townsend and her fancy trunks on the return stage before the ladies were able to get their usual welcome brigade organized.

Once he was beyond the outskirts of Blue Station, Matt backed off, allowing the horse to slow his pace. But he didn't trust himself yet to face the woman beside him. She couldn't have known the true circumstances that led to her invitation, or she never would have come. Though, for the life of him, Matt couldn't imagine any circumstance that would result in a woman who looked like she did traveling from Tennessee to Texas to be a bride.

Lillian Townsend. Lillian . . . There was something about her, something he couldn't quite place. He certainly didn't know anyone named Lillian. Still, there was a sense of familiarity. Then it hit him.

"Lily! You're little Lily Towns!"

"I wondered if you'd recognize me, Matt. Do you still think a strong breeze would blow me away?"

He recognized her. He might have thought she was matchsticks held together with freckles the last time he saw her, but she was a damn-a-man-to-hell-and-back beauty now.

Matt didn't know how, but Lily Towns seemed to have survived her trip across country very well. He wondered if she was still looking for a husband to operate the hotel she expected to inherit from Aunt Dolly. Obviously not, or why would she be here?

He forced himself to think about what he was going to do. How could Aunt Dolly have believed that this elegant woman could be a rancher's wife?

A greater concern was whether or not Aunt Dolly's choice had anything to do with the debt he and Jim still owed her. He'd been the one to insist that the money she gave them be a loan. They'd used it to buy the land that had become, after two failed cotton crops and Jim's marriage, the Double L Cattle Ranch.

And they still owed her for their stake.

Their debt concerned Matt a lot. But there hadn't been much he could do about it, until this year. Now he'd have to use whatever money he'd intended to send to Aunt Dolly to buy Lily a return ticket to Tennessee.

Matt knew from the beginning that Jim had made a mistake in sending for a bride. But now, as Lily settled herself in the wagon, opened her parasol, and peered out from beneath its striped ruffle, he realized how big a mistake it was. When she twirled the frilly creation and gave a light laugh, Matt also knew she was aware of his discomfort.

"This is not a laughing matter," he snapped.

"Oh, I think it is, Matt Logan. Maybe not a deep belly laugh, but your expression is worth at least a giggle. Aren't I what you expected?"

Ten years had made a lifetime of difference in the skinny little girl who'd dogged his footsteps in Memphis. He didn't have to look at her to know that her eyes were as green as shoots of Texas range grass after a rare rain. He'd seen that when she stepped off of the stage.

She still had the same willowy build as when she'd come to his aunt as a child, but that was the end of any similarity. In the years since, she'd filled out, and the flash of stockinged leg, exposed as she'd settled into the wagon, was an intriguing testimony that she would never be called matchsticks again.

The totally impractical saucy little hat she was wearing was designed to show off the glorious golden color of her hair. He groaned silently as he thought about what Emily would say. The child's determined belief in the existence of angels would be confirmed.

"Let's get one thing straight, Miss *Townsend,* is it now? You are most definitely . . . unexpected."

"Really, Matt," she said in an amused voice, "Miss Townsend might be fine for the citizens of Blue Station, but it's a bit formal for a woman who's seen you without your britches."

He'd meant to control his reactions. No point in letting her know that she'd turned up his boiling point by more degrees than was safe. But his words popped out before he thought. "Without my britches?"

She laughed again and pushed the parasol back so that she could lean closer. "Surely you knew."

"Knew what?"

"For a year I followed you and Jim everywhere. Why wouldn't I see you swimming in the river in your altogether?"

His thoughts flashed back to the Mississippi where he and Jim had often cooled off in summer. But it wasn't the swimming that came to mind. It was the conversation. Matt had gone away to war as a boy, but he'd come back a man with a man's desires and speculations.

Jim, already showing signs of the heart condition that would come, had clung to Matt's every word, relishing every embellished tale Matt confided. With a pilfered bottle of Aunt Dolly's blackberry wine and some of the captain's cigars, they'd head for the river where they could pretend the war had never happened. He'd never told Jim about being a coward, about his fear of killing people like him. He only said that he'd had to learn to be tough enough to survive. It was easier to talk about heroism and women and—"Damn!"

"What's wrong, Matt? Surely you're not embarrassed. Even then I could appreciate your physical . . . prowess."

"It wasn't my prowess I was remembering. Our conversations were private."

"You really needn't worry. I found the discussions very enlightening."

What the hell? She'd gotten an earful and an eyeful too. He and Jim had been two randy boys. Matt had shared stories of the camp women and exploits of his fellow soldiers. She'd been eavesdropping, so it served her right. He had no intention of apologizing. "The discussions were private, Miss Townsend."

"Don't worry. I never told Aunt Dolly about them, or the wine. And please, call me Lily."

"I prefer Miss Townsend."

"Suit yourself, but I'm going to call you Matt."

Not for long. And if you do, I won't hear you. Four days from now you'll be back on that stage, heading for Tennessee.

"Gracious, it's warm. Don't you have any trees in Texas?"

"Not many in this part."

"However do people survive the heat, and"—she wiped a bead of perspiration from her forehead, finishing with—"dust? Even the wind's hot."

"First off, the *native women* don't wear so damned many clothes."

"You mean those Indian women in the dime novels, the ones who run about half-naked? I suppose I could take off my jacket, but I'm afraid I'm wearing nothing but my chemise underneath."

His temperature shot up another notch at the thought of her peeling off all those layers of clothing. *Damn you, Jim. You really did it this time.*

"No, I mean the Spanish *señoritas* who wear loose blouses and skirts without yards of petticoats."

"Would that be considered proper for your—for me to wear? I wouldn't want to reflect badly on you."

"How you dress is completely immaterial to me, Miss Townsend, but that gown with the pincushion on your rear is going to be a little hard to deal with on a horse."

"Then I'll make other arrangements. Is there a dressmaker nearby?"

Matt groaned. She'd just given him the second tangible reason for sending her packing. At the rate they were growing, he could barely afford to keep Will and Emily in shoes. He certainly couldn't provide a new wardrobe for a woman who had already brought enough clothes to outfit the entire population of west Texas.

As for the first reason, the tantalizingly beautiful Lillian Townsend was pure temptation. Just sitting on the wagon seat beside her was enough to heat a man's blood. He was even beginning to worry about Jim. His heart couldn't take much excitement, and one good look at Lily was bound to put him in bed for the next four days.

Matt groaned.

Lily wanted to, but she didn't. She hadn't known what to expect, but this rough, angry man wasn't exactly what she'd planned on. Matthew Logan was as grim as a man on his way to the gallows. He wouldn't even look at her. Obviously she was not what he'd been expecting either.

She'd never seen a more reluctant groom.

"I don't understand, Matt. Have I done something wrong?" she asked softly.

"Yes, you have. What in hell made you decide to come out here?"

"A marriage proposal, Matthew Logan. You sent for a bride. Aunt Dolly and I thought you meant me. I guess I can assume by your reaction that you didn't. I know you rejected my proposal ten years ago, but surely I can't be that unacceptable."

"Let's get one thing straight, *Lillian*. I didn't send for anything. Certainly not a bride."

She hadn't expected him to say that. Denying that he sent the request was the last thing she'd envisioned.

"I don't know why you're trying to hurt me, Matt, but I have the letter right here. Don't pretend you didn't send it."

"But I didn't. It was Jim who wrote it."

"Oh. I see. That's all right, Matt. It doesn't matter that Jim put your words on the paper. You need a wife. I'm here."

"I don't need—" Matt broke off his sentence. There was no point in arguing with Lily. Let Jim do the explaining. He was the one who got this mess started. Once she saw the ranch, he wouldn't have to explain anything. She belonged on the Double L about as much as he belonged in the Texas statehouse. He'd just close his ears to her complaints about the heat and the dust. Those problems were nothing compared to the house.

Except there were no complaints. Instead, she shaded her eyes with her hand and studied the landscape with what looked like real interest.

"Matt"—she took a deep breath—"everything is so blue. What are those flowers?"

"Texas bluebonnets," he said. "That's where Blue Station got its name." He could understand her reaction. The stalks of blue flowering plants covered the prairie as far as they could see, blending into a blue sky that cupped the horizon like a bowl. The rims of the wagon's wheels crushed the new range grass, sending a warm, sweet smell into the air. Here and there butterflies went through their saucy mating dances, and birds chirped their greetings.

"Your Texas is very beautiful, Matt."

Damn! Why hadn't she come in winter? This was the best time of the year. "Not always. A storm can come up in a minute and turn this into a living hell. If it's not storming, the heat dries out the land and the wind blows it away. Nothing is as you see it."

He was telling the truth, but more than that, he was trying to make sure that she didn't fall in love with this gentle Texas spring. The unrelenting heat of summer was just ahead.

Matt felt her eyes on him and knew that she didn't believe a word he was saying. On a day like today, neither did he. But all this soft rebirth of the earth was about to end. The reality of life on a ranch was that roundup time was coming. Unless Kitty turned up soon, he'd have to bring in the new calves to be branded—alone. And here he was wasting an entire afternoon fetching a woman who would only cost him another afternoon being returned.

Damn her stormy green eyes!

Damn Jim's well-meant intentions.

"I like storms," Lily finally said. "I don't think we can truly appreciate gentle beauty without a little violence to make us humble. I even like the silence. I rode a long way from Memphis with people who never stopped talking."

He didn't want her to like anything about Texas. He especially didn't want her to understand how the country could get to a man.

"I can't imagine Aunt Dolly allowing you to come out here by yourself."

"She didn't. I had a traveling companion. But I left her at Fort Smith, too sick to continue. By now, she's back in Memphis."

He took a long look at her and shook his head. "And you came on alone?"

"For a time I shared the coach with a Quaker and his wife heading for one of the Indian reservations. Truth is, I liked being alone. I enjoyed watching the scenery. The West is so different from anything I've ever seen. After we left Fort Smith there were miles and miles of nothing but silence."

"I like the quiet, too," he admitted, "but I wouldn't think a woman would. At least Jim's wife, Maria, didn't."

"Aunt Dolly always wanted to know Maria and the children. She loved hearing from Jim. Why didn't you ever write?"

"No time. If I had, I'd have said that Maria liked the excitement of living in Washington City. She hated it that her father sent her home. Coming back to Texas killed her."

"But I thought she died in childbirth."

"That was the official reason," Matt admitted bitterly. "But it was the harshness of the land and the loneliness that did it."

"It won't have that effect on me."

Matt didn't believe that for a minute. "Why did you really come out here? Surely you can see the impracticality of the idea. I don't even have a buggy to fetch you in."

"I'm not marrying a buggy, Matt. I'm marrying you."

"No, Lily, you're not."

She didn't answer at first. Then she turned to face him, those green eyes staring firmly back into his midnight blue ones. "Excuse me?"

"I said, you're not marrying me."

"Give me one good reason why not!" she retorted hotly, at the end of her patience.

He couldn't afford to mislead her. "Look at you. Then look at me."

Lily turned her full attention on him. Looking at him

was definitely not hard to do. "Well, let's see." She ticked off her observations. "You've still got thick dark hair—that needs cutting—and eyes so blue that a cloud could float in them. Your skin wrinkles when you frown, and it's burned brown from the sun. From the size of your arms, you look like you've been lifting some of those cows you raise. And in spite of the fact that you're scowling like a cat with his tail caught in the barn door, you're still the most handsome man I've ever seen."

"That's not what I meant," he said heatedly. "Look at how you're dressed. Then look at my clothes."

"I'm wearing a green travel dress with matching hat and gloves because I wanted to make a good impression." She smiled and whispered mischievously, "I'm also wearing fine lawn drawers and a lacy chemise, which you can't see."

Matt swore silently. She wasn't that innocent. "That's what I mean, Lily. Take a look at your hair; it's silky and clean. And your skin. See how milky white and soft it is? Now look at mine." He pulled up his shirtsleeve. "Is this what you want to look like?"

Lily held her arm next to Matt's and squinted as she contemplated the bands of skin exposed between her gloves and the sleeve of her jacket and Matt's worn brown gloves and the cuff of his shirt.

Silky hair? Milky white skin? So he had noticed her. "You're right," she declared. "I look positively ill, don't I?" She let down her parasol and grinned. "How long will it take for me to turn that color?"

"Now see here, Lily," he tried again. "There's been a misunderstanding about your coming out here. I'm sorry Aunt Dolly wasted her money on your fare, but I'm—I'm prepared to pay for your return ticket."

"No, thank you. Tell me about the children," she said, brushing aside his offer. "I'm sure I'll love them, though I don't have a lot of experience with little ones." She cut her eyes toward him and pursed her lips. "Except I was one, once, so maybe I can remember enough."

Matt had no reply. How could you talk to a woman who refused to listen? You couldn't. So he'd just be quiet and let her come to the truth herself.

The silence stretched between them. Overhead a hawk soared in the air currents, then plunged toward the earth, catching some small animal in its claws and circling away. Matt didn't want to look at Lily. He wouldn't look at her.

She seemed content to ride without conversation. He hadn't expected that. He'd thought she'd be one of those women who insisted on filling up every second with words. Apparently she wasn't.

Finally, Matt let out a deep breath. Maybe talking about Will and Emily would be safer than their other conversation, and it would force him to think about something besides milky white skin and Lily's lawn drawers. Knowing how Emily was likely to react to the sight of this elegant woman, he'd better prepare Lily.

"Will's eight. He's the spitting image of Jim. Or he will be in a few years. He's bright and very good at handling his sister." Matt paused, looking worried. "Emily's almost four. She hasn't adjusted so well to her mother's death. She thinks that Maria comes to talk to her at night."

"And how can you be sure she doesn't?"

He scowled. "And you wonder why I'm not pleased. Emily thinks that angels are real, and you're ready to go along with her fantasies."

"I think a little girl without a mother finds a way to survive," Lily said in a voice that suddenly didn't sound so firm.

Matt glanced at her for a moment, then went on. "Since Jim has gotten weaker, Will has had to do a lot of things that a boy wouldn't normally do."

"After Maria died, Jim wrote that he was ill. What's wrong?"

"His heart condition has gotten worse. He's dying."

She reached out and took hold of his arm without thinking. "Oh, Matt. I'm sorry. We didn't know it was so bad."

"That's what got him started on a search for a wife. He thought it would be better for the children."

"Of course, that's true. I'll reassure him right away. I don't know what you had in mind, but I hadn't planned on our having children too soon. I'll have enough to do as a wife. Learning to have a baby can come later. We'll manage."

"For the last time, Lily, we are not going to have any children."

Lily turned toward Matt. "But Aunt Dolly told me that children were the natural result of a wife lying with her husband." She frowned. "Still, whatever you decide will be fine with me . . . for a while."

"I give up," Matt said, his teeth clenched, his stomach tied into a knot. It wasn't just that Lily paid no attention to his claim that the marriage was a mistake. It was her openness about things that women never talked about.

Talk about having his child.

Of his lying with her.

"Lily," he finally said in exasperation, "what do you know about being a rancher's wife?"

"I know how to be a wife," she said slowly, "or at least I'm willing to learn."

"Can you cook?"

Lily was beginning to see that her future as Matt's wife might not be exactly what she'd envisioned. Aunt Dolly had taught her how to manage a kitchen, but a "real lady" didn't actually cook the food. Still, she wasn't willing to admit defeat. If she didn't know how to cook, she'd learn.

"Of course," she said confidently.

"What about keeping the house?"

There she was on firmer ground. "I can sew, play the piano, plan and serve a simple meal or a fine banquet. I really know quite a lot, Matt. I've been preparing myself for a long time."

"And wash our clothes?"

Lily took a deep breath. As a child she'd learned more than she ever wanted to know about washing clothes, but Aunt Dolly had assumed that Lily would live in a house with servants. "Well, I haven't washed for so many," she said in a quiet voice, "but I'm certain I can manage. What's one more pair of socks?"

Matt could only shake his head. *Wash his socks?* He glanced down at the wagon bottom, catching sight of the shotgun Lily had brought with her. Something about the proud tilt of her chin made him go on.

"I suppose you're prepared to go out and kill a rabbit for our supper, too."

This time she couldn't conceal a stricken look. "Kill a rabbit?"

"Sure. Then you skin him and cook him. The skin we use to make caps for winter."

Matt was having a hard time keeping a straight face. The last time he'd seen anyone wearing a rabbit-skin hat was when a trader passed through several years ago.

"Eh no, Matt. I'm afraid I could never kill a rabbit."

"Then why the shotgun?"

She could have said it was Aunt Dolly's, that she'd brought it for protection, but he wouldn't believe she could shoot it if she said so. Instead, she came up with another reason.

"The shotgun? Oh, that's in case you get cold feet. Aunt Dolly always said that when a man promises a woman marriage and does her wrong, folks have a shotgun wedding." She gave him a stern glance, followed by a wicked smile.

Matt was temporarily stunned into silence.

Not Lily. "You're not planning on being a shotgun groom, are you, Matt?"

Matt let out a frustrated yell so loud that even Racer didn't have to be told to get moving. The wagon picked up speed, finding every prairie dog hole in the area. By the time the ranch came into sight, Lily's hair had lost all its pins and was flying about her head like a golden halo.

As Matt reined the horse to a stop near the house, the front door opened and two children came spilling out.

"Just so you know," Matt said, "before the others swarm around you like honeybees over the comb, there isn't going to be a wedding."

"That's all right, Matt," she said breathlessly. "I don't expect you to be excited about a wedding. But Aunt Dolly said once we do a little courting, you'll be dragging me to the altar. If you don't want to say the words, we'll just jump over the broom like Cook did."

Jump over the broom?

Matt Logan climbed down from the wagon and, behind Lily's back, slammed his fist against the side. What in hell was he going to do with a woman wearing fine lawn drawers? A woman who'd seen him without any? A woman who was set on becoming his wife?

3

Emily walked toward Lily, her eyes wide, her mouth in a small pink circle. "Ohhhhhhh. So pretty."

The boy standing behind her seemed equally awe-struck.

Lily glanced around at Matt, who was more interested in unhitching his horse than helping her down. So be it. She flung her feet over the side and slid to the ground, her bustle hanging on the edge of the wagon and catching her skirt, exposing her bottom for just a second.

Matt remembered his manners and turned back just in time to be granted a clear look at the fine lawn drawers Lily had described earlier. At the sight of her round bottom, he was too stunned to come to her assistance. Instead, it was Jim who appeared in the doorway and rushed to her side.

"Welcome!" Jim said, his face flushed pink in the excitement of her arrival. "Lily? You're Lillian?"

"It's me, Jim. Matt didn't recognize me."

"Sometimes Matt has a way of not seeing what he doesn't want to. But I'd know those green eyes anywhere."

She hugged him. "Are you surprised I'm the bride?"

"Very. I don't know who I expected Aunt Dolly to send, but certainly not such a polished lady."

"No, Daddy," Emily insisted. "Not a lady. She's an angel, just like Mama promised."

Matt watched as Lily straightened her skirt and dropped down to crouch before his niece. Seeing Emily's dirty face and the hole in her stocking through Lily's eyes made him feel guilty about his reaction to Jim's idea.

"I'm not an angel," Lily said with a gentle smile, "but I'm sure your mama had a hand in getting me here. And my name's Lily. What's yours?"

"Emily, and I'm four years old."

Lily raised her gaze to Will, who was still hanging behind. "And this handsome young man is—?"

"That's Willie," Emily said. "He doesn't b'lieve in angels, but that's because he's a boy."

Lily came to her feet, holding Emily's hand in her left one while holding out her right. "I'm very glad to meet you, William."

Matt understood the boy's discomfort. Will shuffled his feet for a moment, then swallowed hard and took Lily's hand in a stilted shake. "Me, too, ma'am."

As Lily swung around toward the house, Matt watched her face carefully. Until now he hadn't spent much time thinking about their dwelling. But not only did Emily's clothing show signs of neglect, the house was downright shabby.

Lily didn't speak, but he could see from the stiffening of her shoulders that this was even worse than she'd expected. Good.

He was certain she'd been accustomed to green gardens and flowers. Their yard was nothing more than hard-packed earth. And the only green in sight was the prairie grass beyond. The house had been upgraded from sod to wood, but the boards hadn't been whitewashed, and the porch was sagging on one corner.

Lily didn't voice her disappointment. Instead she turned toward Jim, who had hung back after his first greeting. "Don't let appearances deceive you, Jim. One thing I've learned is they often aren't what they seem. Are they?"

She didn't look at Matt, but he sensed that she was sending that warning to him as well.

"I really am glad to see all of you," she said softly. "Aren't you going to invite your future sister-in-law inside?"

Inside? Matt winced. Of course she had to stay somewhere. He'd accused Jim of not being honest about their living quarters, but exposing their shortcomings to a woman like Lily bothered him. She couldn't know how far they'd come. She'd think they were a couple of losers. He cursed silently, then realized that the worse things looked, the sooner she'd be gone.

"By all means, Jim," Matt said. "Take the *bride* inside. Show her to her room and have the cook prepare tea and biscuits."

Matt turned abruptly and, without waiting to see what Lily did, took Racer's halter and gave him a jerk. "Come on, old boy. Let's get you some feed." Matt opened the corral and filled the trough with grass, all the while comparing the new posts and fence with the dilapidated state of the porch.

"Don't eat it all, old boy," Matt said loud enough for all to hear as he slapped the horse on the rear. "I might have to share it with you. She said she could cook, but my guess is if I wait for the bride to prepare supper, I'll probably starve."

Bride? Lily took careful note that at least Matt was able to give voice to the idea, even if every other part of him was fighting the plan.

"He's just surprised, Lily," Jim assured her. "He didn't expect anyone like you." He turned and walked into the house, pushing open the front door and standing back to allow Lily to enter. "I'm afraid it isn't much," he said rue-fully. "We've been so busy trying to put up fences and dig a well that we haven't done much with the house."

"The house is fine," Lily said, hoping those angels, with whom Emily was on a first-name basis, didn't report her lie to the man in charge.

Inside the parlor, Lily found evidence of a woman's hand, for there were two glass windows in the front of the house. But it was obvious that a lot of time had passed since a woman had touched the interior.

Beyond the parlor was the kitchen with a cook table and an iron stove. A crude ladder led up to the loft. One door revealed a lean-to that she was told served as a pantry. There was only one other door, and it was off the parlor. "Where is my room?" Lily asked, trying to control her voice.

"I thought I'd let you have the room Maria and I shared," Jim said, opening the second door. "The children sleep in the loft."

Inside the bedroom was a bed and a chest and proba-bly a floor somewhere beneath the clothing and boots strewn about. A washstand boasted a pitcher and basin, and a crude wardrobe completed the furnishings.

"But if you use the bedroom and the children occupy the loft, where does Matt sleep?"

"When he's not out on the range, he sleeps in the tack room in the barn. Unless it's too cold. Then he lays out his bedroll by the fire."

Lily stiffened her back and nodded. "Fine. If Matt sleeps on the floor, so will I."

What she wanted to do was put her arms around Jim and hug him, to ask him how bad it was and what she could do. But she couldn't, not in front of the children.

"I shan't take your bed, Jim."

"Oh, but I'll bunk in the loft with the children," he said.

"No, you won't." Matt appeared in the doorway, dragging the trunk. "He can't climb the ladder, Lily, but you can."

"Of course," she said brightly, trying not to let the sight of the ladder dismay her. "Since it will only be for a short time, we'll manage. Won't we, Emily?"

Matt, appearing more angry by the minute, shoved the trunk against the wall and turned to face Lily. "You're right. In four days the stage will be back through, and you'll be on it."

Lily had been polite. She'd been agreeable and patient. She'd even tried to ease the tension by teasing Matt. Now it was time to make her position clear. "You don't want me, Matt. Fine. I'll go back, but it won't be to Memphis. My agreement with you says that if I prove unacceptable as a wife, you will provide me with one thousand dollars or a year's support anyplace I choose. I choose Paris, France."

Jim bowed his head, Will shuffled his feet, and Emily, picking up the undercurrents inside the house, began to whimper. Matt, who'd already swung around to head back to the wagon, stopped, turned, and with his thumbs hooked menacingly in his back pockets, walked slowly back inside.

"Your agreement with me?"

"Yes. I have it right here. I don't suppose you remember signing it either. Would you like to see it? It's completely legal, filed in the courts by Aunt Dolly's attorney back in Memphis."

She reached into her purse, pulled out the document, and offered it to Matt.

Matt took it and opened it, the crisp sound of the paper cutting through the air like a knife against his ear.

There it was, all written out and legal. If, after due consideration, Lillian Townsend was unable to fulfill the wifely duties as set out by Matthew Logan, she was to be given one year's support in a place of her choosing, or a cash settlement up to but not exceeding the one-thousand-dollar debt owed to Aunt Dolly by Matt and Jim.

Conversely, if Lillian found Matt unacceptable, she agreed to forfeit any claim on the Double L and leave the ranch without compensation. The debt would be considered paid in full. The agreement was signed by Matthew Logan and witnessed by Luther Frazier.

And it was his signature.

Matt looked at Jim.

"I just slid it in with some other business papers you were signing. You didn't know."

Matt felt his blood drain to his feet, leaving him cold and stunned. How could Aunt Dolly and Jim do this? Aunt Dolly's husband had left her well off. Though Matt was always uncomfortable about not repaying the loan, she'd never asked for the money. And one disaster after another had prevented their making good on the debt.

Work, work, and more work was all either man had known, until Jim got sick. Sickness had done what work hadn't—taken away Jim's confidence. Matt had already lost his dreams, fighting a war that had been some grand, foolish illusion. But Jim's health and the children were personal. Every dream he had allowed himself for the future had been for them.

Now Jim had destroyed that dream with one piece of paper. He might have managed to send some money over time, but paying off the entire amount of this agreement at once would ruin them.

"You know I didn't know I was signing this," Matt said in a low, tight voice.

"I'm sorry," Jim said. "I tried to talk to you, Matt, but you seemed determined to manage everything alone. You weren't interested in a wife, and I couldn't see any other way to force you to listen."

Jim was right. Matt had tried to protect his brother by

refusing to let Jim admit he was dying and by concealing the dire circumstances of their finances. Matt had no answers; he just got through one day at a time, hoping that solutions would come. Now Jim had come up with answers of his own.

"You promised her a thousand dollars. That's more money than we'll clear in a year, Jim. There's no way I can pay that, even if this paper were legal, which it isn't."

Emily started to sniffle. "You aren't going to leave, are you, Lily?"

Will took his sister's hand away from Lily's. "Let's go outside and see if we can find some wild berries down by the creek."

Emily shook her head stubbornly.

Jim took a deep breath and caught the reluctant Emily's other hand. "Bring my sitting stool, Will, and I'll help," he said. "Then we'll have berries and cream on our cake for dessert."

Emily brightened. "Okay. Angels like berries, don't they, Lily?"

"Angels love berries," Lily said. "And so do I."

Moments later, Lily and Matt were alone in the house. Until now, Lily hadn't allowed herself to consider that the marriage wouldn't take place. She'd planned on this for too long. And now it seemed that her plans were for naught.

"You really didn't know you'd signed this?" she asked.

"I never saw the letter before."

Lily bit her lip to stop it from trembling. "I see. Then I will leave, of course. I don't expect you to advance me a thousand dollars, but I'm afraid I don't have the fare back to Memphis. You see, things have been . . . difficult. Though Aunt Dolly doesn't really need the money, once I'm settled she plans to sell the hotel to a gentleman who has agreed to let her live there as long as she chooses, with a yearly income as well. Since she won't need it, she insisted on spending most of her savings to buy my wardrobe and pay for my ticket here. So I wouldn't feel right about asking for anything more just now."

"Damn!" Matt grimaced and paced toward the window and back before letting out a deep breath. "She's selling the hotel? What about keeping you safe?"

"Things have changed in Memphis, Matt. The hotel needs repairs so that it will attract a larger guest list. My marrying took a great deal of worry from Aunt Dolly."

"Why didn't she let me know things weren't good?"

"What would you have done?"

"I'd have . . ." He let his words trail off. What would he have done? He'd had to sink most of his money into digging a well. They'd had another year of barely getting by themselves. He had nothing left but their meager savings to send to his aunt.

What in hell made him and Jim think they could become ranchers? They'd been so sure of their plans. Even when he learned that the land they'd bought wouldn't grow cotton, he refused to admit they'd made a mistake. Then Jim met Maria over at the fort. They got married, and Will and Emily came along. By the time Maria died it was too late. They all depended on him.

All he could say now was, "What am I going to do about you, Lily?"

"I don't know," she answered softly. "I don't know what I expected, but you told me to grow up and to be a lady. Then you wrote and I thought . . ."

"It isn't your fault. Jim meant well. I'm afraid he always exaggerated in his letters to Aunt Dolly. You couldn't know the truth. I'm very sorry you had to learn it this way."

"The truth wouldn't have changed anything. I would have come anyway."

Grow up to be a lady? He'd said that. It all came back to him. And she'd done it. Lily had become a beautiful woman. Her green eyes were swimming with moisture, just as they had ten years ago when he rejected her girlish proposal. If he were still nineteen and had it to do over, he might not be so hasty. Back then the futility of his future filled him with so much pain that he hadn't been able to see hers.

But life on a ranch was hard, and he couldn't afford to be sentimental. When the time came, he'd marry a Texas woman, one strong enough to survive this harsh country *and* raise his brother's children.

"It isn't that you won't make some man a fine wife," Matt said. "But surely you can see you're not cut out for a life here."

"I'm sorry you feel that way. Jim said you need a wife. Maybe I'm not the right one, but the children deserve a mother and Jim needs someone to look after him. And I . . ."—she faltered, then went on—"I deserve to be given a chance. I don't want to have to use my shotgun, Matt."

He watched her jut her chin forward in determination. Whatever she'd turned out to be, she wasn't a quitter. "I truly don't want a wife, Lily, but until I figure out a way to get the money to send you back, I'll hire you."

Lily shook her head. "No! I watched my mother work for other people, never having her own home. I—I can't do that. I want marriage, Matt, or nothing."

"But can't you see, Lily? You're a woman who's never done a hard day's work in her adult life. If and when I marry, I'll have to choose someone who can carry her weight on a ranch."

Lily flinched. *Never done a day's work? As a woman?* Maybe not. But as a child who became an orphan early on, she'd done her share of work before her mother died and Aunt Dolly took her in. And she could do it again, if she had to. What gave him the right to judge her without giving her a chance?

"Just what would your wife have to do that you think I can't?"

Matt didn't want to argue. He didn't want to hurt Lily, but she might as well know the truth. After listening to Maria's longing for a life away from Texas, he would never subject a woman he cared about to life on a ranch.

In a steely voice that masked his worry over having another obstacle to overcome, he called out the first chores that came to mind. "She'd have to feed the hogs, look after the orphaned calves, plant and tend a garden, cook and clean and sew. You must see how impossible that would be for a woman like you."

As Matt reeled off his list of chores, Lily felt a knot tighten in her stomach. After all she'd done to prepare herself to be Matthew Logan's wife, she was being rejected again. She glanced down at her fine travel dress and wished she'd never put it on. Lily Towns wasn't some fainthearted, incompetent flibbertigibbet. She'd worked at being a lady, and she could work just as hard at being a good ranch wife. Besides, Aunt Dolly had made her promise that she'd marry Matt. With Lily married to Matt, Aunt Dolly wouldn't worry about Lily's future. And Lily wasn't going back on her word.

If her future husband wanted to be stubborn, he'd just have to learn that Lily Towns didn't give up without a fight.

"You're wrong about me, Matthew Logan. I may not know how to do all those things now, but I can learn," she insisted.

He closed his eyes and exhaled a long breath of defeat. She'd seen him do that so many times. No matter how much time had passed, Matt was still the dark-eyed boy she remembered, the one she'd learned to love so long ago. And he was still in pain. Nothing had changed.

"Why didn't you come back, Matt?" she asked softly.
"Ah, Lily. I only said I'd try. I never thought

you'd wait. Surely there must be someone back in Memphis. . . . If not, there are plenty of wealthy Texans who'd be able to give you the kind of life you always wanted."

She gave him a smile and held out her hand. "I don't want another Texan, I want you. And I want to take care of Jim and the children. I am not going back to Tennessee."

Christ! She was stubborn. He wished Jim was well enough to marry again. He wished she could be strong enough to take care of the children and the ranch. But she couldn't be. And he couldn't give in to the pleas of a woman who dressed like the governor's wife and had hands as soft as a baby's bottom.

"No, Lily. I'm sorry, but I have to say no."

"Read the agreement, Matt. Even if you don't think I can be a rancher's wife, that piece of paper says I have the right to try. Where's your sense of fair play?"

"What do you mean?"

"I mean you've set out the conditions I must meet to be your wife. I accept them. You can't send me back."

"Oh yes I can. I didn't know what I was signing."

"But a judge in Memphis, Luther Frazier, and your own brother's signature says you did. I think you'll have a hard time proving this document is a fraud without hiring an expensive attorney. We have a legal agreement, Matt."

Lily took a step closer and planted her hands on her hips. "Now let's talk about *my* conditions. While I try out as a wife, I insist that you act like my fiancé."

"And what in hell does that mean?"

"It means that when others are present, you have to court me."

"And what happens if I don't?"

She pursed her lips and said seriously, "Well, there's always my shotgun. In Tennessee, if a woman says she's been wronged, the men in town see that a wedding takes place. I think a woman in Texas must have the same rights as a woman in Tennessee, don't you? Of course I could ask your sheriff to be sure."

"We don't have one."

"Then I'll speak to your mayor. What was his name, Ambrose Wells?"

"You wouldn't."

"Believe me, Matthew. I would."

Matt met Jim and the children behind the barn as they returned from picking berries. "Will, you and Emily take the berries and go on to the house."

"I'm pretty tired, Matt," Jim began, using his health as a reason to head off any lectures by Matt.

"I'm not going to argue with you," Matt said. "I just want you to promise me one thing."

"If I can."

"Lily has to go back, Jim. We can't pay her off. I want her to think that things here are hopeless. She has to be the one to give up. Give me your word you won't try to make her stay by telling her anything different."

Jim nodded. Lily was nobody's fool. She'd figure out what their situation was, with or without his help.

By the time Jim reached the house, Lily had changed from her travel suit into a simple cotton day dress and apron.

She was standing before the iron stove still warm with coals smoldering from the breakfast fire. But where was the wood? All she saw was a wooden box filled with dirty clods of straw.

Emily came in chattering. "We find lots of berries for you, Lily."

Lily smiled at the two disheveled children. Taking their pails brimming with ripe berries, she said, "Will, do you think you could take Emily and help her wash her face and hands? Clean yours, too, and we'll have something to eat."

Will nodded, taking his sister to the bedroom where Lily could hear him pouring water into the washbasin.

Jim placed his bucket of berries on the table and sat down on the bench, his breath coming in shallow pants. "I guess you're mad at me, Lily. You have every right to be. It never occurred to me that when I asked Aunt Dolly to send Matt a wife, she'd choose you. I mean, I thought the thousand dollars was an odd request, but I figured it would make Matt agree. Now I understand. I wish I'd been more . . . forthright."

"I'm sorry Matt is so displeased, Jim. When Aunt Dolly showed the signed contract to me, I thought it was an unnecessary precaution. Now I'm not so sure."

"Don't blame Matt. He didn't know. I expected him to fight the idea, but I thought once his bride got here, he'd see it was a good plan."

"Well, he doesn't. He doesn't think I can be a ranch wife. But he's wrong and I'm going to prove it, starting with preparing a midday meal. You haven't eaten since breakfast, have you?"

A smile broke across the worried man's face. "No. We were waiting for you. Does that mean that you're not leaving?"

"Not if you'll help me."

"Of course." Jim looked up as Emily and Will came back into the room. "We'll all pitch in, won't we, troop?"

Emily beamed up at Lily. "I can already dress myself. And I can—I can—" She looked helplessly at her father.

"You can set the table," Jim said, taking in deeper breaths now, "while I build up the fire."

Lily looked skeptically at Jim's wan face. "Then you're going to sit down right here and tell me how to fix the food for our meal."

Dismay crossed Jim's face. "We're pretty much out of

vegetables. There's some rabbit stew over the fire. I'd probably just make a pan of biscuits. We have the cake I made and plenty of milk."

"And our berries," Emily reminded them proudly.

"Wonderful," Lily said. "I love berries with biscuits and rabbit stew," she added dolefully, giving Jim a questioning glance.

"Our garden didn't do so well last summer, and we weren't able to put up as much as usual to last us through the winter. We've already planted this year's crops, and we've got a new well, so we can water what we grow if the creek goes dry."

"And how long will it take this garden to produce?"

"Well, we ought to be getting some greens in about three weeks."

"But there are chickens," she reasoned, "so there must also be eggs."

"Not many. We sell the eggs in town. The chickens we protect. Speaking of chickens, Will. They're hungry too. You and Emily go feed them."

The children went reluctantly out the door.

Lily waited until they were gone, then asked the question that had been hanging in her mind. "Jim, I know that you wrote the letter. You must have known when you wrote the letter that Matt wouldn't agree. Why did you do it?"

Jim waited a long time before answering. "When I first got sick I thought about marrying again, Lily, but it wouldn't have been fair. And Matt needs someone, even if he doesn't know it. I thought he'd change his mind."

"But Jim," Lily began, "a woman would be lucky to have you, even if you aren't well. You're going to get better and then—"

"No," he said, cutting her off, "I'm not fooling myself. I'm dying. It's better that the future of the children be secure before I go. This is the only answer."

Lily couldn't argue with what he'd said. But she could argue with three weeks of stew and biscuits for two growing children and a sick man. That diet didn't sound appetizing or healthy. No wonder Jim was losing his strength. "Isn't there some sort of general store back in town?"

"Yes, but Matt—I mean, we've had to be careful with our money. Our credit is pretty much tapped out. But once we bring in the herd and get this quarter's shipment to the army, we'll be all right." All that was true, even the reference to their credit. But it had been Matt's decision to limit their spending, not the store owner's.

Lily heard his confidence, but she wasn't sure she shared it. Nothing about the Double L was what she'd expected.

Nothing except Matt.

And Matt, Matt was more than she'd expected in every way, including his stubborn refusal to go through with the wedding. She'd spent a lot of years remembering his brotherly good-bye kiss. Nobody would ever know how much she'd cried or how determined she was to be a real lady. The old, tender Matt was still there. She just had to find him.

Of course, the new Matt was exciting, too.

With determination she pressed her hand against her stomach and forced her body to relax. The first thing she had to do was stop thinking about Matt.

And the second.

And the third.

4

Though Lily had watched Aunt Dolly's cook make biscuits, she soon learned that she just might have overestimated her ability to perform ranch-wife duties. Even Jim's caution not to spill their flour didn't stop a fine sifting of it from covering the floor. And Emily's bright smile paled when the overcooked biscuits were removed from the oven as hard as a rock and brown as mud.

Jim grimaced. Their larder was pretty bare now, but with the occasional slaughter of a cow and help from the Comanche, they managed to eat well. New clothes for Emily and Will would come with the sale of their next shipment of cattle. Repairs to the house hadn't seemed important . . . until now.

"These biscuits are pretty bad," Lily admitted as she studied her first attempt.

"Don't worry, Lily. I'll make the biscuits for supper and you can watch. In no time at all, you'll be a great cook."

After the sun moved off toward the western sky, they gave up waiting for Matt and sat down. "Don't worry about Matt," Jim said. "He's usually gone all day."

It shouldn't have mattered to Lily, but it did. This was

her first meal in her new home, and she'd wanted to share it with Matt. When she tried to take a bite of her biscuits, she knew how lucky she was that he hadn't come. There was no way anybody could eat her bread, not unless he had a hammer and a chisel.

Will and Jim were looking at each other, trying to find a way to make her feel better. But it was Emily who came up with the answer when her biscuit fell into her stew.

"I dropped my bread," she announced.

Lily straightened her back and smiled at the child who was afraid she'd made a mistake. "Oh, you know about mountain stew, do you?"

"Mountain stew?" Emily echoed.

"Of course. You take a piece of hard bread and cover it with stew. That's the mountain. Then you eat half the stew, turn the biscuit over, and finish the stew. By that time, your biscuit is soft and you eat it."

"That's right," Jim agreed, turning over his biscuit as an example. "And the bread makes the bowl fuller, the stew lasts longer, and you—"

"Get fuller!" Will added gleefully, as he turned his rock over in the liquid.

They tried. They really did. But, except for the softened outer edges, the biscuits refused to soften. In the end, it was Jim who came up with the next plan: "We'll save the leftovers to dunk in our coffee at breakfast."

"And if that doesn't work"—Lily hefted one, testing its weight—"we can use them as weapons if we're attacked by Indians."

At least they had the cake and berries. Once their stomachs were full, Lily stood up and looked around until she found a pan to wash the dishes. A kettle of hot water sat on the back burner, and a broken saucer held a small sliver of lye soap. Lily glanced at her soft hands, swallowed hard, and submerged them in the water. She might not be able to cook, but she could wash dishes. It couldn't be very different from bathing herself.

Jim sent Will and Emily to make certain the mule had water. "We've been more fortunate than most; we've never been raided by the Indians. That's because Maria's mother was a Comanche."

"I didn't know that."

"Maria was very beautiful. Back east they thought she was part Spanish. But her Indian blood made her life difficult when her father brought her back to Texas. The Indians don't care, they love all children. The white man isn't so kind."

"But Maria's father was a soldier. Is it common for the fort's soldiers to marry local Indian women?"

Jim glanced at the floor for a long time before answering. "In some parts of the West it isn't uncommon for a man to marry a woman who is part Indian, but it is unusual for him to do so in the fort chapel and insist that the marriage be respected as my father-in-law did."

"He must be a very unusual man. What happened to him?"

"He's still the fort commander. Emily takes after him, with her fair skin and Will looks like me, except for his black hair."

"They're beautiful children, Jim. And it sounds as if Blue Station has welcomed all of you. I'm going to do my best to make everyone, including your hard-hearted brother, respect me too."

Jim pursed his lips as if he weren't certain that he should speak, then said, "But you must be careful, Lily. Texas is still a dangerous place for a woman. There's the occasional Mexican bandit or a renegade Indian who leaves the reservation from time to time. It might be better if you keep one of us with you for now."

"I've heard about what can happen to white women out here," Lily admitted. "People on the stage warned me."

"It used to be much worse. Since the army flushed the Comanche leader Rides Fast out of Palo Duro Canyon and moved him to the reservation, the tribes have been pretty quiet. Occasionally they get riled up if the food they're promised doesn't arrive, and you can't blame them for that. But most of them stay on the reservation."

Emily pushed open the door and climbed onto the bench beside her father. "Not Kitty Bird," she said. "Kitty comes to play with me."

Lily washed the dishes and set them on the counter until she could empty her soapy water and fill the pan again to rinse them. "Kitty Bird?"

"Catbird Who Squawks." Jim answered. "He's one of Maria's Comanche relatives. He was wounded when the army ran the renegade Comanche out of Palo Duro Canyon. Matt found him and brought him here."

"I understand he is a relative, but it's hard to believe that Matt brought an outlaw Indian into the house with the children."

"All this probably seems very strange to you after the stories you must have heard back east, but Matt has never been known to turn his back on an injured man or animal."

No, it wasn't strange, Lily thought. That was the Matt she remembered, the one who'd been kind to an orphan, the one who'd suffered over having to fight a war. That man was still here, somewhere beneath that gruff exterior. That man was the one Lily intended to find.

"So all Indians aren't dangerous to whites."

"The Comanche are known to be pretty vicious. But they protect family. And to them, we're family."

"Family," Lily whispered. "I think I like Kitty already."

"Kitty took a liking to us, particularly after Emily was born. She didn't understand his Comanche name, which is after a bird in Texas that makes a sound like a cat, so he became Kitty Bird, or just Kitty. Before Maria died, he turned up occasionally. Now he seems to know when it's time to bring in the herd, or when something bad happens. He just shows up then."

Lily glanced around and wondered about that, then started toward the door with the dishwater.

"What are you going to do with that?" Jim asked.

"Pour it out and fill the pan with clear water for rinsing."

"Uncle Matt says we can't waste water," Emily recited in a mock deep voice, "ever!"

That brought Lily up short. "What do I do with it?"

Jim lifted the lid on a large pot at the back of the stove. "Pour it in here. We'll use it again tonight to wash the dishes. We save the rinse water for bathing."

"Bathing?" Lily glanced around, catching sight of the tin tub hanging from a nail on the wall by the door to the lean-to.

"Sure," Jim grinned. "Every Saturday night, whether we need it or not."

Lily turned to the stove, hiding a look of dismay. She was quickly beginning to understand the hardships a rancher's wife must tolerate.

By nightfall she'd added a cup of water to the stew and stood at Jim's elbow to see what she'd done wrong as he made up a new batch of biscuits. He put them in to bake, then sat down.

Later, when they were done, Lily removed the pan and placed the bread on the table. "When will Matt be here?"

Will reached for a biscuit and dropped it on his plate. "Oh, he ain't coming."

"Isn't," Lily corrected without thinking.

Will blushed. "Isn't. He rode up while I was watering the mule. Said he'd be out on the range."

Lily had almost cried over Matt's rudeness when he didn't return for lunch. This announcement only made her mad. If Matt thought avoiding her was going to make her return to Memphis, he had another thing coming. She might decide to go back, but not until she'd proven that she could perform the chores he'd laid out. Not so long as she still cared for him.

He used to call her a dreamer, and he'd encouraged her. Apparently, now he thought she was living out some kind of girlish daydream. Maybe she had been, in the beginning, but now all she wanted was for him to stand up for her like he used to.

Nobody here was calling her names because her mother was white and worked as a washwoman. But the memory was still buried deep inside, along with the memory of the dark-eyed boy who had made her feel special.

"Jim, do you have a piece of paper and a pencil?"

"I think so. Why?"

"I want to make a list."

"Bring your mama's writing box, Will," Jim instructed. "And give it to Lily."

Moments later she opened a quilted wooden box. Inside she found notepaper, a quill, an ink bottle, and a pencil. The box smelled like the rose petals scattered inside. Lily removed the pencil and gently closed the box.

"I don't want to use this paper. It's too fine. I'll just use the back of my letter."

She unfolded Matt's—no, Jim's—request for a bride and wrote on the other side. She was glad now that Matt had stayed away. It would give her time to get organized. The children might believe her story about mountain stew, but she didn't look forward to hearing Matt's reaction. What she was after now was his respect.

"Let's see," she said, wrinkling her forehead. "What was number one?"

"Number one?" Jim questioned.

"I'm making a list of what I have to learn to do. If I remember right, number one is to slop the hogs."

• • •

Matt unfolded his bedroll on the only ridge for miles. Over an open fire, he roasted the rabbit he'd shot, washing the meat down with water from his canteen. Not as satisfying as a strong cup of coffee would have been, but it meant he could avoid dinner at the ranch house.

Avoid Jim's censuring eye.

Avoid Lily's hurt.

He added another cow chip to the fire and lay down on his blanket. He couldn't stay all night, for he had chores to do in the morning. But he didn't have to go yet. Above him the night sky glittered with stars. He let out a long, deep breath.

No matter how hard the work had been since he and Jim had come west, they'd never given up. Out of nothing, they'd built their ranch, the house, and barns. Year by year, their cattle had multiplied. Now that their hard work was about to show some profit, this girl from the past, a girl he barely remembered, had come to muddle his plans.

No, Lily wasn't a girl. She was a woman, a beautiful woman with more courage than he wanted to admit. She knew what she wanted and went after it. The burning question was, After seeing the ranch, why would she still want him? How could he possibly make her happy?

In the last ten years he hadn't allowed himself to think of her. She'd been a part of the painful past he'd left behind, part of an implied promise he'd made in his youth, one he'd almost forgotten. And now that promise had stepped into the present and added more guilt to what he already carried around.

Guilt over a future he hadn't been able to fulfill for the younger brother who believed in him. Guilt over Maria's death and his brother's failing health, both problems that might have been avoided if he'd allowed Maria to talk Jim into going back east.

Always before, the beauty and peace of a sky full of stars had made this hard life seem worthwhile. When things seemed hopeless, he'd been able to come here, look up, and dream of a time when he and Jim would finally build the new life they'd sought, free of war and pain.

Until now.

Until this afternoon when he'd ridden aimlessly across the land of the Double L, alternately remembering the adoration of a child-woman named Lily, then facing the consequences of Jim's actions. If his little brother had only talked it over with him, he'd have convinced Jim that they weren't ready yet to think about that kind of future. Once they brought the cattle in, branded them, and delivered those contracted for to the army, then they could talk about . . . about . . .

What the hell could they have talked about? There was no way he could say, "Sure, Jim, I know you're dying. But don't worry, I'll take care of Emily and Will." So long as they didn't say it, they could pretend it was somewhere up ahead.

Jim was not only sick, but the years of having an unhappy wife who hated the ranch had eaten away at his optimism. He was no longer the wide-eyed kid he'd been when they first came west. God only knew how he got through the spells of weakness and pain that came almost daily now.

He still couldn't believe that Jim had done this. How could Aunt Dolly have gone along with him? More importantly, how did little Lily Towns turn into the woman who got off the stagecoach in town? And why in the hell had she waited for him?

It made no sense. With her beauty, every man in Memphis must have been after her. Why wouldn't she have married one of them? Why would she come out here?

There were no answers. Only questions. Only cold reality and an unwanted awareness of what a man might need. Of what Lily might give.

Nobody but Matt knew how lonely he'd been. And now he had the temptation of the devil back at the house, sleeping in his loft, determined to learn how to meet his requirements as a rancher's wife.

Meeting his requirements wasn't important. So long as Jim lived, Matt couldn't think about his own needs. If he took a wife, it would be for the sake of the children, and only when Jim was gone. She'd be a strong woman who could survive the hardships of life on the plains—not a beauty with milky white skin and fine lawn drawers.

Matt groaned. Who was he fooling? The only hope he had was in keeping his distance from her and the knowledge that there was no way in hell she could meet his demands.

He closed his eyes and let out a deep breath, trying to let go of the tension in his stomach. Now, in addition to the problems of Jim's health, the ranch, and raising the children, there was Miss Lillian Townsend to deal with.

Matt Logan had learned to be tough. He could handle this. He'd managed to survive everything that had been thrown at him. Nobody else knew about what he'd faced in the war. He'd been a boy when he was thrown into his first battle, when he cowered in fright behind a fallen log when the shooting started and long after it stopped.

He'd never told anyone that he stayed behind that log for two nights and a day before hunger drove him into the woods. Later, when he stumbled into another Yankee camp, he'd been welcomed as a comrade, but he'd felt shame that he'd survived when the rest of his unit hadn't. That's when he knew that he'd either be a soldier or a coward; the decision was up to him.

In the second battle he shot his first man and started to grow old with the weight of his actions. The next three years had been a blur, and the war had finally ended. He'd gone home to find the Logan plantation gone, along with his family, except for Jim, Aunt Dolly, and Lily, the homeless child she'd taken in, the little girl who'd followed Matt's every step.

Jim, still angry that he'd been too young to do his part in the war, made up his mind that they would go west, buy land, and grow their own cotton. By that time Matt didn't care. A new start in a new place seemed as good an idea as any. With a stake from Aunt Dolly, they'd headed out. It soon became clear that Jim would never be able to do an equal share of the work. Two years later they faced the truth: Without rain, the land they'd bought for a dollar an acre wouldn't grow anything but range grass.

Then Jim had met Maria, the fort commander's daughter, and married her. It had never mattered to Jim that she was part Comanche; he'd loved her completely. Matt couldn't begrudge him the happiness they'd shared in the beginning. Three good things came from the marriage: Emily and Will, and Sergeant Major Rakestraw, the fort commander, who, in his efforts to see that his daughter was taken care of, had come to their rescue by providing the Double L the first cattle to start their herd. And later the contract to supply the army and the reservation with cattle. It had taken several years and a lot of searching for unbranded cattle loose on the range, but finally, this year, Matt expected that they would show a profit.

Until Lily.

Until the agreement Jim had tricked him into signing. The agreement he'd have to honor unless Lily failed. God help him if she didn't.

The Double L couldn't afford more silk dresses or another mouth to feed. And he couldn't let himself care for a woman who could never be a ranch wife and proper mother to Emily and Will.

•   •   •

"Jim, I refuse to take your bed. I'll share the loft with Emily and Will."

"No! I may not be much of a man, but I'm responsible for bringing you out here. I knew Matt would be angry, but I never expected him to try and turn you into a servant to prove yourself."

Lily laid her hand on his shoulder. "Jim, it's all right. I came because I wanted to. If I can't sleep on the floor, I'll never be able to prove that I'm tough enough to be a rancher's wife."

Jim shook his head. "I'm sorry, Lily. But Matt isn't going to tell me where I'm going to sleep. This is still half my house, and I won't have you sleep on the floor your first night."

In spite of Matt's orders, Lily finally gave up arguing with Jim about where she would sleep. It was a matter of male pride that he provide the best bed for her. To insist that she have the loft would make Jim feel worse. Determined to make other arrangements the following day, she gave in. Once she took a better look at the bedroom, she was almost sorry she hadn't taken a firmer stand.

It was after midnight when she picked up the last article of clothing from the bedroom floor and piled it on the stack in the corner.

She shrugged her shoulders and looked around. A sorry lot of clothes she'd folded. Holes in the knees and elbows. Buttons missing. Socks with no toes. She'd get started on the repair tomorrow. Not only because it was part of her agreement, but because their desperate need for a woman's touch reached inside and tugged at her heart. For years she'd carried around the picture of the two brothers, laughing and swimming together as they grew toward manhood. Those carefree days were captured there in her thoughts.

Lily had found a home when she came to Aunt Dolly's, but more than that she'd found a family. She'd never known her father. Aunt Dolly's husband was a gruff, demanding man who was away more than he was at home. Jim became the brother she never had. And Matt became the friend who shared her dreams and made her believe they could come true.

Then Matt went away to fight and came back a man. He never talked about what happened, but sometimes she'd catch him with a solemn faraway look in his eyes, and she recognized the pain that he tried to keep locked away. Then he'd give her that melancholy smile that made her feel his sorrow.

All the time she was preparing herself for marriage, she was preparing herself for Matt, for finding him and making that sadness disappear. He'd rejected her girlish attempt to reach him. That still hurt, but she understood that she'd been too young. Still, she hadn't been able to forget, and through the years she'd fantasized about what might have been. But her fantasies had never included two lonely children, one sick man, and another who'd become so much more desirable than she'd ever imagined. She caught the bedpost and leaned her head against it. Could she learn to be the kind of wife he needed?

The picture of Matt's tightly leashed fury came back to her. She'd thought she was prepared to be a wife. He'd said he would ask her when she grew up. She'd never truly believed that Matt would reject her a second time. But he had.

Now, with flour still flecking her hair, and her body weary from both her trip and her failure as a cook, she felt hope falter.

She didn't want to think she'd been fooling herself all along. She didn't want to believe that the best thing for everyone would be for her to pack up and go back to Memphis. It wouldn't matter if that was true, she didn't have the money for her ticket. And she couldn't forget Emily's sweet face and Will's earnest one. She might not be their mama, but she was determined to make things better for these two children.

And Jim, how much longer did he really have? She didn't even want to think about what he was facing in the future without someone to care for him.

Tomorrow, Lily decided. Tomorrow she'd consider what she *knew* how to do. Drawing on a strong sense of optimism, she considered how she'd make use of music lessons in a house with no music. How she'd turn satin dresses into clothes for a little girl. And how she'd prove to the man she'd come to marry that he needed her.

Wearily she moved the candle to the table beside the bed. Eyeing the lumps, she plumped up the mattress, brushed the grit from the bed, and smoothed the sheets, knowing that once she stretched out the stuffing would be squashed into mounds of new lumps. She allowed herself a moment of despair, wishing for her feather bed back in Memphis, and, she thought ruefully as she eyed a split in the covers, the quilt she'd packed in the bottom of her largest trunk.

In the morning she'd make a list of things they needed. It was a dilemma deciding whether to start with the mending or the wash. If Blue Station had a bank, surely it had a general store.

Tomorrow she'd talk with Matt about going into Blue Station.

If he came back.

Finally, she stored her shotgun and her derringer on top of the wardrobe, then, opening her small trunk, pulled out a nightgown and donned it. Over the foot of the bed she draped her house dress and petticoat, and finally, smiling at the memory of Matt's reaction when she'd talked about them, added her fine lawn underdrawers.

•   •   •

But it was neither the mending nor the wash that started her day. In fact, it wasn't even day when she heard a loud knock on her door. She came to a sitting position as the door opened.

"Time to feed the hogs, *Lillian*." It was Matt's voice bellowing orders, but it could have been anybody standing in the inky darkness.

Lily flung her feet over the bed and reached for the packet of matches beside the candle. Moments later, Matt's large body came into view. A half-dressed body wearing no shirt. He'd stepped into his denim trousers and, leaving them unbuttoned at the top, pulled them up over his underwear.

Lily blinked. Red underwear. And suspenders. By the light of the candle she could see that his beard was heavier and his dark hair tangled in wet ringlets that dripped water down his face and made splotches on his knitted underwear.

"Feed the hogs?" she questioned, more from confusion than confirmation.

"That's right. We'll discuss why you're in this bed and Jim is in the attic later."

"It was only for one night," she protested. "Jim insisted. I thought—"

"The hogs come first. I'll do the milking this morning. Then you cook while I'm feeding the rest of the stock. By the time I'm done, you'll have the breakfast pancakes ready."

Lily blinked again. *Breakfast pancakes?* First she had to wake up.

He was smiling at her. His full lips drawn into the suggestion of a dare. Leaning back against the doorframe, he waited, his grin saying that he knew she was not an early riser.

He was right.

So, she'd pretend it was evening and she'd been napping. Now it was time to get ready to go out. "All right," she said with more confidence than she felt, and stood up. "Let me get dressed."

Turnabout was fair play. Wearing only her nightgown, she boldly padded to the foot of the bed and reached for the clothes she'd left there the night before. If he could appear half-dressed, she could do likewise.

Matt's eyes followed her. She knew the exact moment he caught sight of her undergarments. He whirled and left the room, slamming the door behind him.

Lily couldn't hold back a smile as she quickly pulled on a skirt and shirtwaist, shivering in the early morning cold. Spring might have come to west Texas, but the morning chill felt more like the Tennessee mountains. She fished inside the trunk for her shawl, took her candle, and made her way into the kitchen, where Jim was bent over the stove.

"What are you doing?" she asked.

"I'll build up the fire while you're helping Matt," he said.

"That's my job," Lily admonished as she placed the candle on the table. "Tell me how and I'll tackle the fire first." She looked around and determined that Matt wasn't in the house. "There's no hurry. Matt won't expect me for a few minutes."

"Why?"

"I'm a woman, an incompetent city woman. And city women always take a long time to dress."

Jim smiled. "Well, you certainly didn't. Of course, I'll bet city women comb their hair when they dress."

Lily felt a moment of panic, then pulled her hair back and tied it with a piece of string she found on the shelf over the stove. "So, I'm adapting. Now show me how to start the fire."

Jim opened the door to the firebox in the stove. With

an iron poker he swirled the coals around, then added what looked like a clod of dirt to the firebox.

"Is that going to burn?" Lily asked, looking doubtful.

"Sure," Jim assured her. "The only problem is breaking it up without spilling dung on the floor."

"I don't think I heard you right. Dung?"

"Well, some folks call them cow chips. But whatever you call it, it's still dung."

Lily caught her breath. She'd watched the fires being fed along the stage route, but they'd used wood, straw, branches. "Doesn't it smell?"

"Once it's dried, it's not too bad."

"What about plain old-fashioned wood?"

"How many trees did you see driving in, Lily? I know. I had a hard time adjusting to the barrenness. We have to go all the way to east Texas to buy fence posts. Go along now. When you get back I'll give you a lesson in making flapjacks. You'll like the honeycomb Kitty Bird brought last week."

Lily drew her shawl close and moved toward the door. "Where are the hogs?" she asked.

"Behind the barn. Just follow your nose."

"And what do I feed them?"

"Corn, when we have it. The rest of the time it's roots and swill . . . from the hotel."

"And this time?"

"Swill."

"Swill. I'm not sure I like the sound of that." Lily stepped out the door, the cold morning air causing her to pull her shawl closer. A faint light radiated upward from the horizon in the eastern sky as if it were the sun's advance guard, testing the heavens before it appeared. Sunrise. The same sun was rising over Tennessee, she thought with just a quick flash of homesickness. Over Memphis and Aunt Dolly.

Feeling embarrassed, Lily couldn't remember having seen a Memphis sunrise, but she'd seen sunsets so beautiful they made a person cry. She never considered that she'd miss the life she left behind.

"Well?" Matt's impatient voice cut through the darkness. "Are you coming, or have you given up already?"

"Given up? Not by the hair of your chinny-chin-chin. Where are those pigs?" She opened the gate and started around the shadowy building.

"Come behind the barn and watch where—"

"What the—? Yuck!"

"—you step. The pigs like their pen wet."

Lily looked down at her feet. Or she would have if she could have seen them. Instead, all she saw were her ankles disappearing into thick mud that sucked and squished as she tried to withdraw.

"I don't think I want to know what I'm standing in," she said as calmly as she could manage. She could have screamed; Lily was certain that she'd be a champion screamer if she ever let go. But she wouldn't give Matt the satisfaction of seeing her turn into a shrew.

"It's only mud," Matt answered, trying hard to hold back the laugh that managed to escape anyway.

"And how do the pigs manage to get mud in this dried-out dirt that won't even grow a garden?"

"I pump water into a tank and open the sluice so that it soaks the corner of the pen you're standing in."

"And you couldn't have warned me?"

"I tried. But you moved too fast for me. Come on over here and we'll clean your feet."

Lily counted to ten, then forcefully withdrew one foot. There was only one problem: Her right foot was out of the mud, but her right shoe was still in it. She let out a resigned sigh and took a step, finding dry ground. The left foot followed. The left shoe didn't.

"I'll draw some water. Hold out your foot, and I'll pour the water over it."

She walked toward him, slowly. Counting to ten wasn't far enough. Twenty just might be.

"Where are your boots?" Matt asked as the sun climbed high enough in the sky to cast a green-gray touch to the landscape.

"They like the mud, too."

"How in the world did you lose them with all those laces?"

"There were no laces," Lily confessed. "I just stepped into the same slippers I was wearing yesterday."

Matt poured the water into a tin bucket. "Hell, step into the bucket and slosh your feet around and I'll get them." He moved around her and knelt down by the mud-hole.

"Thank you, Matt." Lily rinsed most of the mud away, stepped out, and picked up the bucket. "You say the pigs like mud?"

"Yeah, they do."

"Well, I've learned two things, haven't I?"

"What's the second?" he asked as he pulled one battered, ruined slipper from the mud.

"We save the clean water and the dirty." With that she slung the contents of her bucket toward the mudhole.

Unfortunately Matt stood up at that moment and caught the water square across the back. "What the—?"

"Sorry," she said sweetly. "I would have warned you, but you moved too fast."

Half an hour later, Lily discovered another thing: Hogs really liked swill. Swill was the leftover food that Matt collected from the hotel in Blue Station twice a week. She'd ladled the last of the foul-smelling liquid from the barrel and splashed it into the trough. The hogs knew what she was doing and made a mad charge to get to the food. In the process she was rubbed and snorted on. It was just as well that she hadn't dressed her hair before. She might never get the odor or the mud washed out. She'd lost her shoes, and her skirt would have to be washed before she could stand the smell.

Back at the house she was informed that washing anything meant hauling water to the house from the well by the barn. "You mean the hogs and the stock get piped-in water but we don't?" she asked Matt incredulously.

"Sorry, the stock doesn't know how to draw water. Too expensive to supply the house and the pens, so the animals got first choice."

Lily looked helplessly around as Emily, sitting on the bottom rung of the ladder to the loft, stared wide-eyed at her disheveled appearance. Lily wanted to curse. She wanted to scream.

Instead, she went into the bedroom, wiped off her feet on a dirty shirt, pulled on a pair of men's socks, and tied a knot in the toe of one so that her foot wouldn't slide through. She unbuttoned her skirt and stepped out of it, pulling on a loose wrapper instead. Wrapping a handkerchief around her head she marched back into the kitchen where she used just enough cooking water to clean her hands.

"Now, Jim, let's get those pancakes going."

Matt left the house, whistling. Halfway to the barn he congratulated himself on the outcome of Lily's first encounter with the hogs. Another day or two of chores ought to just about do it. If he could convince Jim to stop mollycoddling Lily. Only because it upset Jim did Matt hold back his anger when he discovered that his brother was sleeping in the loft.

Matt shoved the makeshift sluice from the well back around to the water trough. He'd wasted enough water for the day.

As he fed the rest of the stock he wondered why he

wasn't feeling better about his victory. He'd ruined her shoes, made her look like a fool, and given her a large taste of what was ahead. Why hadn't she lashed out at him, or cried? Most women resorted to tears.

Miss Lillian Townsend would too, eventually.

5

The breakfast pancakes varied in size from a lumpy walnut to a small pie. Somewhere in between was what Lily had been aiming for, but turning the larger ones without having them come apart was another obstacle. Finally, she had them all cooked and on a platter.

While she was preparing the pancakes, Will had appeared with a bucket of milk. "Do you want milk or coffee, Aunt Lily?"

Coffee. She hadn't thought to make coffee. "Milk," she said cautiously. "But I guess I'd better get some coffee going for Matt."

"Already made," Jim said. "I put it on while you were in the—feeding the hogs. Pour the milk, son. Matt wants you to go into town and pick up a fresh barrel of swill."

Fresh? There was nothing fresh about what she'd fed those hogs. The whole idea was dreadful.

She sat down on the bench next to Emily. "Jim, Will's a child. Does he go into Blue Station alone?"

"Twice a week, Aunt Lily," Will explained proudly as he filled the glasses. "Course I don't drive Racer. Only Uncle Matt can make him pull a wagon. I drive the mule."

"I'm surprised you get enough swill from the hotel to make the trip worthwhile," Lily said.

"We don't always," Jim admitted. "When the trail drivers come through there's plenty. Otherwise, we take whatever the manager has left. An occasional piece of pork for the hotel, and the owner is willing to save his scraps. Pigs are rare in this part of Texas. They don't like sun and heat, which we have in abundance, and they like corn, which we haven't had until now."

"You feed them corn?" That made no sense to Lily. The pigs got corn, and there was none for the family.

"Only what the Comanche give us. You see, they like pork, too, and some of them raise corn. It's a good trade."

"I didn't know the Indians were farmers," Lily said.

"They're not, not willingly. Rides Fast, their leader, is a very different kind of Comanche. He saw too many of his people starve when they first moved to the reservation. The agent taught them how to grow crops, and now it's a matter of survival. He's fortunate that Rides Fast is a wise man and that his tribe is willing to be managed. They're no longer the vicious warriors they once were. At least not Rides Fast's men."

Lily remembered Matt's reference to digging a well. "Do they have water on the reservation?"

"They have a good stream. That's another thing the Indians have done, learned to irrigate their crops. That's why they have enough corn to share."

Will swallowed his pancake and added, "It's mostly the cob that the pigs get. We eat the corn. The pigs don't know the difference."

Lily took a sip of the warm milk and smiled at Emily. The child copied Lily's action. This morning Emily was wearing an apron that was much too short and showed obvious signs of wear. Lily didn't know where Matt was, but studying Emily, she began to get an idea. If Matt could barter for what he needed, so could she. While she fleshed out her plan she made general conversation, focusing on Jim.

"Racer is pretty spectacular. He looks like one of the show horses back in Tennessee. Did you bring him out west with you?"

"Kitty Bird bringed him," Emily said. "He wuz a present. For Uncle Matt."

"What a nice present," she agreed. Matt was well thought of by the Indians and, from what she could tell, by the men back in town. "And I'm sure Kitty Bird has been a big help to you, but it's clear that you could use a woman around here. Why hasn't Matt married?"

"He's never even taken the time to look at a woman, not the kind he'd marry, anyway. He's always worked hard, but once I got sick, it seems like he's been driven." Jim reached out and took Lily's hand. "I'm glad you're here. You'll be good for all of us, Matt most of all, even if he doesn't know it yet."

Lily frowned. A truer statement had never been made. He didn't know that he needed her. She had to show him by doing something. Something more than just meeting his conditions.

Maybe she had a way. But first, the morning meal. "Call your uncle, Will. Tell him that I've prepared his breakfast pancakes."

But Will didn't have the chance, for Matt came through the door, his spurs jingling as he stomped his feet, discharging clods of grassy mud from his boots.

Her future husband was too big for the doorway. He had to stoop to come inside. He'd washed his hands and face and droplets of water still hung from his hair and beard. He stopped and looked at her as if he were ready to reprimand her for whatever mistake he could find.

From the kitchen, Lily stared at him, swallowed hard, and searched for something she could use to head off any rebuke. "In the future, Matthew Logan, scrape your boots before you enter the house. I do not intend to clean up behind sloppy men who have forgotten their manners."

Matt's eyes opened wide in surprise. She knew he was about to respond until he caught the big-eyed stares of Will and Emily, and held back what he'd been about to say.

"You're right," he said in a tight voice. "I apologize." He put the toe of one boot behind the heel of the other boot and pried off the first, then the second boot. Completely oblivious to the hole in the end of his sock, he padded to the table.

Emily started to laugh, until a nudge from her father stopped her outburst. "But Daddy, Uncle Matt's big toe looks like it's waving at us. He needs to tie a knot in his sock like Lily Angel did."

"Lily Angel?" Matt laughed. "Where'd you get a name like that?"

Emily scrambled down from the bench where she was sitting and took Matt's hand, looking up at him with worship in her eyes. "It's all right, Uncle Matt. Don't yell. I asked Mama for an angel and she sent Lily."

Matt looked down at the child's small hand entwined in his. "I'm sorry, Emmie," he said, dropping to one knee before her. "But Lily isn't an angel."

Emily tilted her head and smiled. "Uncle Matt, you just don't know 'bout angels. I do. My mommy told me."

Lily's heart was thudding. *Don't destroy her faith, Matt.* She knew how hard he thought he had to be, but with Emily he seemed to soften. Why couldn't he be like that with her?

"No," Matt answered. "I guess I don't."

Emily patted Matt's hand in comfort. "That's all right. I'm going to call her Lily Angel. You can just call her Lily."

Matt shot Lily a dark look as he picked Emily up and put her back on the bench, giving her a kiss on her forehead. "Yes, I'll just call her Lily."

"Do you want her to tie a knot in your sock for you?" Emily chattered on.

"I do not," Matt told the little girl solemnly. "I put the hole there so that my toe can breathe. I like it like that. I intend to keep it that way."

"Not for long," Lily said, smothering a smile. "One thing I do remember is how to sew. Emily and I will be attacking the mending directly."

She knew that she had backed herself into a corner. Either she had to do the mending and sewing, or she would fail to meet his terms and he would send her back.

"I mean, according to my list, Matthew, no respectable rancher's wife would let her men wear socks with holes. So, mending comes right after we do the wash. You do have a washpot, don't you?"

"Sure," Will said eagerly, then frowned. "But we might . . . have run out of clothes-washing soap."

No soap? Lily searched for an answer to that. Even her mother always had soap. Washing clothes for Aunt Dolly became the only way her mother could make a living. Once she went to work for the Yankee's hotel, nobody else would hire her. And Lily had always been allowed to accompany her. Cooking she might not know, but the smell of soap and wet clothes had become ingrained in her hands and back. No need to tell Matt about that. Thinking back, the big sudsy pots of boiling water in Aunt Dolly's washhouse seemed a lifetime away.

"So what do ranchers in Texas use instead?" Lily asked.

Will and Jim looked at each other.

"The Indians use soap root when they can find it," Matt finally answered. "Most of the time we use sand and clean water. It hasn't mattered much out here. I guess you wouldn't understand that." He squared his jaw and let his gaze fall on the table. "What in tarnation are those things?"

"Pancakes," Lily answered. "Sit down and I'll pour your coffee."

"Pancakes?"

"I'll get the honey," Jim said, trying desperately to hide his amusement.

"You stay put," Lily directed. She put the coffeepot down. "Where is it?"

"In the lean-to, in the wooden keg."

Lily opened the door to the western-style pantry and looked around. She saw only one wooden keg, and it was larger than she'd expected. Nevertheless, she lifted it and carried it back to the table, opened it, and let out a startled scream.

"What's wrong?" Jim came to his feet.

Lily dropped the top back to the container. "There are bees in there, dead bees."

Jim opened the can once more. "Kitty always makes sure there are a few bees left inside. The Indians eat them like candy when they're soaked in honey."

"I think I'll just eat my pancakes with butter," Lily said weakly, sliding to the bench beside Emily.

"Don't have butter," Will said, as the others, less reticent than Lily, spread honey over the cakes and began to eat.

Lily was feeling a little better about her cooking until she took a bite from her own pancake. "Oh, my goodness. How can you all eat this? It's awful." She washed the gooey, half-done mess down with a big swig of milk and let out a sigh of genuine dismay.

The table was silent for a long moment before Will cleaned his plate and bravely asked for seconds. "I like them."

Lily stood and turned her back to the others. "You're very sweet, Will, but you don't have to do that. I'll try again." Her voice was thick and tight.

"No time," Matt announced, closing off the guilty

conscience that was trying to assert itself. "Have to get going. Will, get yourself into town to pick up the swill from the hotel. Jim, if you feel up to it, you might see that the garden is watered."

"And me, Uncle Matt," Emily piped up. "What do you want me to do?"

"Just try and keep Miss Lily out of trouble, Emily. Maybe she can teach you some of the things you need to know to become a lady like her."

"Not likely," Lily snapped. "Lady school is closed. According to you there is no market out here for *ladies*. I'll teach her to be tough like me."

Matt took a look at the breakfast table and laughed ruefully. "Like you? Maybe competent would be a better goal."

"Listen here, Matthew Logan. I had to cook and sew before my mama died. It's just that I wanted to be the kind of woman I thought you'd want—a lady who could run a proper house. I may have forgotten how to do some of those things myself, but I'll learn to again and I'll teach Emily all the practical things she needs to know. And I'll teach her to be a lady, too."

Lily tore the apron from around her waist and dashed into the bedroom, closing the door and leaning against it.

"And while you're about it," Matt called out, "move your bed things to the loft."

She heard the outside door slam and the silence that echoed in its wake. What had she gotten herself into? How could she have made Emily such a promise? Emily had looked at her with watery eyes, and Lily knew she'd been thinking about her mother. Will seemed caught halfway between sadness and that kind of false show of maturity that would prove he could handle himself. And she could hear Jim taking deep breaths.

However had she thought she could be a rancher's wife? What on earth was she going to do?

Then it came to her. Lily Towns was going to do what every city woman did when she was without. She was going to market.

"I don't think Uncle Matt is gonna like this," Will observed as he drove the mule across the prairie toward Blue Station.

"With any luck we'll be back before he knows I'm gone," Lily answered.

"But he doesn't like us doing things without asking."

"And he's right. You shouldn't. That's because you're a child. I'm an adult," she said, with a lot more confidence than she felt. "That's different."

Will looked at her skeptically. "I guess."

When they arrived Lily was able to examine Blue Station more objectively than she had before. Matt wasn't there overpowering her with his presence, and she had the time to look.

A single sun-hardened dirt street ran between weathered wooden buildings. There were no ruts. The lack of rain here was obvious, as was the fact that the local trading post hadn't done a big business in whitewash. The blacksmith's shop was little more than an area covered with animal skin. On the far end of the street sat a tent with a sign out front: I Wash U and yor clothes. Shaves extre.

Well, Lily, she thought, looking at her lacy, glove-covered hands with determination, that's what your mama did. You can at least earn a living if Matt throws you out.

As Will drove the buggy into town, one after another of the shopkeepers and citizens stopped whatever they were doing and leaned against the buildings and roof posts to gaze at Lily. The women eyed her with censure, and the men in great awe. Maybe she'd made a mistake. Maybe a woman escorted only by a child wasn't safe here.

Will reached the end of the dusty street, drove around

behind the buildings, and drew the wagon to a stop at the back door of a building whose front was considerably more upright than its rear. The door swung on its hinges, opening onto a stoop that listed to the side like a one-legged sailor.

The boy jumped down and scrambled up the incline. "Mr. Cary, I've come for the swill."

A thin man wearing a white apron over a dingy white shirt and vest stepped through the door. "Who you got with you, Will?"

"This is Miss Lily Townsend, Uncle Matt's new bride," Will announced proudly.

Mr. Cary studied her for a long minute. "Heard about that. When's the weddin'?"

Lily didn't like the suggestion of a leer in the hotel proprietor's manner. "Soon," she answered as she lifted her shopping basket and dropped it to the ground, ruffling up a mushroom of dust. "Will, I'm going shopping while you transact your business. Will you pick me up in front when you're done?"

"Yes, ma'am." Will moved to help Lily from the carriage, deftly turning the hotel manager aside. "The store is two buildings down."

"You want to cut through the kitchen and the hotel, Lily?" Cary asked.

"It's Miss Townsend," she said politely. "And no, thank you, I'll go around." Aunt Dolly had always taught Lily to enter the front door of an establishment. She'd been big on propriety.

Will shot a worried look at Mr. Cary, then back at Miss Lily. From the confusion on Will's face, Lily knew he understood that the hotel owner was not showing Lily proper respect, but he didn't know what to do. Causing a problem for Will was not what she'd intended.

"Mr. Cary," she said with a plastered smile as she paused at the corner of the building, forcing herself to hold the heavy basket without calling her discomfort to his attention, "Thank you, but I wouldn't want to interfere with your kitchen help. I'll see you again."

She thought he nodded, but she didn't wait to see. Setting off whirls of dust with her steps, she rounded the corner and walked down the rough wooden planks that served as a sidewalk in front of the hotel.

The next establishment was Ambrose Wells's bank. Beyond that was the Blue Station Trading Post. Based on the looks of the building, the trading post had been the first building in the town.

Tugging her hamper into the dark store, she came to a stop and looked around. From what she could see by the light sifting through the dusty windows, the post was reasonably well stocked. But not too well, she hoped as she made her way to a small rack of ready-made dresses.

"I'm Willard Tolliver, the proprietor. May I help you?" a round-faced man wearing tiny gold-framed glasses inquired.

"Why, yes, Mr. Tolliver. I'm wondering if you might be open to some trading?"

The man studied Lily with astonishment. "Madam, I am a married man."

Lily laughed. "No, you don't understand. I'm Matthew Logan's fiancée and I'd like to trade this for supplies." She opened her carryall, pulled out one of her more elaborate afternoon tea dresses, and laid it across the counter. "How much will you allow me for this?"

"For that?" he said in astonishment. "Nothing. The women here don't wear elegant clothes like that."

"Perhaps they would if such a dress were available," she argued softly.

The door behind them opened, and the sound of swishing skirts announced the presence of another woman. "Mr. Tolliver, I wonder if you got any calico in on the stage yesterday."

The woman moved around Lily, peering in astonishment at the dress she held, then jerked it out of Lily's hand. "Never mind. I'll take this. How much, Tolliver?"

"It isn't for sale, Mrs. Wells. You see—" he began.

"Excuse me," Lily interrupted, attempting to reclaim the dress. "I've already offered Mr. Tolliver a generous price for the gown."

"Nonsense! Whatever she offered, I'll double it."

Tolliver's initial reluctance gave way to a greedy smile. He pursed his lips and appeared to consider the woman's request. "You know that I've always given you first choice on any new merchandise, Mrs. Wells, but this young woman, Miss . . . Miss . . . ?"

"Townsend. Lily Townsend." Lily gave the other woman a contrived, haughty look designed to prod her, then added, "I was here first, Mr. Tolliver."

"Lily Townsend? Matt Logan's new bride?" the store owner asked in surprise.

"Matt's fiancée, yes. Now, about the dress?"

"I'm sorry, Miss Townsend," he said, removing the dress from Lily's hand, "but Mrs. Wells did ask me to order a special gown for her. As you were just saying, you have an order to fill, so why don't you look around. I'm certain we can supply whatever you need."

Lily managed a frown as she turned away. Mrs. Wells wasn't going to be able to wear the gown as it was, but if she was deft enough with a needle, there was enough fabric to alter it to fit her rounder figure.

While Mrs. Wells paid for her new gown, Lily found a bolt of gingham with enough yardage to make skirts for both her and Emily. She added muslin for blouses, needles and thread to sew it with, soap for washing their clothes, coffee, potatoes, onions, salt, a few cans of peaches, and, remembering Will's valiant attempt to eat her pancakes, two big crackers from a barrel.

"Do you carry kerosene and lamps?" she inquired.

"Of course he does," Mrs. Wells answered. "Bring her one, Tolliver." Mrs. Wells was smiling now that she'd wrestled such a prize away from another customer. "I'm Harriet Wells. I believe you met my husband, Ambrose, on your arrival."

"Why yes. I did. I'm very pleased to know you, Mrs. Wells."

"Didn't know Matt was contemplating marriage," she said shrewdly. "Till I heard he'd sent for a wife. You don't look like the type of woman who'd have to come out here to find a husband."

Lily wasn't used to such direct questions, and she was tired of being considered unfit, for whatever reason. She almost told Harriet Wells to mind her own business when she remembered that she was on trial as a future wife.

"Matthew and I have known each other since childhood. As a matter of fact, we first talked about marriage when I was twelve and Matt was nineteen. He came out west to make a home for us."

Lily might be telling the truth, but Mrs. Wells wasn't having any of it. She cast a jaundiced eye on Lily. "Took you a mite long to get here. Women 'round here would jump at the chance to wed Matt Logan, and they wouldn't have waited years to do it."

The truth of that wasn't lost on Lily. He could put off marriage as long as possible . . . until he was forced to wed. "It wasn't me," she said. "I wouldn't have waited to be married. That was Matt's idea." Let Matt do the explaining.

Harriet Wells studied Lily. "This is a hard life, and Matt needs all the help he can get, especially with those youngins. You know anything about children?"

"Of course. I've had years of experience." She had, Lily decided. She'd been a child. What else did she need to know?

6

By the time Will had loaded Lily's supplies into the wagon, everybody in Blue Station was standing on the street to see the girl Luther Frazier had identified as Matt Logan's intended. But it was Harriet Wells who called out, stopping Will before he drove the wagon away.

"I don't know what I was thinking of back there in the store," she said to Lily, "but I want to be sure that Matt is bringing you to the picnic and dance. It'll be on the first Saturday night of the month."

"Dance?" Lily questioned.

"Yes. It's our second Founders' Day Celebration. My husband and Mr. Tolliver built the first establishments in Blue Station, you see, to service the cowboys on cattle drives and the stagecoach from Wichita Falls," she went on, barely stopping to breathe. "Everybody brings a late-afternoon picnic supper. We hire Lorna's piano player—Lorna owns the saloon—and have a dance."

"Well," Lily began, "I'll speak to Matt, but I don't know—"

"Bring Jim and the children, too. Seems like the only

one we ever see is Will. And I'm certain Matt will want to introduce you to everyone."

Lily didn't know how to answer. She glanced at Will, who shrugged his shoulders as if to say he didn't know. A dance did sound like fun, and Lily had the feeling that it would do Jim and the children good to get out. About Matt, she couldn't be sure.

But Mrs. Wells was right. A dance would put Matt on notice that their agreement was two-sided. He'd have to introduce her to the public as his fiancée.

"Thank you, Mrs. Wells," Lily finally said. "Matthew and I would be pleased to come. I can't say about Jim. It depends on how he's feeling, but we'll bring the children."

"Good. You'll join Ambrose and me, of course. We always have a real table."

"I'm not sure—"

"It'll be good to see Matt. He's always so busy. Now that he's about to take a bride, we expect you to change all that."

All Lily could do was nod as Will flicked the reins to move the reluctant mule forward. They'd left Blue Station behind when he spoke up. "Aunt Lily, I don't think Uncle Matt is gonna be happy about going to the Founders' Day Celebration. He ain't much for that kind of thing."

"Isn't," Lily corrected. "Why doesn't he take part in the community activities? As long as he and your father have been out here, I'd have thought they were the founders."

"Well, I don't exactly know. Uncle Matt and my daddy were here before the townspeople came. There was just us, the Indians, and the army. But Uncle Matt never spent much time with anybody but Mr. Kilgore. He's the Indian agent. Course there is Kitty and my grandpa. Grandpa's the commander over at the fort."

"It must be nice to have your grandfather nearby. I guess you must see a lot of him."

"No, not so much. It's a long ride and I have chores."

Lily could tell that there was something wrong. She changed the subject until she could talk to Jim. "Tell me about Kitty Bird."

"He's Rides Fast's cousin. Daddy says that all this land used to belong to the Indians. Well, they didn't own it cause Kitty says nobody owns the land. But this was their hunting grounds before they got sent to the reservation."

"I can understand that your uncle Matt is tied down with running the ranch, but what about you and Emily? Don't you go to school?"

"When I can," the boy answered. "Before Daddy got so sick he would take me over to the reservation for lessons from Mr. Kilgore."

"Why didn't you go to school in town?"

"They—some of the townspeople didn't like having me there."

Lily took a quick look at Will. "I can't imagine why anyone would not want you in school, Will."

He squirmed for a moment, then admitted, "It was just one boy. He said something about my mama, and I—I hit him."

"Good for you. I'd have done the same thing."

Will grinned. "Mr. Ambrose came to see Uncle Matt, said I was welcome to come back, but Daddy said no. He could teach me more than I could learn in town anyway. I didn't care. I like Mr. Kilgore."

Lily was beginning to understand why Matt didn't go into town. "Did what that boy said bother you?"

"Not much. Besides, that was a long time ago."

Lily suspected it wasn't that long ago. She suspected, too, that Will's not going to school might have more to do with Jim's health than with animosity. "But you don't go to see Mr. Kilgore anymore."

"No, ma'am, but Papa makes me do my sums, and I read the Bible on Sunday."

Lily made a mental note to speak to Jim about that, too. In the meantime, she could help. "Matt, why don't you and I make a deal? I'll get you some lesson books and teach you if you'll help me learn what I need to know about the ranch."

"Books? Storybooks, too?" Will looked a little embarrassed, then added, "Emmie likes stories."

"Storybooks, too."

Will grinned and gave the mule a little slap with the reins, hurrying him along. "Storybooks, potatoes, and peaches," he said. "It's been a great day."

"It's been a long time since breakfast," Lily said. "Maybe one of these crackers would taste good." She pulled out one of the hand-size biscuits and gave it to Will, whose eyes almost popped out.

"A store-bought cracker?"

"One for you and one for Emily."

Will took a big bite and closed his eyes in pleasure. "Aunt Lily, it sure is going to be good to have you in our family."

It would have been better if she and Will had gotten her supplies into the house before Matt came home. She would still have had to explain, but the explanation would have come a lot better if Matt had had a full stomach. Unfortunately, that didn't happen.

Just as they drove into the yard, Matt came out of the barn. He walked over to help Will unload the barrel of swill.

"What's this?" he asked, nodding toward the parcels.

"Miss Lily bought some things, Uncle Matt. She's going to get us lesson books and—"

"You'll have to take them back," Matt erupted, fury etching his face.

"I'll do no such thing," Lily said in return. "I only

bought soap, and fabric, and some supplies, which we badly need."

"Tolliver let you have all this?"

"Why yes. So far I've only purchased necessities. And I didn't pay for them. He let me put it on my account."

"Your account? I see." Matt squared his jaw and motioned to Will. They began to slide the barrel down the planks he'd laid from the back of the wagon to the ground.

Lily fumed as she watched. The nerve of the man! He just assumed that she'd run up a bill at the store on his account. And, what if she had? She knew she was going to be a part of this family, even if he didn't. And she intended to make some decisions on her own.

They rolled the barrel to the fence by the pigpen before he spoke again. "Will, I'm sorry, but you'll have to take Miss Lily back to town. It'll mean you'll be late finishing your chores. In the future, Lily, don't buy anything without asking me."

So much for Lily's plans to surprise her new family with a change of diet. Not to mention the gingham she'd bought to sew a new apron for Emily. She could understand Matt's concern if he was really as broke as he'd said. Any money he spent had to be for necessities. But he'd automatically assumed the worst of her, and there was no way she'd let him do that.

Lily forced herself to count to ten, then climbed down and waited, her foot tapping.

Once the barrel had been stored in the barn, Lily met Matt as he headed back toward the wagon. She spoke out, forcing herself to be pleasant. "Will, take our supplies into the house while I talk to your uncle."

"There will be no discussion about this, Lily. Whatever you bought, I can't afford."

"You didn't pay for it, Matt. I did."

He looked at her in disbelief. "You said you had no

money. Would you like to explain how you paid for all that?"

"I do have a little money, not much, but a little. However, I didn't spend any money. I got this by bartering, Matthew, a method of exchange people have used since the beginning of time. A practice you engage in when you swap pork for corn. I swapped one of my dresses for merchandise."

"Dammit, Lily. You went into town and traded for goods? What do you think the town will say about that? They'll think I'm too stingy to spend money on my— my . . ."

"Your unwanted bride? Go ahead, say it. I expect everyone in Blue Station is gossiping about the *warm welcome* you gave me when I arrived."

Lily hid her hurt by turning toward the wagon. She lifted the basket filled with the cans of peaches and potatoes. Trying to stop the moisture welling up in her eyes, she didn't see the end of the board sticking out. As she whirled around, it caught the basket, and the contents went flying as she pitched forward.

Right into the man responsible for her frustration. Right into a chest so hard that it knocked the breath out of her. Right into arms that caught her and held her even closer.

"I'm sorry," he said. "I shouldn't have yelled at you. You have no way of knowing the situation here."

"No, I don't. How could I? You've been very careful to avoid talking to me, and you avoid the people in town, giving rise to heaven-only-knows-what kind of speculation. Are you having trouble getting to know your neighbors?"

"Let's just say that I have good reason to avoid them."

"Particularly the women. Mrs. Wells said every woman in town wanted to wed you."

He started. "She said what?"

"Well, I can understand that. If what I saw of the men

in Blue Station is any indication of Texas's husband material, you're a definite improvement. I hope the women are better."

"I never noticed."

But Matt had noticed Lily and concluded that every part of her was spectacular—if a man were simply looking for a beautiful woman. But he wasn't looking for a beautiful woman. He wasn't looking for a woman at all. Not even if Lily did give up one of her fancy dresses to provide things his family needed.

He was still holding her, feeling the soft fabric of the dress she was wearing, feeling the pressure of her hands against his chest. "Why'd you do it, Lily? Come out here when you could have stayed in Memphis and been the kind of lady you always wanted to be?"

"I never wanted to be a lady for me, Matt. It was for you and Aunt Dolly. She thought it would help me to have a better life. And I thought you wanted your wife to be a lady. I learned and I waited, but you never came back, not even to see Aunt Dolly. Why?"

"I couldn't," he said quietly, seeing the confusion in her eyes, breathing in the smell of her, and cursing the response of his body. They were standing in the yard, in full view of the children and Jim. But he couldn't let her go, not yet. "I didn't want to admit that we'd failed."

"But you haven't failed, Matt. How can you say that? You have this ranch, Jim, and you have Will and Emily. That's more than a lot of people have now. You should be celebrating."

"I have Jim now, but you and I both know he's dying. Celebrate? I don't feel much like celebrating."

"Not for yourself, Matt, but for the children. For Jim. Celebrate life, every day that comes. Jim is, and he's trying to do the only thing he can for Will and Emily, secure their future."

Lily straightened and stepped out of his reach. "Will

and Emily need to feel safe, too. They may not understand how ill their father is, but they know he's sick and they're scared, at least Will is."

Damn her. How could she find his guilt and shame him? In all his efforts to make a new life, he hadn't found a way to deal with his brother's illness. He'd ignored it, refused to discuss it, forcing Jim to find his own solutions.

"Don't you think I understand what he was trying to do? I do."

"Then stop being such an old bear. Let him at least think he's contributing to his children's future."

"And you have a suggestion about how I should do that?"

"I do. When we go into town for the picnic I expect you to make all the citizens of Blue Station think I'm your fiancée, including Jim."

"Picnic?"

"We're going to the Founders' Day Celebration, and you're going to introduce me to your neighbors, just like I asked."

"Like hell I am. I told you, I avoid any unnecessary friendship with the good citizens of Blue Station."

Lily folded her arms across her chest, jutted out her chin, and said, "Matthew Logan, hell will be an improvement on your situation if you don't go. We have an agreement. I'll learn to be a rancher's wife, and you'll treat me like one. I realize I've only just started, but so must you. On the other hand, if you decide to send me back, I could get used to France. I'll bet they really know how to celebrate in Paris."

Matt swore again, balling his hands into fists. There was no way she was going to Paris. He wouldn't have that. He couldn't afford it. "All right, Lily," he agreed reluctantly. "You want to go to the picnic, you'll go. Jim can take you. And you can celebrate all you like."

He wasn't going to give in. At least not completely.

"Jim isn't my intended," she said, picking up the potatoes and peaches.

"He ought to be," Matt said, and turned to unhitch the mule, then led him to the corral.

"Please, Matt. Being a family would mean a lot to your brother and Will and Emily," she said to his retreating back.

"I'll think about it."

Lily watched him go, a tiny spark of joy loosened by his reluctant promise to consider the picnic. "Will you be joining us for the noon meal?" she yelled after him, pleased to note the stiffening of his back.

"No. I may not even be back for supper."

"Whatever you say, Matthew, but I brought home something special for supper. And I have to prove to you that I can cook. Remember?"

"I remember. I also know that until we deliver our next shipment of cows, we can't afford special treats. I don't want Will and Emily to be disappointed."

Lily started to argue, then held back the words. Matt was right. She hadn't thought. Any bartering she did had to be for necessities, not special treats. But it wasn't fair. Why hadn't she saved some of the money Aunt Dolly had spent on her education and her trousseau? She'd been so intent on making sure Matt was impressed that she hadn't thought any further.

But by golly, the dresses were hers, and she could do what she wanted with them. She wouldn't apologize.

"Matt, I'm sorry you're upset. But we have an agreement and I'll keep my part of it. How I do it, is my business. I bought soap because we need it, for health reasons if nothing else. And I bought gingham to make Emily a new apron. The other things, well, perhaps they are frivolous, but Will and Emily deserve a treat. If you don't want to eat with us, that's your choice."

He stood still for a long time, his back to her, before

he answered. "I won't make any promises, but maybe I'll be back in time. Help Will feed the stock and . . . if you think it's that important, you might use some of that soap on Emily." He disappeared into the barn.

"You mean feed the pigs?" she called out.

"No, the pigs are fine until tomorrow. Just give the mule and the cow some hay."

Moments later Matt appeared on Racer, ready to ride away.

"About Emily," Lily delayed, "shall I put her in the horse trough, or can we spare water for the house?"

"There's a tub in the lean-to, and yes, we can spare the water. Just don't waste it when you're done."

"I wouldn't think of it. Maybe I'll even use it myself. A hot bath would be wonderful." She caught Matt's expression and, hiding her smile, started to the house. Maybe a little whitewash would be next on her list. And some flower seed, and some curtains, and some lumber to build another bedroom. She didn't know how many dresses that would take, but she hoped she'd have enough. By the time she reached the porch she'd forgotten her guilt over buying luxuries instead of necessities.

At the door she met a whirlwind with ginger hair. "Lily Angel! Lily Angel! Will says you bringed me a cracker." Emily flung herself around Lily's knees. "Did you? Did you?"

"I certainly did. And some soap, and some gingham for a new apron."

But Emily wasn't interested in anything but the cracker. Matt was wrong. Children needed an occasional treat. Emily was so excited that Lily didn't have the heart to make her wash her face and hands first. But, on closer examination, that bath Matt had ordered was definitely on her afternoon duty list.

Maybe the bath for herself was important, too.

And for Matt.

She picked up the bar of fancy bathing soap she'd brought from Memphis and took a deep breath, drawing in the rose fragrance.

Yes, she'd heat some extra water for Matt.

Inside the kitchen another odor permeated the air.

"Chicken?" Lily asked Jim, who was stirring the contents of the iron cook pot.

"Close enough. Prairie hen. Kitty brought two birds just after you left. He was sorry to miss you."

"Oh, I'm sorry, too. I want to meet him."

Lily unpacked her goods and set to peeling potatoes and onions to add to the stew. When she finished she looked around the room, glancing through the open bedroom door. Jim had been busy. The bed was made. He'd swept the floor, and from somewhere he'd found a faded cloth for the kitchen table. In the center was a crockery pitcher filled with blue flowers.

"Oh, Jim. How pretty. I saw these flowers along the railroad coming into Blue Station and on the way here. Matt said they are bluebonnets. They are very beautiful."

"Texas bluebonnets," he said with a pleased smile. "One of the few things about Texas Maria liked."

"Could we plant some in the yard?" she asked.

A bleak expression swept over Jim's face, and he walked slowly to the window. "Maria wanted flowers. Back then there was no water for anything like that."

"But there is water now, isn't there?" Lily asked. "We have a well. We'll plant bluebonnets for Maria."

"Yes, we will." Jim smiled sadly. "Thank you for coming, Lily. The Logans need you. Matt needs you. Even if the stubborn fool won't admit it."

Emily finished her cracker, asked for a glass of milk, and started up the ladder. "Where're you going, sugarplum?" Lily asked.

"To talk to Mama," she said, and climbed over the end of the loft, disappearing from sight.

"A nap," Jim explained. "That's what she always calls her nap time, talking to Maria. Sometimes, I think she really does."

"What about something for you to eat?" Lily asked.

"No, thanks. I think I'll wait for supper. Besides, I finished off your pancakes this morning."

Lily laughed. "I don't know why. They were truly awful."

"With honey they weren't so bad. I promise you, we've eaten worse before I learned to cook a little."

And, until I learn to cook a little better, you still might, Lily thought.

Matt rode west, toward the river in the hazy distance. Once again he wished his land touched a year-round creek, but it didn't—a fact he hadn't known until after he bought it. He hadn't known they had so little rainfall either. Last summer it didn't matter that the creek dried up; there was a river on the border between his land and the free range still under government control. But how long would it remain free?

The land on both sides of the river and all the way to Palo Duro Canyon had once been under the control of the Comanche—before the American government, bowing to the pressure of John Austin and the Texas statehouse, rounded up the Indians and moved them to the reservation. Now it was about to be gobbled up by outsiders. Bigger cattle ranches were coming, ranches owned by wealthy men who'd never been to Texas.

What was worse was that he'd heard barbed wire was coming with them. If he couldn't come up with money to buy the land between his spread and the river, the Double L would die.

The heat beat down on Matt, reminding him of the summer yet to come. For now, the grass was green. An occasional shower moistened the earth. But all that could change without warning.

He'd ridden for half an hour when he saw them, four fat black birds circling lazily in the distance.

"Turkey buzzards. Damn!" He touched his spurs to Racer's haunches, and the stallion took off.

Matt squinted, trying to see what had attracted the birds. Once it might have been a buffalo, but that time was gone forever. The range belonged to the cattle now: those wearing the Double L brand and the mavericks who interbred with them, and the cattle belonging to ranchers to the south.

The most famous maverick in the Texas Panhandle was One-Eyed Jack, a huge rust-colored beast with horns that spanned almost eight feet. Matt had seen him only twice, both times at a distance and both times he'd been unsuccessful at capturing the prized bull with only one eye. A bull like that would increase the size and strength of any man's herd. Many had tried to capture Jack, none had succeeded. So far, One-Eyed Jack had avoided Matt and Jim's ranch.

The buzzards squawked and hopped away as Matt rode up to the remains of a small heifer, one wearing the Double L brand. A few feet farther, he found a second cow. Both had arrows buried in their necks. The best parts of the meat had been hacked crudely away and skinned, leaving much of the carcass.

Matt frowned. It didn't make sense. The Indians wouldn't have killed the cows and butchered them like this. They needed food too badly. The Mexicans might have, but they were worth more to the bandits alive. Matt studied the ground carefully. No sign of hoofprints, shod or not. Matt climbed down from his horse and studied the dead animals more closely. Something was wrong. He just couldn't put his finger on what it was.

Two dead cows, dead too long to salvage for food. Food desperately needed by so many, including his own family, and it had just been wasted.

Climbing back into the saddle, he directed Racer toward the fort. Another hour's ride southeast and Matt was entering the gate. If something was going on, Maria's father, Sergeant Major Rakestraw, would know.

When Matt told him what he'd found the old man's expression showed his concern.

"Sorry, Matt. If there is new trouble in the area, I don't know about it. I'm not surprised, but I'm worried."

"Why?"

"Well, you know Washington is thinking about closing the fort."

The idea of closing the fort put a wrench in Matt's gut. The reservation depended on the army to keep the Indians in feed, and Matt needed the beef contract for both the fort and the reservation.

Matt didn't know how old the sergeant was, but he'd spent his entire life in the army. An old horse soldier, he'd accompanied the surveyors sent from Washington to map the West, then migrated to Texas when it was reaching for statehood. He hadn't wanted to return to Washington City during the War between the States, but because of Maria, he had agreed to become Lincoln's western adviser.

His skin was leathery and wrinkled now. His salt-and-pepper hair was more white than the brown it had once been. The word on the post was that he still slept on his horse more than he slept in his cot.

Though Jim had been married to the old man's daughter, it had been Matt who most often sought his advice, Matt who'd learned to respect the soldier's instincts. "No, I hadn't heard. Why would they do that?"

Rakestraw stood and began pacing behind the desk,

his back arrow straight and his uniform inspection ready. "Because the Indians have settled down, Congress thinks we don't need so many forts in Texas. I've tried to tell them they're wrong. The Indians never give up, they're just waiting. Once word gets around that the army is pulling out, the raids will start all over again."

"You really think so?" Matt asked. "Rides Fast may not like it, but he seems to be trying to make the reservation work."

"Yes, and for that I hold you partly responsible, you and Kilgore. But Rides Fast's tribe is only a small group, and the reservation was never meant to be permanent. Once they're moved, trouble will come. And there are still the Apache and the more aggressive Comanches. They are ready to rise up, given the chance."

"What about the Texas Rangers?"

"Rangers handle criminals, bank robbers, and rustlers. The army handles the big problems. Always has, always will. But that's not all I'm worried about," he confided, taking his seat again.

"What then?"

"New settlers are ready to come to Texas. Once the railroad's in, there will be no stopping them. But what is worse are the large conglomerates being formed to claim millions of acres. Between them and the farmers, open ranges will disappear, and the Indians and small ranchers will revolt."

"I can't believe anybody is going to try to farm here," Matt argued. "It's too dry."

The sergeant gave a short laugh. "You and Jim were set to try—until you found out there was no water. You almost starved."

"We would have if you hadn't given us the beef contract for the fort and the reservation. I thought you were crazy. The range was full of strays."

"And Indians, too," Sergeant Rakestraw said.

"Soldiers aren't cowboys, and only half of the supplies sent to the men ever arrive. A controlled herd is the answer. I don't want to have to send my grandchildren back east to protect them. Sending their mother was a mistake that I've lived to regret. The Double L Ranch will be their future. That's why I don't like this incident."

"You think settlers killed my cows?" Matt couldn't keep a little skepticism from his voice. He hadn't heard anything about new settlers in the area.

"I don't believe Comanche did it," Sergeant Rake-straw said. "Could be Apaches trying to stir up trouble, but it doesn't feel right."

"It does seem more like something a white man would do," Matt agreed.

"I'll do some looking around," the sergeant said. "Now, let's go to my quarters. I've managed to get a hold of some good Tennessee sipping whiskey."

Matt followed the wizened old man, and they spent a few minutes filling glasses and sampling the familiar liquor before Rakestraw asked, "How are my grandchildren?"

"They're growing like weeds."

"And Jim?"

Matt couldn't hold back a frown. "Good enough to get me and him into trouble."

This time it was Rakestraw's eyebrows that lifted. "Jim? That's hard to believe. Never thought the boy had enough gumption for that. What's he done?"

"Sent for a bride."

There was dead silence following Matt's bombshell statement before the sergeant responded. "What in the hell for? I know the children need to be seen to, but hell, boy, why not get him a local girl?"

"That's what I said. Until I learned that the woman he ordered wasn't for him."

"Then who?"

"Me."

There was no holding back the sergeant's laughter. "That's splendid! I don't know why I didn't think of it. I don't know why you haven't done it before."

"Because I have no wish to marry," Matt said angrily. "Certainly not some yellow-haired society girl who loses her shoes in the pigpen."

"Am I to assume that the bride has arrived?"

"Yes! Got off the stage and introduced herself to everyone as my future wife."

"So you don't like her."

"Yes. I like her. But it isn't a matter of liking her or not. She's too soft, gentle. There's no way she's tough enough to be a rancher's wife. You know what happened to Maria, and she was born out here. No, I would never put another woman through that kind of hell."

Matt winced when he thought about classifying Lily as a gentle woman. She might be a lot of things, but so far, gentle wasn't one of them.

The old soldier waited a long time before he asked, "And the children? Do they like her?"

That stopped Matt. "Emily's already named her Lily Angel. She thinks Maria sent her. Will's quieter about it, but I think he'd like her to stay as well."

"What does Jim think?"

"If, and I repeat if, I don't strangle him, he thinks he's going to teach her to cook, to feed the animals, to weed a garden. If you could see the clothes she arrived in you'd know she'll never be able to survive the heat."

Sergeant Rakestraw took another sip of his whiskey. "Is Jim well enough to help the woman learn?"

Matt swallowed his reply. "I don't know. He does seem a little stronger. I hate to say it, but I think she might actually be good for him, once she moves out of his bed and in with the children."

The commander looked startled. "His bed?"

"You know Jim," Matt explained. "He gave up his bed

and moved into the loft. He can hardly walk across the room and yet he's climbing a ladder. But I've put a stop to that."

"Well, the idea sounds farfetched, but if you aren't interested in a bride, Jim could be."

"But he isn't physically able to . . ."

"Maybe that won't matter. And if the worst happens, well at least the children will have a mother."

Matt bit back his objection. The sergeant was right. The children had to be the determining factor, not what he or Jim wanted.

It was full dark when Matt caught sight of the house in the distance. There was a lamp in the parlor window that hadn't been there before. It cast a warm glow in the darkness, a glow of greeting. Matt caught his breath. It had been a long time since anything about the house had been welcoming.

With any luck he'd missed supper. He'd just feed and brush Racer and bed down in the barn after he stood under the makeshift shower he'd rigged next to the windmill's water tank. His shower was the only luxury he allowed himself. And that would stop if the water level dropped.

It took some manual pumping to move enough water to the barrel he'd attached to a platform on the back of the windmill, but a cool brief shower was worth it. This was his private moment at the end of the day.

He might have followed through on his plans if he hadn't seen Lily emptying a bucket into the barrel by the front door. Wearing nothing but a wrapper, she appeared as a silhouette against the light inside the house. The door closed and reopened as she brought a second bucket, then a third.

Emily must have been given a bath. Apparently Lily had taken one too.

Matt felt his skin flush. He held on to the corner of the barn, listening to Racer as he munched on hay in his stall. She had bathed Emily and the stock had been fed. He didn't like this. Lily wasn't supposed to be able to meet his conditions.

He remembered Sergeant Rakestraw's suggestion about Jim marrying Lily. The thought made his entire body tighten as if he'd sucked on a green persimmon. Lily stood on the porch and tied the sash of her wrapper tighter. He didn't have to see her body to imagine what it looked like.

Full and warm. Feminine. Sweet-smelling.

She continued to stare across the hard-packed dirt as if she'd heard something or knew he was there.

Matt froze, holding on to every ounce of control he possessed to keep himself from crossing the yard and jerking that loose garment away.

He knew then that she *must* go. Children or not, he had to find a way to send Miss Lily Townsend back to Memphis—without the one thousand dollars Jim had promised.

Kitty. Kitty would know what to do. He was wise in the ways of nature and women. Tomorrow, he'd find Kitty. In fact, tomorrow he might even introduce Lily to Kitty. She wanted to meet the neighbors. He'd do what she wanted.

Across the yard, Lily felt his gaze. She couldn't see him and there was no movement, but she'd known instantly that he was there, watching. Her body told her that Matt Logan was spying on her.

So, she might as well reward him. Carefully she closed the door and walked toward the window in the light of the lamp. After glancing behind her at the closed bedroom door where Jim was sleeping and up toward the loft where the children were, she slowly moved between the lamp and the window, knowing the outline of her body would show through the thin fabric.

Just a second. No more. Then she stepped away from the window into the shadows and smiled.

That's what he got for being a Peeping Tom. Any other man would charge across the yard and rip open the door. Any other man would put his arms around her and kiss her senseless.

But Matthew Logan wasn't just any other man.

Lily smiled.

She wasn't just any woman either. And she'd just begun to fight.

7

The breakfast pancakes the next morning weren't perfect, but they did taste like pancakes. Once again Matt didn't show up, but she noticed that someone had taken flour and bacon from the lean-to.

Will ate and left to do his chores. Jim, pleased with her cooking progress, pretended to enjoy his breakfast, though what he really did was push the cut-up pieces of pancakes around his plate. He was thin, too thin, and no matter what Matt said, Lily was determined to get some better food in his diet.

Emily, still in her nightdress, her uncombed hair looking like a bird's nest, crawled down from the table and put her arms around Lily's leg. "Will you tell me a story, Lily Angel?"

Lily stacked the tin plates and grimaced, realizing that in her attempt to impress Matt with her progress, she had neglected Emily. "Later, sugarplum. Jim, would you—no, never mind," she said quickly. Jim had already given her a cooking lesson. She couldn't keep depending on him to do her job.

"What, Lily? I'll do anything I can to—"

"Oh no, you won't," Matt said, entering the house. The threat in his voice stopped his brother's offer. "Either she does her work on her own, or it doesn't get done. And if it doesn't get done . . ."

The threat was obvious.

Jim looked stunned. He sat for a moment, then stood slowly. "Now just a minute, Matt. I realize that I haven't been carrying my load around here, but I'm still a full partner in the Double L . . . with equal say. I'll decide what I am able to do."

Will, who'd preceded his uncle inside, backed up against the ladder to the loft, surprised at his father's tone.

Silence filled the room. Matt didn't move from where he stood in the doorway.

Then, as if he'd decided to make a truce, Matt let out a slow, deep breath and leaned against the doorframe. He might appear relaxed, but Lily knew that his pose was a facade.

"Of course, Jim, you're right. If you choose to help Lily, I can't stop you, but," he said softly, "if she does anything to cause you to overextend yourself, she'll be on her way back to Memphis . . . on that mule out there."

He was talking to Jim, but his gaze never left Lily's face. She knew he was waiting for her to show some sign of weakness. Well, he could wait till hell froze over before she'd do that. And hell, so long as Matt was anywhere around, would never cool.

Jim glanced uneasily at Lily and took another step toward Matt. Jim might be fifty pounds lighter and a head shorter, but it was obvious to Lily that he intended to protect her.

Emily sniffed.

Lily glanced down at the little girl's scrunched-up face and knew she had to do something. Not only was she responsible for two brothers about to come to blows, but she was frightening a child. How could it have come to this?

She slid around the table and moved in front of Jim to face Matt. "No. I don't need Jim's help. I can get what I need myself."

Matt took a menacing step toward her. "And exactly what is it that you need?"

She wondered how she managed to set him off. Did every meeting have to be a confrontation?

"What do I need? I need hot—" she began, then faltered. Hot was one thing she didn't need right now. There was enough heat coming from Matt's eyes to scorch a custard, if she only knew how to make one.

He was doing it again, backing her down. "Hot water," she snapped. "To wash the dishes." She picked up the water bucket, pushed her way past him to the porch and into the yard, hoping that distance between them would cool off the situation.

Distance didn't help. She'd just stepped into a different kind of heat.

It was barely seven o'clock, and unlike the morning before, the sun was already beating down on the yard. The hard-packed earth was etched with spidery cracks, like the quilting stitches of some mad housewife. Even the pigs had disappeared from their pen.

Halfway to the water pump Lily stopped and shaded her eyes, searching the horizon for something, anything to break the endless blue overhead. In the distance the horizon blurred into a dusty blue-green haze. She almost couldn't tell where the earth met the sky.

Texas was so big, so overwhelming. When she'd stepped on the train heading west she'd never imagined space that went on forever. No wonder Matt had changed: He spent much of his time out in that emptiness. Without boundaries or points of reference in which to exist, he seemed to have lost touch with any kind of restraint. He no longer knew how a man should behave.

For the past ten years the men back in Tennessee certainly had been guilty of the same thing. First money-hungry carpetbaggers had come in. Then the freed slaves. But the soldiers returning from the war had been left out of the new South. Their lands had been burned, sold for taxes, or left in such a state of disrepair that men without spirit or money gave up.

Was that what happened to Matt and Jim since they'd come to Texas?

Lily folded her arms across her chest and stiffened her resolve. She wouldn't let this raw land intimidate her. She might fail, but it wouldn't be from giving up. Going back wasn't an option. She wouldn't do anything to burden Aunt Dolly. Besides, she and Matt Logan had a deal. She'd prove herself capable of becoming a rancher's wife, and he'd treat her as his fiancée.

She knew he was behind her before he spoke.

"I know this place isn't what you expected, Lily. If you're ready to give up the idea of marriage, I'll find a way to get you back to Tennessee."

She almost believed his concern was for her, but she'd learned Matt Logan cared about only one thing—the Double L Ranch. "No thanks, Matt. I'm staying. I've made my bed, so to speak. Now I'll have to sleep in it."

"Your bed better be in the loft."

She didn't answer.

Matt had made his own bed as well. And it looked as if he was taking up permanent residence in the barn. From the set of her back it was obvious that Lily was having no part of his offer. If the ranch hadn't disappointed her enough to make her want to leave, he'd have to find something else—something bigger than the obvious problems. What were women afraid of out here?

Indians.

Catbird Who Squawks.

He'd already toyed with taking her to the reservation. Now he'd use Kitty and the rest of the Comanche to send

Lily packing. Eastern women were terrified of *wild Indians*. Preparing herself to be a lady wouldn't have prepared her for savages as neighbors.

"I have chores to do this morning, Lily, but after the midday meal, be ready. You want me to act like a bridegroom? We're going calling on our nearest neighbors. In fact, we may stay the night."

"We're what?"

Matt knew he'd surprised her. Good, that's what he'd intended.

Matt looked over at Lily. She could feel his gaze, and she tugged at the skirt of her striped afternoon gown with buttons to her chin and a sassy bustle that hung over the back of the wagon seat. She hoped that she was properly dressed. Being brought up in Tennessee she should be prepared for the heat, but the intensity of the Texas sun was worse than anything she'd experienced. Without a hat to protect her face, she could already feel her skin begin to tingle.

Defiantly Lily opened her parasol to shade her face. She'd get used to the sun. She'd let her skin turn dark like Matt's. But not all at once. To take her mind off her discomfort she tried to engage Matt in conversation. "What about my chores, Matt? I thought you didn't want Jim doing my work."

"He isn't. Will is. Until you came, most of the cooking and cleaning had become his job, under Jim's supervision."

"But he's only a child."

"He'll manage."

She started to argue, then hushed. Men could always justify their actions. Women had to explain theirs. Besides, riding alone in the wagon beside Matt was nice. She was pleased that he'd accepted their situation and had decided to do something to indicate good faith. She'd let him do the talking. She had the feeling that he wouldn't expect that.

Matt watched a smile spread over Lily's face. A brisk wind sprang up, tugging tendrils of her hair away from the severe knot she'd twisted at the base of her neck. The frilly umbrella she'd opened was whipping so in the breeze that she finally lowered it to protect its fragile fabric.

"How do you know where you're going?" she asked. "There are no roads, no trees, nothing to use as a landmark."

Matt almost smiled. There was a route, about a hundred yards over. But he wanted the solitude of an unmarked trail to make Lily uncomfortable and uneasy. "Racer knows. He'll take us where we want to go."

The sudden, unexpected sound of gunfire shattered the peaceful afternoon. Two quick shots were fired, then silence.

"What was that?" Lily asked.

Matt looked around. No signs of trouble. "A hunter maybe, or perhaps one of the Indians taking potshots at some tumbleweed. We're too close to the reservation to be in any danger."

Lily wasn't certain she believed him. "If you're certain."

"I'm certain," he said in a gruff voice that told Lily he didn't appreciate her lack of trust.

The mood suddenly turned cold. Maybe it was because of the gunfire, or maybe it was his harsh rebuke, but the air between them became strained. For a moment Matt missed the warmth, then told himself that, except for the gunshots, everything was working out the way he'd planned. In the silence a low murmur began, a steady moan that meant the Indians were aware of their presence.

"Matt, what is that sound?"

He made a show of listening, though he'd heard it for

some time. "Drums. Looks like our hosts know we're coming."

She looked confused. "But I thought you said we were going to call on our nearest neighbors."

"These are our nearest neighbors. Just up ahead is Chemaw, the reservation where the Comanche have been confined by our wise government back in Washington."

"You don't sound like you agree with their decision."

"I don't. There's room for all of us out here."

"Why were the Indians confined?"

"Because," he remembered his plan and quickly changed direction, "they rustle cattle and kidnap white women. Haven't you heard about the bloodthirsty Comanche?"

"Yes. I've heard about the rustling," she said. "I also read that the Indians are starving because all the buffalo have been killed . . . by white men. I don't know about the kidnapping, but I don't believe that you'd put me in danger."

Matt turned toward her and said seriously, "Being kidnapped by Indians is a fact, Lily. Any woman out here is afraid, or she should be."

"Maria wasn't afraid," Lily said.

"You don't understand. Maria was part Comanche."

"I know, Jim told me."

"Did he tell you that her father was a Yankee soldier who sent her back east to school, to learn to be a white woman?"

"Apparently she learned."

"Oh yes. She learned . . . too well. When she came back here, she was always unhappy. And after they married, she was always nagging at Jim to take her back east where no one knew about her past."

"But Jim didn't want to go?"

"I was never sure. He felt responsible for our being in Texas. Because he'd convinced me to come, he wouldn't leave me to shoulder the entire burden of the ranch. I let him think that. I'm sorry for that now."

That didn't surprise Lily. Matt probably felt as much guilt over keeping Jim in Texas as Jim felt for not taking Maria away.

"Aunt Dolly always says you can't live with guilt. It only grows."

"I'm sorry Maria never learned that. She hated her shame over her Indian heritage. But she hated being part Indian even more. For years she hid her heritage from everyone, pretending to be Spanish."

"I'm sorry it had to be like that," Lily said softly, better understanding the woman who'd given birth to Emily and Will. "And the children? How do they feel about their Indian blood?"

"Emily's too young to understand. But Will does. After Maria died there was some trouble with the town children calling him 'Injun.' Jim stopped sending him to school in town. He decided to send Will to the reservation for private tutoring instead."

"What kind of education does he get there?"

"Allen Kilgore is the Indian agent, and he teaches the children, too, though he stays in hot water over that. Folks think that the more ignorant the Comanche are, the easier it is to take advantage of them."

"In the future that won't be necessary," Lily said. "I'll teach Will."

"You're going to weed the garden, do the cooking, sewing, feed the stock, care for Emily, and teach Will?" Matt smiled skeptically. "I don't think so, Lily."

"I'm already cooking—not well, but it's getting better. I can feed the stock—"

"With Jim's help."

"And I gave Emily a bath."

"Yes, you did that."

She caught the odd inflection in his voice. "Why shouldn't I?"

"No reason. Emily just isn't real fond of water."

It hadn't taken her long the night before to figure out Emily's reaction to water. A discussion was required about the purity of angels and how they were dismissed if they didn't exist in an aura of cleanliness before Emily reluctantly agreed to get in the water. Washing her hair was another matter.

"But she let me give her a bath," Lily said nonchalantly.

Matt looked doubtful. "Emily willingly *let* you bathe her?"

"Well . . ." she hedged, ". . . we did have a small disagreement about the necessity, but once I let her hold my bath soap, she decided to try it. She wanted to smell good, like an angel."

Lily smelled good, like flowers, Matt decided. Maybe all angels smelled like flowers. They seemed to have some connection with lilies, if he remembered his churchgoing days.

Lilies.

Angels.

Maybe Emily was getting to Lily with all that angel business. The scent of Lily was sure getting to Matt.

The bath. Matt's mind cut back to the previous evening, re-creating the sight of her standing in the doorway, emptying the remains into the barrel to be saved for other uses. Unnecessary now, he guessed. But he couldn't seem to forget the years of hauling water for even the simplest chore and the parched earth of the previous summer.

And he couldn't forget how she looked standing there in the darkness, with the glow of lamplight behind her.

"I saw you emptying the water."

"I thought you did."

Dammit, she was getting to him, reaching him on a level he couldn't control, forcing him to see her, smell her, and create an image that wasn't real.

What was real was Lily standing in the mud in the pigpen, losing her shoes, complaining of the odor. Except she hadn't complained. The only constant grouch around the Double L was him.

His constant distraction by thoughts of Lily had to stop. She didn't belong here. She was no more equipped to be a rancher's wife than Maria had been.

Jim had fallen in love and married a woman of the West who should have been used to the hard living conditions out here. Matt didn't have to try to imagine what kind of life Lily had led back in Tennessee; he knew. Lily would have had a private maid who did nothing but make her life pleasant. There would have been a seamstress, a cook, house servants to clean, a gardener, a washerwoman, a coachman. Lily might have been taught to sew a fine seam, but an entire garment?

Matt hadn't been there, but he was sure that when the hotel business improved, Aunt Dolly would have provided Lily with riding instructors, piano teachers, and lessons in elocution and other skills required of a true Southern lady. He'd seen the results of that kind of schooling the moment Lily stepped off the stage. He saw it now.

"Do you come out here often?" Lily asked curiously.

"No, visiting is a luxury to a rancher," Matt answered.

Lily felt the intended prick of guilt at his statement. She was taking him away from his work. "You didn't have to do this," she reminded him.

"Didn't I?"

"I'll help when we get back this afternoon," she offered.

"If we get back this afternoon," was Matt's terse reply. "We may have to stay the night."

Lily blew a wisp of hair away from her forehead. "Stay?"

"It happens. When the Comanche entertain a guest, they expect you to feast and celebrate with them. It isn't like a picnic in town, but it's their custom. That's what you wanted, isn't it? To meet our neighbors?"

Something about Matt's body language as he drove said he was more alert than he wanted her to know. Maybe he was expecting trouble. Maybe the gunfire was more than just a hunter's random shot. He obviously wanted her to believe that she could be in danger, otherwise why all the warnings?

Lily was beginning to understand that Matt might have some kind of ulterior motive for making this visit. If he was going to introduce her to neighbors, why not the ones in town? Except Jim had told her that Matt had little patience with the attitude of the good people of Blue Station toward Maria, and knowing Matt's way of looking after people he cared about, she understood his preference for the Comanche. Still, she felt a prickle of unease.

"When we go onto the reservation, stay close to me," Matt warned. "Indians don't see many white women. And their idea of hospitality won't be what you're accustomed to back in Tennessee. They're friends, but you might not understand their ways."

Obviously he was trying to scare her. She refused to let him do that to her. He'd decided that if being a rancher's wife didn't scare her away, the threat of danger from the Indians would. Maybe she'd go along, just to see how far he'd go.

"You think they'll try to scalp me?"

"No. Women are too valuable for that," he answered seriously.

She adopted a wide-eyed, fearful look. "Then what do you think they might do?"

Matt turned toward her, letting his gaze travel up and

down her body. "I'll let you figure it out," he said in a voice that was deliberately cold.

Part of her wanted to gasp at the implication. The other, more rational, part admired his cleverness. The sad condition of the ranch hadn't sent her back to town. The hogs, while unpleasant, hadn't deterred her. She hadn't really learned to cook yet, but she would, eventually. And the children and Jim seemed ready to accept her.

Now Matt was counting on the unknown and her fear of it to do what nothing else had: force her to give up. Well, that wasn't going to work, and he might just as well understand. Instead, she'd give him something to worry about. It was only fair.

"I've never seen Indians up close, Matt, but I've read about them. Bringing me out here was a wonderful idea," she said enthusiastically. "You're right. I should learn about the people and the country where I'm going to live. Do I shake hands?"

"No." The word came out as a growl.

She reached into her pocket, pulled out her silk hand fan, and waved it vigorously. "Gracious, this heat is going to take some adjusting to, but I think you're right. Lighter clothes will help." She paused her fan and covered her mouth with it conspiratorially, leaning forward as she spoke. "Oh, when I was in town I bought muslin to make new drawers for everyone, including you."

Matt's flushed face was more than she'd hoped for. "You did *what?*"

"Bought material for new drawers . . . cooler drawers."

That did it. Matt was momentarily stunned. He sputtered. "This is serious, Lily. My bringing you to meet Rides Fast is a risk. If he should take a liking to you, he could ask me to—to share your favors. I'd have a hard time refusing him. You might keep that in mind instead of worrying about drawers!"

What in hell was Lily up to? She seemed wholly unconcerned about meeting Indians. Unless she was turning the tables on him, drawing mental pictures of something he couldn't allow himself to see.

He forced himself to think of Maria. He'd wanted Jim to be happy, wanted to believe that they could be a family. But he'd watched Maria's hopes dry up until there was nothing left, and Jim's joy turn into pain.

Matt regretted what he was doing to Lily. She didn't deserve it, but he couldn't let Jim and the children suffer any more pain. And he couldn't let himself take a city-bred wife, no matter how lonely he was.

Lonely? Where'd that come from? He didn't have time to be lonely. He didn't have time to spend half a day visiting Indian reservations either, but he was doing it. And, as far as he could see, Lily wasn't concerned in the least. Instead, she was rattling on about drawers.

"Like Tennessee mountain men, I understand ranchers wear long drawers year round," she was saying. "But I think you'll like what I have in mind much better. I just have to figure out the particulars." He saw her venture a quick look at him.

She was waiting for his response. He forced himself to relax the white-knuckled grip he'd fastened on the reins. "Forget the particulars," he said.

Matt flicked the reins sharply, forcing Racer into a gallop. His vocal urging to the horse didn't completely block out Lily's laughter. The wheels, bouncing over the clumps of range grass, brought any more conversation to a close.

As the sun beat steadily down on her, she wished again for a wide-brimmed hat like the one Matt was wearing and made a mental note to add that to her list of supplies the next time she went into Blue Station.

Even with the heat and the silence, the movement of the wagon was like one of Aunt Dolly's rocking chairs bumping over the warped boards on the hotel's front porch. Except on Aunt Dolly's porch she could see the mighty Mississippi. Here there was only a small stream and a vast emptiness. And the steady thrum of the drums. "How many Indians are there on the reservation?"

Answering her questions about Indians was safer than discussing his particulars. "Too many to live comfortably. But at least this reservation is better off than most. Because it was set up to be temporary, there are fewer Indians here. At the Washita reservation they have more land, but the government has herded Kiowa, Apache, and Comanche together. They expect them to put aside their differences and turn into farmers like white men. And they're fighting it every step of the way."

Lily frowned. "But not Rides Fast. He's learning to live like a white man. Still, that seems unfair since they were here first."

Matt couldn't stop himself from turning toward her. She was surprising him again. "There aren't many whites who feel that way."

"Not the people in Blue Station?"

"No."

"Maybe they're just afraid. People do cruel things when they're afraid."

Matt didn't want to think about that. It was too close to home. He didn't want to change his mind about the people in town. They'd shunned Maria out of jealousy because a woman with Indian blood had snared one of the two most eligible men in west Texas. And they'd let that disdain spill over onto the children. But Matt knew, and he refused to socialize with them. They didn't deserve compassion. He grunted an indistinguishable answer and flicked the reins once more. "People are what they're raised to be."

"Not always, Matt. People grow and change. Just look

at you, what you've done out here with the odds against you."

"Yeah, just look at what I've done. Damn little."

"I don't believe that. You've built a home and a future. And if you'd let me, I could help change the attitude of the townspeople. You stood up for me once, Matt. Let me do that for you."

Matt didn't answer. Lily thought she might just be getting to him, and she pressed the issue. "About the Founders' Day Celebration, Matt, I wish you'd go."

"I already told you . . . no."

"Well, suit yourself, but I'm going to the picnic, with or without you."

"Fine."

"If Jim feels well enough, I'm sure he'll accompany me. And I'll take Will and Emily. Social occasions are an important part of their education, and I won't allow them to be looked down on."

"Fine," he repeated.

Lily gave him a quick look and added, "If you don't want to live up to our agreement, you certainly can do whatever you like. But, Matt"—she reached out and laid her hand on his arm—"I wish you'd reconsider."

This time he brought Racer to a full stop. There was no anger in his voice as he said, "You might as well understand now, Lily. I have no intention of going to any celebration in town, now or ever."

She suspected he was simply being stubborn about changing his mind.

"This wasn't a good idea," he finally said. "But you insisted that I introduce you to our neighbors and present you in public as my fiancée, and that's what I'm about to do. But I'm afraid you're not taking this seriously."

A flush of outrage tinted Lily's cheeks. He really thought she'd be afraid, that she'd be ready to take the next stage back to Tennessee. "I'm not giving up, Matt. If the Comanche are your friends, they'll be mine."

"What if you have to choose between them and the people in town? I saw how it affected Maria." His voice softened slightly, "I wouldn't want it to happen to you."

Lily looked down at her hands, already showing the evidence of harsh soap and dishwater. "I was looked down on once, and I'll never accept that from anyone, ever again." She paused. "I don't know why you won't trust me, Matt. I'm still unwed because I waited for you. Is that so hard for you to understand?"

Matt shook his head. "You shouldn't have waited for me, Lily. I would never have come back."

"Yes, you would have. You think you're a different man from the one I knew back then, but you're not. Inside, you're still the same gentle, caring person."

"You're wrong, Lily. There's nothing left inside."

"I don't believe that. You just need to learn to be happy. Once we're married, I'll teach you. And I intend to marry you, Matthew Logan. You might just as well give up trying to scare me off."

He didn't answer.

A thin sheen of perspiration beaded her upper lip as the morning sun moved up the western sky. She opened her fan once more. In spite of the heat, cicadas sang through the prairie grass and wildflowers. Racer moved steadily along, scaring up a blue quail now and then. With no mountains or trees the land rolled away toward the horizon in swells of heat, until there seemed to be a veil of dusty blue in the distance.

They rode for a while in silence, the distant murmur of drums growing louder, though the reservation was not yet in view. Lily let the silence drag on as she searched the horizon, trying to regain some sense of composure.

A spindly legged bird with a long black, white-tipped tail darted out of a clump of grass and raced ahead of the wagon, breaking the spell of silence that had fallen over them.

"What's that, Matt?"

"A roadrunner."

The bird suddenly stopped short, used its tail like a rudder, and turned back, soaring across the prairie inches above their heads.

Lily watched the bird until it disappeared, then turned back to check their progress. "I've never seen one before. And those?" She pointed off to her left. "In Tennessee we called them buzzards."

"In Texas we call them buzzards, too." Matt frowned and pulled on the reins, turning Racer toward the circling birds.

"Matt, what is it?"

He yelled at the buzzards, chasing the one on the ground away, and climbed down from the wagon. "A cow," he said. "One of ours."

"How'd it get out here?"

He glanced at the ground and the chewed-up grass around it. "I think it may have had help."

This time whoever had killed the cow had made no attempt at blame. It hadn't been dead long enough for the flesh eaters to attract others to their prey. Two arrows protruded from the cow's chest. A closer examination showed that they'd been fired into fresh bullet wounds. Damn! He'd been so preoccupied with Lily that he'd paid little attention to the gunfire he'd heard earlier. Something must have scared off the shooter before he could cut away at the carcass. Racer and the approaching wagon could have stopped the butcher.

Or the drums.

Matt climbed back on the wagon and stood on the seat, studying the surrounding rangeland. It didn't make sense for anyone to shoot a cow so close to the reservation anyway, unless whoever it was wanted blame to be cast on the Comanche.

He'd chosen his spot wisely. A line of cottonwoods just ahead and to the right bordered the stream that flowed through the reservation. Still, there was a trail, bent grass left by horses, herding other cattle toward the trees.

Rustlers? Maybe, but why kill one cow?

"What's wrong, Matt?"

Lily's voice was calm, but Matt could no longer ignore the potential danger. Reluctantly he flicked the reins, forcing Racer into a brisk trot. He'd get Lily to the reservation, then he'd go after whoever had killed one of his cows. "I don't know yet. But I'm going to find out."

Lily held on to the sides of her seat with both hands, trying not to bounce off. A dull glow in the distance turned into the orange flames of campfires, and the drumbeats intensified. He could tell she was finally beginning to worry.

"I don't know whether those drums are welcoming me, or announcing that the tribe is going on the warpath," she said. "But until you know, I'd just as soon you didn't hurry."

From the cottonwood along the stream, the rider watched Matt's hurried ride. For a moment he'd been afraid that Logan would come after him. He could always outrun a man in a wagon, but he didn't want to take a chance on being recognized. He rode through the small herd he'd gathered, covering his tracks, then pushed his horse into the stream. Logan would follow him here, but maybe, with a little luck, he had time to get away.

Turning back, he pulled his whip from its strap on his saddle and unfurled it, then snapped it against the haunch of the nearest steer. The frightened animal dashed away in the opposite direction, drawing the rest of the herd with him. Quickly, the rider whirled and rode downstream, using the water to cover his escape.

He'd managed to kill only one of Logan's cows, but one might be enough. All he wanted to do was remind the rancher that his range was no longer safe. From the pace the wagon was setting, he could assume that Logan understood the message.

The rider let out a sigh of relief and rode swiftly away. If Logan hadn't elected to get the woman to safety, there might have been a confrontation. A confrontation could have ruined everything.

Then another thought came. If this didn't bring the results he needed, Logan's concern for the woman might.

The lone rider smiled.

8

Suddenly, a party of Indians splashed across the shallow stream and, amid a cacophony of raucous yells and screams, charged toward the wagon.

Lily screamed.

The riders laughed riotously, surrounded and fell in beside the wagon. "Greetings from our chief, Rides Fast, friend, Matthew Logan," the obvious leader of the welcoming committee said, then turned his attention to Lily, grinning and exchanging comments with his associates in their language, accompanied by much slapping of thighs and laughter.

Matt's sudden sharp comment, spoken in Comanche, brought the ribaldry to an immediate stop, and the Indians pulled their curious attention from Lily and turned to Matt.

Now Lily was really worried. It was obvious that whatever Matt had said was more startling than Lily's appearance. Their conversation continued until they reached a well-trod path that led across the creek and into the center of the village.

One of the Indians slid from his saddleless horses and

watched as Matt drove the wagon into the encampment and climbed down. He took the reins of one of the Indian's ponies and climbed on.

"Lily, stay here. The women will look after you until I get back."

"But Matt, I don't speak their language. What will we talk about?"

"Well," he said with a hint of a grin, "if all else fails, you can show them your fine lawn underwear." With that statement he rode off, taking the welcoming party with him.

"Wait! Where are you going?"

But he didn't answer.

The Comanche women hung back, stirring food over open fires or caring for the children who hid shyly behind their legs. They all stared at Lily, but they did not speak. The women had short hair, rather than the braids Lily had seen in the picture books. Covering their bodies completely were long voluminous cloth tunics embroidered with flowers or animals.

It was the men in the village who were dressed magnificently. They wore earrings of silver and gold. Their hair was plaited into two queues that hung down below their waists. Into the braids were woven bright strips of cloth, fur, or feathers. Shirts of animal skin hung open over breechcloths drawn from the front to the back and fringed with silver and beaded ornaments. They wore tight leggings that reached from their moccasins to their waists. A few were bare-chested.

"Hello," she finally ventured. "My name is Lillian—no." Lillian Townsend would never make it out here. "Lily." From now on she was Lily Towns, the woman she'd always been. She held out her hand, prepared to shake hands with the woman leading a small group of the curious. To her surprise, the woman slapped it away, reached out, and tugged viciously on a strand of Lily's hair.

"Ouch!" she cried, then realized her mistake as two other women also pulled her hair.

"Now just a minute," Lily snapped. "Is this the way you welcome someone to your home?" She glanced around, growing angry at Matt. He probably arranged the entire episode just so she'd be frightened.

The scoundrel. He'd known what would happen. He warned her about the men. He could have warned her about the women. He hadn't. It would serve him right if she embarrassed him before his *friends*. If being nice was pulling hair, she could do it with the best of them. Before the women surrounding her knew what she was about to do, she reached out, grabbed two handfuls of coarse black hair, and yanked.

Then she let go, lowered her right hand to grab the right hand of the woman standing before her, and proceeded to give her an exaggerated handshake.

"Hello," she repeated, pointing to herself again. "My name is Lily." She reached into the pocket of her skirt, withdrew the silk fan, and handed it to the woman.

The Indian woman examined the fan, spreading its accordion length open, then closing it. Seconds later she grinned, exposing two missing front teeth.

"Welcome, Lily Towns," she said. "My name Little Hen, first wife to Catbird Who Squawks."

"Catbird Who Squawks? Kitty?"

Little Hen spoke broken English, but apparently the others did not. After much gesturing, Lily understood that she was to sit on the ground near the fire in front of one of the tepees. As if it weren't hot enough. She glanced in the direction Matt had disappeared with the others and decided that she was on her own.

"Thank you," she said to Little Hen, and sat down as best she could, a feat that remained almost impossible, considering the stricture of her skirt and the torture of the bustle beneath it. At that moment she decided that it was time she changed her attire. Matt was right. Out here, comfort was foremost. Fashion seemed a million years away.

"Your house . . . home?" Lily questioned, pointing from the tepee to Little Hen and back. If they'd allow her inside, she'd remove the hateful appendage.

The woman nodded, gestured to herself, and back to the tepee. Lily then patted her chest and pointed toward the dwelling. A puzzled expression crossed Little Hen's face.

Once again she indicated that Lily was to sit.

"Well, if you won't let me go inside and take it off," Lily finally said, "I'll just have to get rid of this thing out here."

With that she backed up against the tepee, put her hands underneath her skirt, unfastened the wire bustle, and let it fall. "There."

The women chattered in shocked wonder as she stepped out of the fabric-covered device and one of her heavier petticoats, dropping them both to the ground.

Little Hen approached the bustle as if she expected it to spring to life and attack. She poked it with her toe timidly at first, then more forcefully. When it didn't react she reached down and picked it up by its ties. The other women crowded around, examining the object curiously.

At first Little Hen looped it around her waist and walked gingerly about, frowning as it bumped against her bottom. Then she smiled and placed the round frame on top of her head, retying the strings beneath her chin.

The oohs and nods of the other women seemed to indicate that this was acceptable. Little Hen grabbed the petticoat and ducked into the tepee, returning moments later holding out a string of small blue-green stones.

"Take it," a feminine voice said in perfect English. A light-skinned woman appeared from behind Lily and came to sit beside her. "She thinks you brought her a gift, and she's returning your kindness."

Lily took the necklace and placed it around her neck, smiling as she said, "Thank you, Little Hen."

Little Hen and the others crossed their legs and sat in a circle, beginning with Lily and ending with the woman sitting beside her.

"You speak English?" Lily asked the newcomer.

"Yes."

"And you're white. Why are you dressed like an Indian?"

"I am an Indian. My name is Kianceta. I was captured by the Apache when I was ten years old. Rides Fast, the chief of this band of Comanche, stole me. I've lived with them ever since."

"But the Indian agent . . . Mr. Kilgore, can't he help you escape?"

She laughed lightly. "You don't understand. I don't want to escape. Rides Fast adopted me. He is my father now, and Mr. Kilgore is my husband."

Lily didn't know what to say. She could only stare in amazement at the beautiful woman dressed like the other wives. She'd been warned about what happened to women stolen by Indians, and yet this one stayed by choice.

Kianceta went on, "And you're Matthew's wife?"

"Eh . . . no. I mean, not yet."

"But you care for him deeply. I can see it in your eyes. And he cares for you."

"I wish," Lily heard herself saying. She felt an understanding in this woman and the possibility of friendship. Perhaps it was because Kianceta told her what she needed to hear, or perhaps there was something about the woman that drew Lily's confidence. For whatever reason, she trusted Kianceta, and she badly needed to talk to someone.

"If he cares so much for me, why would he drop me here and ride off like some kind of crazy man?"

"I'm not sure, but I think he's after the man who killed his cow."

"Oh." Lily felt foolish. "I'm sorry. I'm too preoccupied with my own problems. But, I just don't want to go back to Tennessee."

Kianceta looked at Lily curiously. "And Matt wants you to go?"

"Yes. I'm afraid I'm not what he wants."

The other women continued to talk around them, touching Lily and her dress.

"You do not please him?"

"That's putting it mildly. He's furious that I've come."

Kianceta smiled and took Lily's hand. "I think that you are wrong, Lily. I think that Matthew is very drawn to you. Perhaps he does not know how to be with a woman like you. He is a man who conceals his feelings, except with the children. Tell me how you came to be here if he does not wish it."

Lily found herself telling Kianceta how she came to Texas expecting to wed the man she'd fallen in love with when she was a child, only to find out the proposal had been sent by Jim.

"Jim? I don't understand."

"Oh, he slipped the letter in with some other correspondence so that Matt didn't know what he was signing. Matt didn't know about me until I got here."

"But you came. Why?"

"Because . . . because I believed that when I grew up he'd marry me. I know it doesn't make much sense, but I waited for him to come back. When the letter came, I thought he was sending for me."

Kianceta nodded. "That is the way of love sometimes. Once a woman chooses, she closes her mind to all others. Men are more practical."

"Apparently Matt is. He doesn't believe that I can be a rancher's wife."

"But you think he's wrong," Kianceta observed.

"He's wrong."

"So now you must prove to him that you are worthy of being his wife," Kianceta said, pursing her lips thoughtfully.

"I'm not sure that anything I do will prove that."

"Then perhaps you're going about this the wrong way. Love is a matter of the heart, not deeds performed. Maybe you need to make him desire you so much that he forgets to look for your shortcomings. Once he is truly bewitched, he will love you. And you will be what he needs."

"Is that the Indian way?"

Kianceta laughed. "No, that is the woman's way."

"How do I bewitch Matthew Logan?" Lily studied the native women who sat quietly now in their circle, watching and listening. Obviously they respected Rides Fast's daughter.

"Tonight we will have a celebration of welcome in your honor, Lily. Tonight you will observe and learn the way of the Comanche women. But first we must prepare you."

By late afternoon Matt had returned and joined the men inside Rides Fast's tepee to smoke and hear any news. Matt knew Lily would expect him to check on her, but that would have to wait. Finally, when the pipe was emptied, cleaned, and put away, the chief signaled that the time for talk had come.

Matt tried to keep his attention on the old Indian, but his mind kept drifting back to Lily. He hadn't expected her thoughtful observations about the Indians. On the drive over, she'd seemed more interested in the Comanche than frightened. And after her initial scream, she'd been calm when the welcoming party surrounded their wagon. Mired in mud, covered with flour, or planting her bustle on his wagon seat, nothing stopped her. But then, nothing about Lily was working out the way he had planned.

Now, instead of worrying about not catching the man who was killing his cows or paying proper attention to Rides Fast, he was being distracted by thoughts of Lily's bright smile, her coquettish glances from beneath her parasol, and her determination to prove that she was a Texas woman. He forced himself back to the present, shifting uncomfortably and attributing the heat to the closed tepee and the presence of so many men inside. He glanced enviously at the bare-chested warriors. The Comanche had the right idea. No shirts. No wool drawers.

Drawers.

He groaned silently. She actually intended to take *his* measurements, to sew drawers for *him*. Lily had a way of capturing his thoughts and diverting them. Matt shifted his knees. It didn't help.

He was further tormented by what might be happening outside.

He wondered how she was surviving the curiosity of the women. He had heard no screams or loud voices to indicate the crisis he'd expected. Knowing Lily, maybe he ought to be worrying about how the other women were faring.

Finally Rides Fast spoke. "Matthew Logan, you have come about the trouble?"

"Trouble?" He wasn't sure what the chief was referring to. He considered Lily trouble, but he didn't think that the Comanche would. An Indian would simply move Lily into his tent for a month. If their being together proved satisfactory, they'd consider themselves married.

"Trouble for you, Matthew," the chief said, "for your ranch."

Matt searched for his meaning. "You mean the dead cows?"

This time the chief frowned. "Cows? More than the one beyond the stream?"

"Yes, there've been others killed in the same way so that I would think Indians did it."

Rides Fast considered for a moment, then said, "I know nothing of dead cattle. No, my friend. It is the man with a woman's skirts who brings trouble."

Matt glanced at Kitty, who merely nodded. "What man who wears skirts?" Matt asked.

The chief looked puzzled. "He has not come to you?"

"About what?"

"He covets your land."

Now Matt was really confused. "I don't understand."

The chief studied Matt for a moment, then said to Kitty, "Take Logan to Kilgore. Kilgore will explain."

Kitty stood and waited outside for Matt to follow him. Matt glanced over at the circle of women squatting before the tepee of Little Hen, Kitty's first wife. He searched the circle until he found Lily. She looked wistfully at him for a moment, then quickly turned away and engaged the wife of Allen Kilgore in conversation.

Matt hesitated. He'd expected Kianceta's life with the Indians to bother Lily, but from what he could see, they were getting along just fine. Leaving her to find the man who'd killed his cow had been a necessity. But now, he was uncomfortable with leaving her behind while he visited Kilgore. This new information about a stranger who coveted his land was as disturbing as the recent dead cattle, and he needed to find out more. He took one last look. It bothered him that Lily had adjusted so easily.

Kitty led him quickly across the village, past the center of the tepees and beyond, to a crude log house flying an American flag. As they approached, a thin, sandy-haired man came out to meet them.

"Greetings, friend," he said, and held out his hand.

Matt took it. "Kilgore, good to see you. Rides Fast said

you could tell me about some outsider who is here to cause trouble."

Kilgore nodded. "I'd intended to come over earlier this week and warn you, but the government supply wagons are late again. I don't dare leave until they come, or the drivers could short us more than they already have. Please, come inside."

Matt and Kitty followed the agent into the building that served as office, warehouse, and living quarters. The empty shelves that lined the walls stood testament to the village's need. Government supplies to the reservation rarely arrived on time, and were never enough to feed and clothe the entire reservation.

Kilgore poured three cups of coffee and handed one to each man, then settled down behind a battered desk. Kitty took his cup and stepped back, making it evident that he was simply there as an observer. Matt's coffee was hot, but weak. That Kilgore served the hard-to-come-by brew was testament to their friendship.

"I heard about your cattle. I don't know what to make of it. Doesn't make any sense," Kilgore began.

"Neither does a man in a skirt," Matt said.

"His name's McConner. From Scotland."

"Scotland? That explains the skirt," Matt commented. "I'm assuming he wore his kilt onto the reservation."

"That he did. Caused quite a stir, I understand. But not as much as his mission."

"The chief said he wants my land."

"Yours and the reservation's. He must have somebody important in Washington listening because I received instructions to let him look the place over."

Kitty made a sound that announced his displeasure without speaking.

"Surely," Matt said with more than a hint of sarcasm, "our wise white fathers in Washington don't intend to sell government land to a foreigner. What do they plan to do with the Comanche?"

Kilgore looked troubled and sighed. "Move them to the Washita reservation."

"There are already too many Indians there."

Kilgore didn't have an answer. Both the politicians and the Indian agents had debated the problem often and long, with no resolution. Finally Matt asked the question that most worried him. "Why would a Scotsman want so much land?"

"For cattle," Kilgore answered. "He represents a group of outside investors who want to raise cattle in Texas."

Sergeant Rakestraw had mentioned conglomerates that were formed by wealthy foreigners to raise large numbers of cattle. There were already a few Texans, like Goodnight, who ran herds in the thousands. But for someone to take his land, the land that he and Jim had struggled to turn into the Double L? That couldn't happen.

Matt would have to find the Scotsman and set him straight. As a foreigner, McConner couldn't understand the ways of the free range, which worried him. The man Kilgore described could be a real threat to the Double L.

"If he's interested in buying my land, why hasn't he approached me?" Matt asked.

"I understand he's just looking over the area, trying to decide exactly what he wants, and how much it will take to get it."

Matt stood. "Even if I wanted to, I couldn't think about selling while Jim is ill. He's refused to go back east before. Selling now would make a mockery of Maria's death. Jim wants some kind of future to leave to his children. We've worked too hard, we can't give up now. Where's the Scotsman staying?"

"He's gone down to Austin. But he'll be back in Blue Station for the Founders' Day Celebration. I guess he wants to meet with Wells. You'll see him then."

"Wasn't planning to go," Matt observed wryly. It looked as though fate was plotting against him—in Lily's behalf.

"My wife heard that you brought your woman to meet us," Kilgore said, smiling. "The Comanche are planning a special welcome for her. They'll expect you to stay the night." He gave Matt a curious look. "Didn't know you got married."

"I haven't. Getting married is the last thing on my mind. All this is Jim's idea."

Kilgore laughed. "Marrying was the last thing on my mind as well. Kianceta decided, and before I knew what was happening, we were . . . together."

"Not me," Matt said emphatically.

He was uncomfortable with Kilgore's suggestion that a woman could have that much control over him. But he was more uncomfortable with the way his thoughts kept drifting back to Lily when he ought to be worried about the ranch.

Kilgore drained his cup and placed it absently on his desk. "I hear she's a real beauty."

For the first time Kitty joined in the conversation. "Logan's woman golden-haired. If Logan not want, Kitty pay many ponies for her."

"Lily is not for sale," Matt said emphatically. Not want Lily? That was the trouble. He did want her. He wanted her too damned much, and he didn't know how much longer he could conceal his need.

"I meant to speak no disrespect," Kitty said.

Matt looked at his old friend. "Don't worry. It isn't you who shows a lack of respect. It's me. I think I'd better check on my fiancée." He left the house and started back toward the village.

Damn his soul.

Jim had always accused him of being an old grouch. Now he'd turned into a snarling bear. All because of Lily.

First she set Jim against him. Matt didn't even want to think of what she may have done in town with her bartering. Now she had the Comanche bidding for her.

He was caught up in a Texas whirlwind.

Instead of Lily being out of place as he'd planned, she seemed to fit in everywhere. What was he going to do? Miss Lily Towns was surely the devil's handmaiden, sent here to make his life hell.

And she was doing a damned fine job of it.

"And," he added loudly, to no one in particular, "no matter what Emily thinks, she's no angel!"

He wondered who he was trying to convince.

9

The sun was a fiery orange ball resting heavily on the edge of the horizon as Matt walked back toward the center of the Indian village. Kitty joined him as he made his way to Little Hen's tepee.

The women had disappeared. He couldn't see them, or Lily. What had they done with her? To worry Lily, he'd warned her that their idea of welcoming a white woman might be different from what she'd expect. But he was the one who was worried now.

"You tell chief about dead cows. There were other dead cows, Matt?" Kitty asked.

"I found two of our herd slaughtered. Whoever did it only took enough of the meat to make it look like they'd been killed for food."

"But you don't believe it?"

"I don't know what to believe, Kitty. Rustlers would have stolen them to sell—alive. Indians would have taken the whole animal for food. It doesn't make any sense."

"You think it man in skirt?"

"I can't figure out why he'd kill cows. That's not going to make me sell him my land."

"Maybe it's sign," Kitty suggested.

Matt thought about what he'd just learned. "Or maybe it was a warning."

"You think somebody is trying to scare you?"

"I don't know, but if so, I'm going to have to make it clear that it's not going to work."

"How you do that?"

"The first thing I'm going to do is go to a picnic."

Kitty looked puzzled. "I don't understand this . . . picnic."

"The celebration held by the people in Blue Station."

Kitty nodded and smiled. "Celebration? Yes. We hold celebration for Matt's wife."

"Not my wife," he corrected sharply.

Kitty only smiled.

Inside Little Hen's tepee, Lily had stopped smiling. Exchanging her dress for the embroidered tunic worn by the Indian women hadn't been so bad. Except the tunic was scandalously short. Removing her chemise and drawers had given her cause for concern, but the loose garment was certainly cooler and the moccasins were a definite improvement over her own shoes. Finally, in spite of her concern, she began to appreciate the freedom of movement.

But when the women had her sit on the floor, and then began to weave feathers and beads into her hair, she decided they were going too far.

"Kianceta, do you really think this will work?"

"Do you mean will it make Matthew feel desire for you?"

Lily blushed. "I don't know what I mean. It seems almost like I'm actually getting married."

"No. In the Indian ways, this is part of the choosing. The woman presents herself to the man, and he either responds or he does not. She cannot ask, but this will tell her how he feels. The marriage comes later."

"And you think Matt will respond?"

"In his mind, Matthew has a picture of the woman he believes you to be. Only you know what that picture is and only you can change it."

She knew all right. First she'd been a skinny little girl held together by freckles. Then he thought she was a silly woman who was nothing more than a fashion plate. She couldn't be certain what he thought now, only that he was determined to send her away.

"When you change this picture," Kianceta went on, "Matt will be confused. A confused man forgets to hide his true face."

"I'm not sure I can convince him otherwise, even by wearing your lovely dress."

"You don't have to do it by yourself. Everyone will help."

Lily was beginning to feel apprehension. "I don't understand. How will everyone help?"

"You'll see," was Kianceta's mysterious answer.

Finally Little Hen stood back and smiled broadly, motioning the others away. "Good." She reached into a pouch hanging from the frame of her tepee, and pulled out a mirror with a handle, extending it toward Lily.

Lily took it. Worried now, she held her breath and looked.

The woman staring back at her was a stranger. She was mysterious, almost mystical. Around her neck hung the string of blue-green stones that turned her already green eyes even greener. Her lips were a soft peach color, and her hair hung down her back in a thick braid interwoven with beads and feathers. Lily decided that if Matt was as affected by the change as she, anything could happen. She just wasn't sure how she wanted him to react.

Life had been so different back in Tennessee. In the

beginning she'd been shunned. Then later, when she'd started to mature, the men of Memphis had started taking notice of her. In spite of her questionable parentage and Aunt Dolly's Yankee husband, they'd swarmed around her. But she'd turned them away. Matt had been the only one for her. She'd used her suitors to make herself over, for Matt.

For the Matt she remembered.

In the past ten years, she'd become a different woman, without considering that the years and this hard land would make Matt a different man. He'd been a gentle boy, forced into adulthood by the horrors of war. Then later, he'd had to take on the responsibility of running the Double L. Now he was as hard as the land he was trying to tame, and she couldn't seem to get through that hard exterior.

Lily looked at the women waiting expectantly, and smiled. "I don't know what to say."

"Neither will Matthew," Kianceta said. "Now, you must wait inside until I call for you. Then step out and follow the path."

The women backed out of the tepee, carefully closing the flap behind them. Inside, the shadows hid the corners, and Lily knew that it was growing late. She tried peering out through the crack between the flap and the side. She could see a large fire blazing in the center of the village, sending tongues of red-orange dancing into the early evening sky. The smells of cooking food and wildflowers filled the air.

Where was Matt?

The drums started again, slowly at first, then intensifying, changing the beat. As Lily watched, the men entered and began a slow shuffle around the fire. Their faces were painted, their clothing brightly colored and decorated with stones and the shells they'd traded for from the coast. Their moccasins made a rough, sliding sound against the hard-packed earth. Finally they came together, forming a circle. At the closure of the line, the men froze in place. The drums picked up the rhythm, and the dancers began a series of thrusting and parrying movements that seemed to portray some kind of imaginary hunt.

Lily could hear conversation and laughing. She thought one of the men speaking was Matthew, but the chief's tent was just out of her field of view and she couldn't be sure.

She wished for Aunt Dolly. She wished for Jim and the children. She wished for her shotgun . . . just in case.

Just as she was about to push the flap aside and run out of the tent, the men dropped into squatting positions around the perimeter of the circle and the women appeared, having shed their long fringed skirts. Their movements around the fire produced bell-like sounds that added urgency to the beat. After several turns around the circle, they formed an arrow with the point leading to Little Hen's tepee.

Once again the drums' pulsating rhythm changed, rising to a rapid beat that became a crescendo of sound. Then suddenly the drumming stopped. Kianceta jerked back the flap to the tepee, and Lily forced herself to step forward into the light.

All conversation ceased.

Across the open space, Matt caught sight of Lily and was stunned. She looked around frantically for a moment before she found him. Then she moistened her lips and smiled. He drew in a sharp breath in response to the unconscious movement. She straightened her shoulders proudly, lifted her head, and stepped forward.

The women standing beside Lily took her hands. Like the ribbon carriers at a Tennessee Maypole dance, the women began to bob and weave, pulling Lily first in one direction, then in another, as they moved around the circle to the beat of the music.

"Close your eyes," Kianceta whispered. "Let yourself feel the music of the night. It will move your feet and reach out to Matthew, calling him to you."

Closing her eyes was the easy part. She couldn't look at Matt any longer without revealing her growing desire. At first she felt like a fool, standing there in Kianceta's dress, feeling herself being manipulated by the pattern of the dance. Then, responding to the drumbeat, her body began to absorb the rhythm and step in cadence to the sound. Lily didn't know how long they'd moved when the drums suddenly stopped.

"Now, open your eyes, Lily," Kianceta said.

It took Lily a moment to regain her senses and comply. As her eyes focused, she realized she was standing directly in front of Matt.

"Lily?" he said in a tight voice. "You're beautiful."

His eyes never left her. Full, high breasts strained against the buckskin fabric of her dress. She crossed her slim, pale arms over her chest and swallowed hard, revealing that she was as caught up in the moment as he.

"Sit," commanded Rides Fast, as he pointed to the vacant place beside Matt. "We will make celebration in honor of our friend and his woman."

Kianceta urged Lily gently toward the space, helping her to sit on the ground. Sitting cross-legged in the tunic exposed much of her legs, and she tried in vain to pull it over her knees, then gave up and simply waited.

"Do you know what kind of dress you're wearing?" Matt asked in a low, strained voice.

"It's Kianceta's," she said, not allowing herself to look at him.

"It's also a Comanche wedding dress," he said, surprised at how his pulse raced. His mouth was dry, and he knew that whatever happened the following day, tonight he was seeing the woman Lily had promised him she'd grow up to be—not the grand lady, the real woman inside.

A man's voice began a haunting song.

Shocked, she could scarcely speak. "Wedding dress?" Her heart beat faster. "I didn't know."

"Don't look at me like that, Lily. Your eyes tell me things better left unsaid."

"What do they say?"

"That you're ready to share my tepee."

"And your eyes?" she whispered. "What do they say?"

"I don't think you want to know."

But she did. She needed to hear him give voice to the longing she saw there.

Little Hen and the other women brought pots of food to the chief and the others sitting beside him. Kianceta handed Lily a wooden bowl, moving forward to whisper in her ear. "Remember, Lily, he must see you in a different light. Make use of this opening to his soul. Offer him drink to soothe his mind and repeat the words I am about to speak." Lily took the bowl and nodded.

Kianceta turned to Rides Fast, holding out a second bowl. She spoke first the Indian words, then repeated them for Lily. "As a sign of my obedience, I bring you this drink of the spirits, my father."

She stood back and waited, her message clear. Lily was to copy her action.

As if in a dream, Lily held out the bowl. "As a sign of my—" she couldn't say obedience—"friendship, I offer you this drink of the spirits, my . . . my . . ." What was he? She dared not put a name to this fragile connection, for she truly did not know what it was. "Matt."

Matt hesitated, then took the bowl, his entire being focused on Lily. He'd attended special ceremonies before, but never one like this. Kitty had confided that outsiders were rarely allowed to participate. Were it not an insult to his host, Matt would have changed his plans and taken Lily back to the ranch that night.

Rides Fast looked at Matt and Lily, then lifted his cup

in the air in a toast. Lily couldn't understand his Comanche words, but when the other men lifted their vessels, Matt joined them. Each man took a sip, then handed his cup to the woman beside him. Matt did the same, motioning to Lily that she should drink.

The first swallow made her mouth pucker, and she blanched for a moment; then after a glance at Matt, she drained it. Curiously, her thirst remained only partially quenched, and when Kianceta brought new cups to them, she didn't refuse.

Matt accepted a dish of food, which he tasted, then, selecting a morsel of meat, offered it to her. Time seemed to stand still. She opened her mouth and turned her face so that she touched her cheek to his hand.

A shiver ran through her as her lips brushed his fingertips.

"Are you cold, Lily?" Matt slid closer.

She thought she nodded. As their thighs touched, the muscles of her stomach clenched and ripples of heat raced through her. "I mean, no. Suddenly I seem to be getting warmer."

"So am I. Must be the chief's special elixir. He says the spirit world speaks to us. It makes us reveal our true selves and put away masks of deception."

His eyes were as dark as the night sky, catching the dancing firelight and keeping her prisoner. A passageway to his soul, Kianceta had said. "How does it do that?" she asked breathlessly.

"Look around."

She forced herself to look away and saw all the men swaying in rhythm to some unseen music. They seemed more vibrant, more alive. Then the drums began again, and both the Comanche men and women rose as one and moved around the fire. They stood so close that they could have touched. Instead they began to move sideways, stepping together, twisting their bodies in a teasing motion.

The intensity of their connection gave off such heat that Lily felt it permeating her body. When her cup was filled again, she drained it without thinking, more aware of Matt than she'd ever been as they sat beside each other, barely touching, her body aching to be closer.

"Join us, Lily," Kianceta said, stopping before them. "It is time."

Almost as if she were sleepwalking, Lily rose and stepped into the circle. She held out her hand for Matt to join her. The dancers waited, moving their feet in place. They were waiting for him.

"Dance with me, Matthew," Lily invited softly.

Matt stood, shaking his head in disbelief as Kitty made room for him in the circle. Then they began to move. The dancers' arms hung loosely beside them. Their clothing brushed against their partners'. Their breaths intermingled, but they never touched.

"You're very different tonight, Lily," Matt said.

"And do you like this Lily?" she asked, leaning closer to be heard over the low chanting of the dancers.

"Yes, God help me. I do."

Lily looked at Matt. He was the same man he'd been from the moment she saw him in Blue Station, but his usual anger seemed to be gone. Instead, there was a hunger about him that was almost hypnotic. He was dark, male, intense. Even his scent was distinct. She knew that years from now she would be able to close her eyes and recognize this man. Her breathing came in short breaths, and her legs could barely support her. Desperately she moved closer, allowing their garments to brush against each other with every step.

With each shuffle step around, the drumbeat changed, becoming more seductive, more enticing, until suddenly the drums stopped, and their dance ended. The Comanche dancing continued after they had taken their seats, but she and Matt only watched.

As the night wore on the dancing grew more frantic, and the sounds of the dancers rose and fell as some left the circle and others returned. The open desire between the Comanche men and women became more obvious, increasing Lily's awareness of the man next to her. She tried desperately to focus on something else: the children, Jim, Aunt Dolly. Matt was right. She'd never known what real passion was until now. She wanted him, but deep inside she knew that Rides Fast's elixir wasn't the way. If he changed his mind about marrying her, it should be because he wanted Lily Towns, not because he was caught up in a fantasy. And if they proceeded now, she'd never truly have all of him. She had always been the dreamer. Now she had to break the spell or risk losing Matt forever.

"I think we'd better go, Matt," she said, or tried to say. Her tongue seemed suddenly thick.

"Go?" he repeated, as if he didn't understand.

"Yes."

Lily turned to the chief. "I thank you for the lovely celebration, but we are leaving now. We've a long ride ahead of us."

"No! You stay. Have tepee ready for Matthew's woman."

"Tepee? I'm sorry, but we have to get back to—to the children." She was suddenly desperate. "Please, Matthew. Will you take me home?"

Home. Matt liked the sound of that. He stood carefully. He'd drunk the chief's elixir from the spirits before. Though he'd paced himself, he still felt the effects. In his rational mind he knew that Lily was right, but he was caught up in the vision of her dancing seductively around the fire. Did she even know that the dance had been one of invitation? All he really wanted was to carry her off and find the tepee Rides Fast had made ready for them.

But he realized that would be a mistake.

"Let's go," he said.

Lily tried, but her legs refused to support her. "I can't," she finally said weakly. "My body seems to have decided to stay. Please help me."

Matt knew that touching her would be a mistake. But there was no other way. Drawing in a deep breath, he took her hand and pulled her to her feet, too hard. She fell into him, grabbing him around the waist to keep from collapsing.

"Oh, hell!" Matt groaned.

Lily couldn't even stand. The feel of Matt's body pressed against the length of hers took her voice away. Without her chemise and petticoats, she felt as if she weren't wearing anything at all. Every line of his body was imprinted on hers. She could feel his chest rise and fall as he breathed. She instinctively moved closer.

"Matt," she whispered, her voice heavy. "Matt . . . I feel so strange, so warm. Do you think I'm coming down with a fever?"

"You have a fever all right, and I think we'd better get out of here before we both do something we'll regret. Hold on to me, Lily, and I'll try to get you to our wagon."

"My clothes, Matthew. I ought . . ."

"You ought never to have taken them off." He turned her around and with one arm around her waist, walked her away from the dancers to the horses tethered by the stream. When they finally reached the wagon, Matt propped her against the wheel and let her go. Lily began to slide down the side.

He grabbed her, pulling her back into his arms. "Stand up, Lily. I have to hitch up the horse."

"I don't think I can."

Her breath felt like fire against his chest, left bare by his open shirt. He didn't remember unbuttoning it. When he'd grabbed her to stop her fall, he'd caught a handful of fabric, drawing her tunic above her knees. He had to get his other arm beneath her to lift her into the wagon. That hand, operating on its own, reached around, touching first her bare bottom, then sliding down to her knees. Bracing himself against the wagon, he leaned down and picked her up. That brought his chin to her chest.

His lips to her breast.

"Put your arms around my neck, Lily."

As she did, her nipple brushed against his lips. There was no mistaking the pucker of the hard little bud. Nor was there any mistaking Lily's moan.

"Oh, Matt."

"Ah, hell," he swore, his blood boiling white hot. He let her knees drop, pinning her body against the wagon with his while he took her lips.

With the kiss, Matt lost all attempt at control. Desire flowed between them and seemed to wrap around them like a second skin, until he was ready to explode. Like ignited gunpowder, his body felt a shock that flashed from his head to his toes.

Even as he was kissing her he knew it was wrong. She was moaning softly and moving against him as if she were trying to get inside his clothes. This was a mistake, a mistake that could have disastrous consequences. If he made love to her, he'd have to marry her. If he kept her overnight at Rides Fast's village, he'd have to marry her whether he made love to her or not. She was right, they had to get home.

Matt forced himself to think of the children, of Jim; to remember how Maria had hated her life on the ranch. Drawing on his last ounce of willpower, he pulled away. "Forget the wagon, Logan," he told himself.

"Matthew? Kiss me again," Lily invited, pressing closer.

Matt fought for control of his body. It had been too long since he'd been with a woman. A little longer and he wouldn't be able to stop. Still cradling her, Matt whistled.

As Racer responded, Kitty suddenly appeared in the darkness.

"You go?" Kitty asked in disbelief.

"I go. Will you bring the wagon? It's too much trouble now." Matt asked, pushing Lily into Kitty's arms while he mounted Racer. Kitty nodded, and together they managed to lift her up.

"Matt," she whispered, and with a big smile slid her arms around his neck, laid her head on his chest, and went to sleep.

The ride was pure torture, the longest return trip from the reservation Matt had ever made. Lily's skin smelled like bath soap, intensified by the heat of their closeness. Her hair, soft and silky, tickled his chin. The feel of her breast against his rib cage and her bare legs moving against his thighs as Racer cantered across the plains made him know that his need for Lily had reached far greater proportions than he wanted to admit. His plan had backfired. Once again it became clear. The whirlwind intensified. He was the one who was trapped.

Matt had to find a way to send Lily back to Tennessee before he gave in to his desire. He had to keep her from knowing that he wanted her. Wanted to feel her body beside him when he waked. Desire wasn't enough. Desire didn't last. Neither did dreams.

Then he remembered Kilgore's words. *Suddenly I was with Kianceta.* Even as he wrestled with his desire, he realized that this was what Lily and Kianceta had planned. The witch. Kianceta knew that once they'd made love he was honor-bound to marry her. Well, that wasn't going to happen, no matter how much he might want it. The throbbing hardness against the seam of his Levi's was his punishment. It would remind him of what he'd almost done.

When he reached the ranch, he rode Racer into the barn. Using the last of his strength he lifted Lily and let her slide down into the pile of hay. She didn't wake. From the amount of Rides Fast's elixir she'd put away, she'd be lucky to be awake by tomorrow night. Matt could have stopped her. He'd paced himself, while he let her learn the hard way.

But he hadn't thought this far ahead. Now he had to protect her from being discovered by the children. That meant Miss Lillian Townsend had to spend the night in the barn. He'd slip in the house before they woke and get her some clothes.

After Matt unsaddled Racer and turned him into the corral, he pulled a horse blanket from the stall wall and covered Lily.

If he went inside, he'd have to explain everything to Jim. That was, *if* he could explain. He might not be as far gone as Lily, but he wasn't sure he wanted to face Jim now.

Better for him to sleep in the barn as usual.

He looked down at the woman asleep in a beam of moonlight. Somewhere along the way she'd lost her moccasins. Her hair had come loose from the braid and spilled across her shoulders like a shower of gold. A half smile tugged at her lips, and even in sleep there was a magic about her.

"And that's another thing you have to learn, Miss Lillian Townsend," he said. "Any rancher's wife would know not to drink liquor. And she'd know not to get a man riled up, either."

He lifted the blanket and crawled in beside her. As she turned and moved naturally into his arms, he knew it was going to be a long night.

Lily groaned and tried valiantly to open her eyes.

Tried and failed.

There was a roaring sound setting off waves of pain. Her head was going to explode, and there was nothing she could do to stop it.

Something seemed to be poking her thigh. A rough hand caressed her breast.

Hand?

Her eyes flew open. Where on earth was she?

It was almost daylight and the smell of animals was strong. A prickly itch attacked her bare legs.

Bare legs?

She tried courageously to focus. She was in the barn, lying on her side in the hay. Beneath her thigh she could see a man's long tan fingers encircling the buckskin dress at the spot where her breast was throbbing painfully.

A man?

Forgetting her pounding head, she skittered away, then tried to identify the man who'd been fondling her so intimately.

"Matt Logan," she said hoarsely, "what have you done to me?"

He opened his eyes, smiled that familiar, quirky, devil-take-it grin she remembered so well, and said, "Nothing, Lily. I've been a perfect gentleman, even if you did ask to be ravaged."

"I did no such thing." She grabbed her head as fresh waves of pain washed over her and blurred her vision. In truth she couldn't be certain of anything. Except for some vivid dreams, she didn't want to remember. Last night was pretty much a blur. She remembered being dressed by Little Hen and the others. She remembered following Kianceta's instructions and dancing with Matt. Beyond that, everything seemed clouded in a fog that still made her body weak.

"No? You lie in my arms, your leg across my body, your lips against my chest. I call that an invitation. You asked in every way a woman asks a man. I only responded. What did you expect?"

She gasped, jerking herself farther away. "I didn't expect anything, certainly not that I would wake up in a barn with you!"

Matt raised himself to his elbows, knowing exactly how she must feel and sympathizing in spite of his own mixed emotions. Maybe he should stop her before she roused the children. Maybe he should let her know how much she'd aroused him. He never should have taken her to the reservation. No, damn her, he thought. She deserved this and worse for the hell of sexual frustration she'd put him through last night. He might just as well give her more to think about.

He reached out and touched her nipple with his fingertip. "In spite of your plan, I swear I didn't accept your invitation. But, my little witch, you are very good at seduction. However, being good at seduction isn't on my list of requirements."

Lily attempted to stand, caught her head, and cried out, "Ohhh! You and Rides Fast's elixir. I thought you said they were welcoming me. Your friends tried to kill me and you—you—low-down son of a coyote, you let them!"

Matt wanted to laugh, but he was too strung out with his own emotions to follow through. "And I suppose you had no ulterior motive in wearing that dress. Where are your fine lawn drawers now?"

Splitting head or not, Lily gritted her teeth and started climbing down from the pile of hay. By the time she reached the floor she knew she'd made a mistake. She was barefoot in a barn built for horses.

Too late to do anything now but keep moving.

The only other choice was to lie down and die. If death was her fate, she wouldn't leave this world with hay and feathers in her hair, and manure between her toes. She headed toward the house.

"Lily Angel, Lily Angel!" Emily's shrill voice shattered Lily's composure. "My daddy made pancakes. Do you want one?"

She held out a mangled pancake, offering it to Lily. Lily could only groan.

"Did you sleep in the barn with Uncle Matt?"

"Yes," she snapped. "Sleep is exactly what I did."

Jim appeared in the doorway, a towel about his neck to catch the dripping water from his face. His eyebrows lifted when he caught sight of her. "You all right, Lily?"

"Of course." If she moved very, very slowly, the pounding was reduced to a dull roar.

But Emily wasn't going to make it easy. "Why are you walking so funny? Where are your pretty shoes? Daddy doesn't let me go barefoot until summer. And where did you get that dress? Kianceta has a dress like that. She showed it to me once when she came to look after Mama when she was very sick. Could you make me one like it?"

Lily reached the porch and caught hold of the post holding up the roof. "Emily, sweetheart, do you think you could be very quiet for a minute? I seem to have a headache."

"Hangover, you mean." Matt's amused voice corrected her.

At that moment Will rounded the corner of the house. "Uncle Matt! Uncle Matt! Come quick."

At the urgency in his voice, Matt broke into a run. "What's wrong, boy?"

"It's One-Eyed Jack. He's in the pasture. I saw him. He's headed this way. And he looks really mad."

Lily groaned. "Company? Please, God, not now. I can't entertain anyone now."

Matt glanced at Lily's white-knuckled grip on the post and ignored his conscience. This opportunity was too good to pass up. "Lily, take Emily in the house and bar the door. I don't know what One-Eyed Jack will do."

In spite of her pounding head, Lily heard the concern in his voice. With the little girl in tow, Lily went inside, dragged the wooden bar across the door, and dropped it into its fittings. She closed the inside shutters except for a small sliver through which she could peek.

"Do you see him, Lily Angel? Will says Jack only has one eye," Emily whispered, still holding the pancake.

"Not yet, Emily." Lily wanted to say, Don't talk. Don't move. Don't even breathe. She wanted to ask who Jack was, but the smell of food was beginning to make her queasy. Her stomach groaned ominously. She was going to be sick. She swallowed it down. *If I don't think about it, I won't embarrass myself.*

The sound of pounding hooves matched the dull pounding in her head. One-Eyed Jack must not be alone. He must have brought his gang with him, she thought. Then she saw the biggest bull she'd ever seen charge into the middle of the yard, and come to a sudden stop. He was rust-colored, with horns as long as a room. As if he knew she was watching, he strode toward the porch and stopped directly opposite the window.

"It's One-Eyed Jack," Emily whispered. "It's really him."

The turmoil in Lily's stomach was quickly escalating. "You mean Jack is a cow?"

Emily giggled. "No, silly. He's a bull. Uncle Matt says he's the biggest, orneriest, meanest bull in the state of Texas. I guess he's come to marry our cows."

Lily was beginning to wish she were behind the house instead of inside it. Her stomach had the same idea. The situation had become urgent. Swallowing weakly, she prayed that Jack would move out. He didn't, so Lily finally did. She lifted the bar, dashed out the front door, and leaned her head over the porch rail. If Jack had evil intentions, he'd just have to wait.

By the time Lily had emptied her stomach, Jack had stopped opposite her. He seemed to be watching curiously. Behind her, Lily heard Emily chattering brightly. Seconds later she felt Emily cling to her leg, peeking out at the bull.

"What happened to your eye, Jack?" she asked. "Does it hurt? Do you want some of my pancake?"

"Emily," Lily said quietly. "Step back slowly, into the house."

"But Lily Angel, I want to see the bull."

One-Eyed Jack was breathing hard, moving his head back and forth so that he could watch Lily and Emily.

"Don't move," Matt called out. "Don't spook him."

No one moved.

The standoff continued, the bull watching and Emily chattering. At that point Lily reached the end of her patience. She reached down and took the pancake from Emily and threw it toward the bull. It landed in the dirt at his feet. He sniffed, looked down at the mangled food, then back at Lily.

"Lily, what are you doing? Get back inside!" Jim yelled from the barn. "Use the rifle, Matt, before he kills them."

Jack might be a killer, but at the moment he was more interested in Emily's breakfast. When he leaned down to sample it, Lily slowly pushed Emily back toward the door and into the house. Standing down a bull wasn't on Matt's required list of accomplishments, but protecting Emily was.

Jack made no move toward the cabin. Instead, he gave one last snort and backed away, turning his head so that his one yellow eye glared back at her one last time. Then he turned and ambled leisurely away.

"Miss Lily." Will charged around the corner of the house where he'd retreated.

Jim started toward her. "I don't believe it."

"Neither do I." Matt's voice was tight with anger as he came up on the porch. "What in hell were you doing? If I'd had to shoot Jack, I might have hit you . . . or Emily."

"Throwing up," she said as another wave of nausea washed over her. She grabbed the doorframe. She wasn't about to faint now, she told herself even as the sky seemed to tilt.

It was Matt who picked her up and carried her into the bedroom. "Don't fool around, Lily. You're not going to faint. You're too tough for that."

"How do you know?" she managed. With her cheek against his chest she could feel the rapid beat of his heart.

"I know that Jack has killed a dozen men who've tried to catch him, and you took him on. You may be Tennessee's second-biggest fool!"

He was angry, but she heard his concern. "Second-biggest fool? Who's the first?"

"According to Jim, if I don't marry you, I am."

"Jim's a very smart man, Matthew. Now take me to the loft and go away. If I'm going to die, I want to do it in peace."

"No loft this time. You need to be where we can watch you for a while."

Lily closed her eyes as her head hit the pillow. Being close to Matthew was what she'd wanted, but her response to his body was too much. Matt wasn't the only fool in the room, and he certainly wasn't the most stubborn.

When Matt pulled a quilt over her, Lily sighed. Her future husband might not know it, but when he'd danced with her last night she knew she'd found a small chink in his defenses. She knew now the dream she'd had last night was real. She'd touched him during the night and she'd known the degree of her success. Now all she had to do was make the chink in his defenses bigger.

She didn't believe he wanted her to leave now. He'd put her in Jim's bed. That meant he was concerned about her. Whatever had put the concern in his voice, Matt had let her see his true face. Now all she had to do was make him see it, too. She wasn't certain how to go about that, but she was sure she'd find a way.

For now, the Founders' Day Celebration was coming up. She had to devise a way to get Matt there. The Indians didn't touch when they danced, but a waltz could be entirely different.

As she drifted into sleep, the memory of being in his arms came back. She'd thought she was dreaming. He thought she didn't know what she was doing last night. They'd both been wrong, Lily decided. Matt would soon discover the next step in her plan. There were lots of possibilities.

10

Jim waited for Matt outside the bedroom. "Is she all right, Matt?"

"She doesn't think so now, but she'll live."

Jim looked at Matt reproachfully. "What happened, big brother?"

Matt looked at Jim's frown, saw his wan face, and decided not to tell him about the dead cow. For now, he'd keep the information about the Scotsman quiet, too. "Nothing much. Lily just did a little too much celebrating."

"And that's why she came to the house with a hangover and hay in her hair? I don't believe you, Matt."

"Believe me. She got the hangover from too much of Rides Fast's elixir, and the hay in her hair from sleeping in the barn. I thought it would be better if she didn't come inside . . . in her condition. The children wouldn't have understood." Matt looked around. "Speaking of the children, where are they?"

"I sent them to feed the chickens. Don't try to get out of this, Matt. Lily leaves here wearing her best afternoon gown and comes back half-intoxicated, wearing a buckskin wedding dress with hay in her hair."

"There was no wedding, Jim. Kianceta just loaned Lily her dress. I swear it."

Jim leaned against the table. "What I want to know is whether I should *arrange* a wedding before Lily pulls out her shotgun?"

"Hell no! I already told you I'm not getting married. When you get better, you can take a wife." But his statement was just an automatic response. Even he didn't sound convinced.

Jim sighed. "Why are you being so stubborn? No matter what you say, marrying Lily is a reasonable solution to the problems we're facing."

"I have too much to deal with to take a wife. Certainly not a wife like Lily."

"Matt," Jim said carefully, "Lily is nothing like Maria."

Matt scowled. "But she is. And she'll want to leave, sooner or later. And I don't want the children to see her turn into a bitter, unhappy woman."

Jim took a long, measured look at Matt. "I knew Maria didn't want to be a rancher's wife, but I thought loving her would be enough; that, once we were married, she'd give up her idea of going back east. I always thought the people in Blue Station would have accepted her if she'd given them a chance, but she couldn't stand them knowing. Back east, she felt like she was as good as anyone else."

"I never understood why she thought the people in Blue Station judged her."

"Neither did I. I thought I was being strong by staying here and building our future. I know now I should have taken her back east. Matt, we all have our regrets and we all share the guilt."

Matt felt suddenly sick. He hadn't looked at it from Jim's point of view. "You should have gone. I should have made you."

"Texas was my idea, Matt. I couldn't leave you because life was hard. At least I had Maria and the children. Now you have someone. Lily."

"Lily?" He groaned. "Lily with her fancy dresses and silk parasols?"

"Yes, Lily, who doesn't let a wild bull intimidate her. Lily who puts herself between that bull and Emily. You're wrong about her, Matt, and you're too stubborn to admit it."

"She's got you flummoxed, Jim. If Maria couldn't survive, what makes you think Lily can?"

"There is a big difference," Jim argued. "Maria didn't want to be here. Lily does."

Matt took a deep breath and slowly let it out again. "You loved her, Jim, and she knew it. And once she learned you weren't going back, she tried to be a good wife."

Jim nodded. "Yes, she did, didn't she? But I know the truth, Matt. In the end, I don't think she cared; she just gave up."

And after she died, so did you, Matt wanted to say. He should have seen what was happening. But he'd refused, because he wanted his brother with him in Texas. And the weight of his selfishness fell heavy on his shoulders. It wasn't Maria's fault. But it had been easier to blame her than accept his own part in what happened to them.

Jim said softly, "Don't be a stubborn fool. If you let Lily go, you'll lose something special."

Matt knew he was being stubborn. He knew it better than anyone. But that was the only way he'd gotten through the hard years. The only way he'd been able to live with Jim's illness. The only way he'd survived facing the responsibility for Maria's death.

"Maria wanted to be a lady so much that she forgot how to be a survivor, Jim. In the end, it killed her."

"And because Lily is a lady, you think she won't make

it," was Jim's reply. "You're wrong. Lily is beautiful and smart and passionate about what she wants. And she's as stubborn as you."

She's passionate, all right, and damned irresistible, Matt thought. He'd learned that last night. He shook his head.

"What's really the matter, Matt? You can't fool me. You like her."

"I do like her," he admitted. "It's just that Lily Towns is as dangerous as One-Eyed Jack. In fact, she's a lot like him. All the years we've been here we've tried to entice him to visit our herd, and that bull has avoided our cows like they were poison. Now, Lily arrives, and suddenly he turns up in our front yard."

This time Jim grinned openly. "I think you're the one who's like Jack." Then his expression changed. "What did happen in the barn?"

Matt swore and pushed past his brother. "Nothing happened in the barn," he said through clenched teeth. "Nothing!"

Matt slammed out of the house and headed toward the barn.

He was sorry now nothing had.

Unless that was what she'd counted on.

That thought left him reeling. The witch! What if her innocent touching of his body in the barn had been deliberate? He was the one who'd set up the afternoon to accomplish his purposes, but his plan had backfired. Instead of sending Lily back to Tennessee, he was the one storming furiously across the yard. Not only that, but he was going to take Lily to the Founders' Day Celebration.

Not because of Lily, he told himself. He was going to the celebration to confront the Scotsman. And if he had to play the part of fiancé, he'd have to make the sacrifice. He could dance with Lily; it was the touching and the courting he might have trouble with. Unless he figured out a way to turn the tables on her. Courting and touching worked both ways.

Yep, this could be a way of getting back at her for turning his life into a hell of frustration. He might create consequences for his intended that she hadn't counted on. Nothing else had worked. Maybe he'd change tactics and just torment the hell out of her. He'd make certain she appreciated all his talents.

So what if dancing wasn't one of them?

Lily heard the bedroom door open and groaned quietly. She just wanted to be left alone. Maybe if she kept her eyes closed the intruder would go away.

"Is Lily Angel still sick?" Emily asked in a whisper.

"Nah. She's just sleeping," Will whispered back.

"But it's time to eat. I'm hungry." Emily's voice was plaintive.

"Shush, Emmie. You're going to wake her. Uncle Matt said she got her wings clipped and she needs time to mend."

"Lily don't got real wings, Willie. I looked to see."

Will nodded. "Come with me, Emmie, and let her sleep till she's feeling better."

"No, Willie. I have to stay here with her." Emily's lip trembled.

"What can you do, silly? I don't see why you're so upset."

"Because . . . because, I don't want her to die and go to heaven like Mama."

"She's not dying," Will said in a strangled voice. "Uncle Matt promised."

There was a sound of a scuffle, followed by a sniffle that Lily couldn't ignore.

"Come here, Emily," she said, holding out her hand.

Seconds later there was a thud, and Emily's small body slammed into Lily. "Easy, Emmie."

"You wake up now, Lily?"

"Will? Emily?" Jim's voice brooked no argument. "Come out here right now."

Instantly the weight of Emily's body disappeared and the door slammed, leaving a thrumming echo in the room. Lily tested one eye, forcing it open. She groaned and closed it quickly. She felt as if someone were holding a bright torch in front of her face.

If everybody who drank Rides Fast's special brew was as sick the next day as she was, she couldn't imagine why they'd seemed so willing to take part. Matt had to have known the potent aftereffects. Why hadn't he warned her? Because he wanted her to make a fool of herself. Well, she'd done a good job of that. If she lived long enough, she'd make Matt pay.

If she could just manage to sit up.

And open her eyes.

Inch by inch she forced herself upright, every movement setting off arrows of pain. Finally, she was sitting on the edge of the bed. She slowly opened her eyes again. The torch appeared to have moved slightly so that she focused on the bare legs in front of her.

"Ohhh!" she groaned, wincing. She stared at the legs until she could identify them as her own. They were as bare as the rest of her body. The beautiful Indian wedding dress was gone. "Where are my clothes?"

Then she remembered. Her own clothes had been left behind in Little Hen's tent. When they left the reservation, she'd been wearing Kianceta's dress. She didn't want to think about how she'd reached her present state.

Groaning, she pulled the quilt from the bed and draped it around her shoulders. Marshaling all her strength, she stood and grabbed on to the bedpost, her limbs as liquid as the honey Kitty had brought. She had other clothes in her trunk. All she had to do was get to it . . . if the floor would just stop moving.

"Be still, you varmint," she threatened the trunk that seemed to be sliding back and forth by the floating wardrobe. "Or I'll take you out to the barn and shoot you with my shotgun."

"Try not to kill any of the furniture," Matt's amused voice responded.

She hadn't heard him come in. Her senses were so scattered that for the first time she hadn't even felt his presence.

"What happened to my dress?" she demanded.

"I didn't think you'd want to sleep in it . . . after your little episode on the porch."

Lily closed her eyes and bit back another groan. He'd undressed her, and she hadn't even known. The tension between them escalated.

"Let me help you, Lily," Matt finally said.

"You've already helped me enough."

"No, I haven't. And I should have." Two strong hands clasped her shoulders and turned her back toward the bed. "I don't suppose you'd believe me if I said I'm sorry."

"No, I wouldn't. And don't talk so loudly."

Matt lowered his voice to a whisper. "Sit down and I'll bring you whatever you need."

Lily let herself be pushed back to the edge of the bed. "Fine. I'll take a new head."

"Sorry, don't have one. Ask for something else."

"Some water, a wet cloth, my chemise, and drawers."

"Are you particular about the order?"

She had to put some distance between them. "The only thing I'm particular about right now, Matt, is proving to Emily that I'm not going to heaven to be with her mama."

She heard an exasperated sigh.

"Just be still. I'll bring you your . . . drawers."

To prove her words, Lily straightened her shoulders and stood. "Never mind. I don't trust you." What she really meant was that she didn't trust herself. In the space of a few minutes everything had changed, and she didn't know how to react to this new, gentler Matt. "Just leave. I'll get what I need. Including a fiancé who doesn't try to kill me."

"I hate to tell a proper lady like you—"

"No," she interrupted. "I'm just plain Lily Towns, Matt, or I will be . . . if I survive. I'm sorry, Matt."

He'd been prepared for Lily's anger. For admonishments, perhaps for her even to threaten him with her shotgun. But the strangled threat of tears touched him in a way he hadn't counted on.

Before he realized what he was doing, Matt reached out and touched Lily's cheek with one finger, pushing a strand of hair behind her ear. "There's nothing plain about you, Lily Towns. It's me who should be sorry. I should have warned you about Rides Fast's drink."

Without thinking, she leaned against his hand for a moment, then raised her eyes to his face, struck by the tenderness she saw there. "Yes, you should have."

Matt smiled. "I'm sorry. And I did bring you home safe and sound."

"Did you? What about last night?"

"Nothing happened. I thought it was time that I kept you safe," he said, a welcome softness in his voice. "That's why we slept in the barn."

Lily didn't argue with him.

"We only slept," she said, trying to sound confident, but she heard the hesitation in her voice. As if she weren't quite sure.

"We slept," Matt repeated, "though if I were not a gentleman, the outcome might have been different."

"Why?"

"Because," Matt answered with a grin, "I didn't think you'd want Will or Emily to see you pie-eyed."

"I was not . . . pie-eyed."

He grinned at her again. She almost smiled back, until he added, "You were out of your skull."

She forced herself to step away from him, lest he see her weakening. She wasn't sure where this new tenderness was coming from, and she didn't trust him yet. "And I suppose you didn't plan to get me inebriated?"

"No, I didn't. I thought you'd run screaming into the night. Most—no, any other woman would have refused to take part in their celebration, Lily. You were magnificent."

Matt hadn't intended to say that. Until the words came out, he hadn't even admitted it to himself. But it was true. Suddenly his plan to torment Lily fell by the wayside in the wake of his admission.

He backed up until he was leaning against the wall, hanging his thumb in his belt as if that had been his intention all the time. Clearing his throat, he replaced the gentleness in his voice with an amused rebuke. "Of course I didn't expect you to take on One-Eyed Jack."

I wanted to keep you safe, he'd said. You were magnificent. He'd really expected her to faint or behave in some silly fashion. She hadn't, at least not until later. Still, he seemed to approve. She hadn't expected that.

Lily covered the flush in her cheeks by tucking the quilt around her and marching stiffly to the now still trunk. She reached inside and pulled out the first garments she touched, swallowed hard, then lifted her gaze to Matt in a dare.

When he didn't turn away, she fastened the quilt across her breasts and stepped into her best pair of fine lawn drawers, pulling them up and tying them at the waist. Turning her back, she dropped the quilt and donned her chemise, forcing herself not to react to his presence.

Why should she show any modesty now? He'd undressed her. He'd already seen every part of her body. Let him be embarrassed; she wouldn't be.

She wasn't certain she believed what was happening. For now, his abrupt, harsh behavior was gone. This man was a stranger, not the gentle boy she'd known, not the defeated one who'd returned from the war, and not the angry one she'd known during the past week. Maybe she was hallucinating.

Beyond the door, Emily's worried voice rose and fell, jerking Lily back to reality. Whatever might be happening between her and Matt would have to wait. Emily needed to know that Lily was all right.

"Thank you, Matt," she whispered finally. "I liked your friends, and I hope they'll come and visit us. But for now, you'd better go. I have food to cook and, according to my list, clothes to wash, a garden to plant, and a new apron to make for a little girl who needs to know I'm not leaving her."

An immediate wall fell between them. Matt's mouth was suddenly drawn into a grim line, and the illusion of new intimacy vanished. Reality had returned. Lily swallowed hard. So be it. At least she knew where she stood with the old Matt.

"The garden has already been planted," he said. "You just need to hoe out the weeds."

"Fine, I'll hoe out the weeds." Retrieving a dress from her trunk, Lily quickly pulled it over her head. That seemed to do the trick. Matt turned and left the room. As the door closed behind him, Lily let out a long breath and sat back down on the bed. She couldn't have stood a moment longer. And she couldn't have held back the tears of frustration.

"By the way, Matt," she called out, determined to let him know that she hadn't changed her mind, "get ready for the Founders' Day Celebration. I'm going with my fiancée.

If you don't want that to be you, I'll take Kitty. Kianceta said he made you a generous offer for me."

Lucas McConner stared in astonishment at the Greek columns supporting the upper veranda of the governor's house. "I was told that Texas was uncivilized and unclaimed. It seems I was misinformed on both counts."

Governor Hubbard bit back a sharp retort. This Scotsman wasn't the first outsider to run into the finer aspects of Austin society with surprise. Though he was the first one to do so wearing a kilt.

"You have to understand, Mr. McConner, the plains have always been shared. First the Indians hunted buffalo. Then when the buffalo disappeared, cattle took over. But every rancher uses the prairie freely."

"Aye, but much of the land is being used by men who don't own it. And sooner or later, that will end," McConner warned.

"No Texan is going to give up use of the range willingly. The Land Bureau may have approved your leasing Texas land, but you can expect trouble if you try to fence it." The governor looked grim.

McConner took a sip of his drink and looked out over the green lawns. The sound of music drifted from the house into the cool air of the Texas twilight. When he'd come to Texas to buy land, he hadn't expected this kind of evening or this kind of resistance.

"You know I have friends in Washington," McConner said.

"So do I, but they're a long way from Texas, and Texas has always made its own decisions," Governor Hubbard responded dryly.

"So you won't support me?" McConner asked, deliberately keeping his voice casual.

"I will not, and I have to tell you that I've made a

serious protest to Washington about their plans to close the reservation."

McConner frowned. "Look, I was told that Chemaw was never meant to be a permanent site. I'm only taking advantage of plans already made. You can't blame me for that."

"The people of Texas don't need any more outsiders claiming their land. And I can blame you for trying."

"But what about Mr. Goodnight? I understand he owns over a thousand acres, not counting what he leases or the government land on which he grazes his cattle." It was becoming clear to McConner that his mission was in danger.

"It's Colonel Goodnight," the governor corrected, "and he earned the right to every square mile he uses. If it weren't for him, his soldiers, and the Texas Rangers, we'd still be fighting Indians and bandits. You wouldn't understand about that."

McConner could have told the governor that he'd worked for Grenville Dodge. He'd engineered the building of the Union Pacific Railroad, fighting the weather, the Cheyenne, and the Sioux. When the Chinese were brought in to replace the workers who had deserted, it had been McConner's job to deliver them from California. He understood far more about the West than he wanted anyone to know.

"I noticed quite a few small farms on the way down," McConner said casually, "particularly around a little place called Blue Station."

"Ranches. In Texas, they're called ranches. And yes, now that we've got the Comanche and the Apache on the reservation, we're settling the northwest part of the state. Blue Station began as a stagecoach stop, but it's really starting to grow."

McConner drained the last of his whiskey. "I'm surprised at the number of cattle through that section. I wouldn't have thought they'd survive the drought last summer. I heard it was bad."

"Droughts come and go, but Texans and their cattle are tough, Mr. McConner. Now, I think I'd better see to my other guests. Come by my office one day, and we'll look at a map. There may be a few acres not claimed."

McConner nodded. He'd been warned that Texans were clannish. He understood that better than most. He'd never dreamed they'd refuse to sell for cold hard cash. But the first ranchers he approached had done just that.

He smiled. He'd just have to find another way. For now, he'd head back to Blue Station. Along the way, he'd do a little more looking around. Just to be sure.

He reached down, broke off a bare stem from a plant, and stuck it in the corner of his mouth. This time he'd look like a Texan.

"Lily, you don't have to make supper," Jim insisted. "I'll feed us tonight. Why don't you stay in bed until you feel better?"

She tied on the apron she'd snatched from a nail by the door. "I'm supposed to be pulling my own weight around here. Feeling bad doesn't stop responsibilities, Jim. You of all people know that."

Lily's voice was sharper than she'd intended, and when she caught the expression on Jim's face she was sorry she'd said it. Impulsively she reached out and caught his arm, the leanness of it registering as she tried to turn an awkward moment into something uplifting. "Jim, I bought peaches when I went into town. I want to make a pie for supper. Will you help me?"

Jim closed his eyes and drew in a deep breath, as if he were smelling the pie already. "Peach pie? You bet, I'll help. If you're sure you're up to it?"

She wasn't. But she intended to do it anyway.

Emily planted herself at the table, chattering brightly as Jim instructed and Lily carried out his directions.

Only during the moments when Emily was tasting the peaches did Lily manage to get in a question: "Tell me about Kianceta, Jim."

"Kianceta is her own woman. She chose her life. You know she adopted Maria as a sister. If it hadn't been for Kianceta, Maria would have given up a long time before she did."

Lily hadn't known that. "What about Maria's family?" she asked.

"Maria's mother, Night Wind, was the child of Rides Fast's half-Indian cousin. The cousin and his war party were killed by the army when they tried to steal military supplies from a supply train. The army sent a troop of buffalo soldiers after them, and Night Wind was wounded in the encounter. The soldiers had no trouble killing the men who were firing back, but Night Wind was a woman, a mixed breed who was more white than the others in the village. They took her back to the fort, intent on making her one of the fort women used for their pleasure. But Sergeant Rakestraw put a stop to that. By the time she recovered from her wounds, they'd fallen in love."

"Night Wind. What a lovely name."

"I was told that she was a lovely woman. But the wives at the fort never accepted her."

"I know what that is like, living somewhere you don't belong."

"Yes. Living at the fort was a problem, but being married to an officer was even harder. She was still a Comanche, and the Comanche attacked the soldiers at every opportunity. Once they were sent to the reservation, it should have been easier, but it wasn't. Night Wind was never comfortable. Finally, she gave up, took Maria, and went to the Chemaw reservation to live with Rides Fast's people."

Lily rolled out the pie dough, peeling it from the rolling pin where it stuck and mashing it back into the lump of dough. She'd seen Aunt Dolly's cook do this a hundred times. It hadn't looked so difficult. Learning about Night Wind made her feel better. She'd had as hard a time being a soldier's wife as Lily was having trying to learn to be a rancher's wife. Finally, she got the crust rolled out and pressed half of it in the bottom of the pan. After mashing it together where it had split, she cut the remainder into strips.

"Can I do it, Lily Angel?" Emily, leaning across the table, picked up a strip, stretching it into a long strand that broke.

"Of course, sugarplum. Lay it across the peaches."

If the strips were lumpy and uneven, Lily decided nobody would mind. After all, Matt didn't expect anything from her. This would be enough of a surprise so that, with any luck, he wouldn't complain.

"What happened to Night Wind?"

"When Maria was about five years old, Night Wind died of smallpox. Soon after that, Sergeant Rakestraw was called back to Washington. He took Maria with him. When the attack came on Fort Sumter, he put Maria in boarding school and took an assignment as western adviser to Mr. Lincoln. At the end of the war he was sent back to Texas as the commander of the new fort set up to protect the soldiers who'd been given land grants to settle the frontier."

"But Maria didn't like it here any more than Night Wind."

"No. But for different reasons. She'd gotten used to the comfort of the city. She was accepted there. Out here, even after all those years, she was still part Comanche. When new people came into Blue Station, they snubbed her. She couldn't live with the stigma."

"And because of Maria's death, Matt thinks I won't be

able to survive either," Lily said, blowing a strand of hair off her forehead. "Well, he's wrong."

"That's what he says, but I'm beginning to think that Maria doesn't have anything to do with his dragging his feet. I'm beginning to think part of Matt's trouble is that he's afraid you will survive; he'll have to marry you and let you inside that hard shell he's built around himself."

Lily wasn't sure what she thought about that. There was a hard shell around Matt right enough, but she couldn't see him letting her or anybody else break through. Though she didn't know quite how to explain his actions that morning. Her aching head made her decide she could better deal with Matt's change of heart in the morning.

Finally, they got the pie in the oven. By the time the smell of cinnamon filled the air, she'd put on a pot of beans. That and a pone of corn bread was as much as she could manage before she walked out to the porch and sat down on the bench beneath the window. Emily followed her, sitting on the edge of the porch, letting her legs swing over the side. The late-afternoon air swirling across the open yard was hot and heavy. There was a different feel to it today.

"I'm afraid to even think it," Jim said from behind, "but it looks like we might get some rain."

"That's good, isn't it?"

"Maybe."

An hour later she was beginning to wonder, too. Dark angry clouds swept across the sky, accompanied by brisk winds that tumbled small limbs and dried grass along the hard earth. Jim had taken the pie from the oven, put the corn bread in to cook, and moved the beans to the back of the stove to stay warm. Will fed the stock and began closing the barn doors and the shutters on the inside of the house.

Still Lily continued to sit. She ought to pick up the sewing box and attack the mending. There were still clothes to be washed and the garden to hoe. But until she saw Matt riding toward the barn, she hadn't known how worried she was.

"Uncle Matt!" Emily cried out, jumping off the porch and starting toward him.

"Emily, go back to the house. Lily, take her inside. Now!"

His words were swept up by the rough wind and carried away. Emily was almost blown away as well. Lily ran toward her, caught her, and turned back to the house, just as the rain began to fall.

Lily realized quickly the raw power and violence of a Texas storm. Will came inside, too, and it took both of them to close the door.

"Where's Matt?" Lily asked.

"Letting the pigs out of the pen," Will answered.

He and his father collected pots and pans to catch the rain leaking through the roof. Emily pressed firmly against Lily's side, immobilizing her. Beyond the house Lily heard the water rushing across the yard like a river. She didn't have to look out to know that it swept through the pigpen and into the corral beyond.

Will found a spot by one of the windows and peered intently through the crack in the shutters at the darkness beyond. The sound of thunder rolled across the plains as the rain slashed at the house, whipping against it, making the building groan and tremble. Emily started to cry. Distracted, Lily lifted her up and held her close.

Something cold and wet hit Lily on the forehead. The roof had sprung a new leak. Jim continued to empty the pans into the barrel by the stove. Soon water played a new song on the metal pans, the furniture, and the floor, the stove sizzling as drops spattered on the hot iron surface.

Unconsciously Lily hummed and rocked the child, all the while her mind was focused on Matt and the storm.

Where was he? Was he all right? Her stomach felt as if it were tied in a knot.

Then, just as quickly as it had come, the main fury of the storm was gone. Cautiously, Will opened the door, and they all walked onto the porch, Emily resting on Lily's hip. Jim leaned against the post, his forehead drawn into a frown as he searched for Matt, who was nowhere in sight.

The sun came out once more and the damp earth steamed.

"Where's Uncle Matt?" Emily asked.

"He probably went looking for the pigs," Will said, and started toward the barn. "One of the sows is ready to have babies."

Lily didn't know where Matt would put them if he found them. The pigpen was gone. Only the trough was left, overflowing into the already soggy ground beneath it. Lily could see no sign of Matt. She comforted herself by noting that Racer was missing, too. At least Matt wasn't alone, wherever he was. The big horse would bring him home.

They finally sat down to eat a cold supper, saving the pie until Matt came back. When time passed, and Matt still hadn't returned, Lily's concern grew. Finally, Jim decided that they couldn't look until morning and that they needed a good night's sleep. Will climbed the ladder to his sleeping place in the loft, and Lily followed, putting Emily down on her pallet. She lay down beside her but couldn't sleep. Finally, Lily gave up, wrapped her shawl around her shoulders, and crept down the ladder to wait.

The house grew cooler, and Lily regretted not wearing the pair of socks with the hole in the toe.

She made a pot of coffee. Matt had missed supper and he'd need something hot when he returned . . . if he returned before morning. Unless he decided to sleep in the barn. No, the barn wasn't the best choice tonight. She was reasonably certain that that roof leaked, too. Besides, he'd need dry clothes.

Lily filled her cup and dragged Maria's rocking chair next to the front window. She rocked as she sipped the hot, strong liquid, thinking about what had happened to her since her arrival. It seemed unbelievable that it had been only three days since she stepped off the stage. She'd been rejected by Matt; revered by Jim, Emily, and Will; and offered for by the Comanche.

Until this morning. Maybe she'd read more into Matt's concern. Was he fighting marriage because he didn't want a wife at all or because he didn't want her?

But then she remembered her list, the pigpen, Emily's dress, Matt dancing with her. She remembered the fleeting look of pride in his eyes as she'd taken part in the celebration at Rides Fast's village, and the way he'd felt when she awoke during the night with her head on his arm and her leg thrown across his thighs. Remembered the brief flash of tenderness he'd shown in the bedroom that morning.

That Matt was the one she'd come to marry. She just had to find a way to draw him out. This was her home now. She'd win the bet, and Matt would stop fighting her. Lily touched her cheek in the same place Matt had. She smiled, pulled the quilt over her, and closed her eyes.

A moment later she sat straight up.

Suppose he was dead?

"No," she whispered, "he wouldn't do that. I haven't measured his particulars yet."

11

As he rode into the yard, Matt could see Lily silhouetted in the window. She sat in Maria's rocking chair, a quilt draped around her shoulders, as if she were waiting for him.

He'd planned to catch a few hours' rest in the tack room, then head out again to look for the sow . . . until he saw Lily.

Matt reined Racer into the barn, removed his saddle, and let him go. The last thing Racer needed was more water, and the last of the winter hay was stacked in the corner of the barn in easy reach.

As if he were still caught in the aftereffects of Rides Fast's elixir, Matt was drawn toward the house. He stepped up on the porch and stopped outside the window, simply looking at Lily.

Her cheek rested on one cupped hand as her chest moved slowly up and down with each sleep-drawn breath. She was so lovely, so fragile, so incredibly appealing. Her golden hair lay loose across her shoulders, reflecting the lamp's glow like a streak of fool's gold he'd once seen. Like a miner desperate for a strike, Matt allowed himself to yearn for what the scene offered. Tonight, alone here with no one to see, he could let himself drink in the picture of what he could have if he allowed himself to marry this woman and make her his wife.

Lily, who smelled like wildflowers and danced like an Indian maiden.

Damn! That word again. Marry. He was surrounded by people trying to convince him that marriage was the answer to all his problems. Kianceta, Jim, and—even in sleep—Lily.

What was she doing, sleeping in that chair? Was she waiting up for him? His Lily was a woman who went after what she wanted in spite of everything he'd done to discourage her. He'd deliberately allowed her to think the worst. Granted, their larder was almost bare, but they had a herd of cattle that would feed them until their garden began to produce. Except now the garden was gone. Now he'd have to dip into his savings to buy food.

And the children did need more clothes. They were growing like weeds, and he knew it was time to hire the seamstress in town to come out. That would take more money.

But none of that seemed to deter Lily. Instead of throwing up her hands in defeat, she was waiting up for him. For a long, unguarded moment he allowed himself to watch her.

Watch, nothing more.

Finally, the lamp burned down, sending a wisp of smoke into the air as the flame died, closing out the picture, reminding him that he toyed with an illusion.

He was no dreamer. He was wet, muddy, and tired— too tired to face this kind of honesty. Daylight would arrive soon enough, and with it would come the reality of their situation. The rain had come, replenishing the range grass for now, but it had also come close to washing everything away. And he'd been unable to find the sow.

If he'd learned anything about Texas, he'd learned that

every season was a gamble. Who could tell about the long hot summer ahead?

What could he offer a wife?

Nothing but hardship and an uncertain future. Wearily he turned and headed back to the barn. No need to wake Lily. His own defenses had collapsed, and he was too vulnerable tonight to trust himself inside the house.

Inside with Lily.

The next day was Sunday. Except for Will reading a Bible verse at breakfast, it came and went with no change in the routine. Lily had never been one to relish her time at worship, but she found that she missed attending church. She prepared a simple meal of bread, cheese, and potatoes. Her joy in successfully making the pie had washed away with the storm, and, although Emily climbed up in Matt's lap and explained in detail how she'd *helped,* the lumpy crust and thick strips of dough seemed to catch in their throats.

By Monday the hot Texas sun had sucked up all the moisture, and Matt surprised everyone by announcing that he was sending Will and Emily on Racer to the reservation for lessons with Allen Kilgore. They'd gone for schooling periodically, but never on Matt's horse. Lily wondered, but she didn't ask. She knew Matt would never put them in any danger. Instead, she packed the rest of the breakfast bread and cheese and, whispering secretively in Emily's ear, gave it to the children "for a snack."

She watched them leave, the big horse moving slowly and carefully, as if he understood his responsibility. After they had gone, she gathered up their soiled clothing and heated a washpot of water to start on the laundry.

With the soap she'd bought in town, she washed their dirty clothes just outside the kitchen door in sight of the garden. Through the morning, she felt Matt's eyes on her, but each time she looked up he was nowhere in sight.

Once she rinsed her wash, she was faced with the task of drying it. Back home, their clothes went to the laundry house, with its boiling tubs of water, and finally to the lines where clean garments dried. Here there were no lines and no poles on which to string them, and with her small hands, she couldn't even squeeze all the water out.

Lily gathered up an armload of her clean clothes. The corral had the only fence in the area. It would have to be her clothesline. With a sense of determination and humor, she stretched out her drawers on the fence. As she hung the last shirt, Matt appeared in the corral, hitched up the mule to a plow, and drove him behind the house.

"What's he going to do?" she asked as she walked back toward Jim, who'd left his spot on the porch steps and was pulling on his boots and a flannel shirt.

"Looks like he's decided to replow the garden."

"Replow? But I thought the garden had already been planted. He said I was to hoe the weeds."

"Unfortunately the storm washed everything away, weeds and vegetables."

"Oh." Lily watched, chagrined that Matt was doing what he'd instructed her to do—work the garden. She had no intention of losing what she'd gained by letting him do her job. "Do you have an extra hat?" she asked.

"Maria left an old sunbonnet in the lean-to," Jim said. "It may still be there."

It was, though it looked like nothing Lily had ever worn before. She plopped the flowered creation on her head and tied the strings beneath her chin. "Will you show me what to do?"

"You don't need to do anything now, Lily. I'll plant the seeds. When Matt is done plowing, I'll show you how to hoe the weeds away."

"Jim, I know Matt expects me to fail. But I won't. I can work just as hard as he does, no matter what he thinks."

Jim grimaced. He hadn't agreed with Matt's treatment of Lily from the beginning. "I don't know what Matt wants anymore." Jim slung a seed sack over his shoulder and headed out to the garden.

Jim dropped kernels of corn into the still-moist earth.

"Is this corn for the hogs or for us?" Lily asked.

"Hogs first, I'm afraid. Then us."

Lily didn't know why she asked when she already knew the answer. "Please let me help, Jim," Lily said. "I don't know much about gardening, but I'm willing to learn."

"All right. You cover the seed."

Lily knew that Matt heard the exchange, but he never looked around. "Of course. I can do that." She reached for the hoe and fell in behind Jim, smoothing the earth across the row as he'd been doing.

By midmorning Lily's hands were stiff and sore, and her face was smeared with dirt. Though the ruffle of her bonnet covered most of her face, her nose tingled from the heat of the sun bearing down. Even the brisk wind blowing across the flat landscape and down the garden rows didn't help; it only picked up the layer of dirt on top and swirled it. Her back seemed permanently bent as she forced herself to keep up with Jim, who doggedly put one foot in front of the other.

Ahead of her, Jim suddenly stumbled, then fell to one knee and began gasping for breath.

Matt dropped the reins and came running. "Jim, you've done enough," he said with concern. "It's time to quit. We'll finish tomorrow."

"No, I need to help, Matt. The garden has to feed us," he protested between gasps. "Let me rest a minute, then I'll be all right."

"I said you've done enough," Matt insisted more softly now, including Lily in his worry. "Both of you. Look at Lily's face. She's as bad as you."

"I am tired, too, Jim," she said. "At least let's go inside and get a drink of water."

Matt nodded gratefully, helping Jim to his feet.

Lily couldn't be certain whether Jim agreed to go inside to pacify her or because he was exhausted, but the result was the same. For once, she and Matt, on either side of Jim, were a team. As they helped him to the porch, Kitty drove up in their wagon. Taking in the scene, he quickly climbed down, nodded toward Lily, and took Jim's arm.

"I see to him," the Indian said.

Once they got Jim inside, Matt unhitched Kitty's horse and turned him into the corral, then turned back to the garden. Lily followed Matt. This time she dropped the seeds into the ground as she'd watched Jim do, and covered them. When Matt reached the end of the row and headed back, he came to a stop alongside her.

"I thought I told you to get out of the sun."

"You did. You also told me I had to prove I could be a rancher's wife."

"You'll end up sick and I'll have to nurse both you *and* Jim. Stop trying to be something you aren't, Lily."

"Get back to the plowing, Matt, and leave me alone. I can do what I have to do, and sooner or later you're going to believe that."

Matt swore, picked up the reins, and slapped the mule's rear. Lily fell in behind him, resuming her work.

The sun rose higher. Kitty brought them water, but Matt didn't stop. Lily didn't stop either. She refused to look at her hands. She knew they were raw. Finally, when the handle of the hoe became blood-smeared, she stopped, lifted her skirt, and ripped the ruffle from the bottom of her petticoat. Grimacing at the pain, she wrapped her palms and fingers in the muslin and turned back to the planting.

Moments later two large gloved hands grabbed hers,

took the hoe, and slung it away. She looked up into Matt's frowning face.

"Christ, Lily. Look what you've done to yourself. Don't you have any gloves?"

"Yes, but not the kind that protect your hands."

"Come with me," Matt said, then yelled for Kitty to take the mule to the barn as he pulled her by the arm to the horse trough. "This is going to sting." He plunged her hands into the water.

Biting her lip, she kept from crying out by concentrating on her clothes, still on the corral fence.

Directly behind the garden, they'd caught the dust flung by the wind and were now streaked with dirt. She wanted to cry. Why hadn't she noticed? They'd have to be washed again. Another strike against her in her struggle to prove her worth. Why hadn't she moved them?

Why didn't Matt move away?

She was so tired that, for now, she didn't care. He seemed so angry that she'd tried to become the kind of woman he demanded.

"Keep them in the water," he said, "while I get rid of some of my dirt." He let go of her arm and stepped away.

She heard the ruffle of water at the end of the trough. And looked over to see Matt submerge his face, then rub it vigorously and sling the water away.

Matt came over to her, then swore. He untied his bandanna from around his neck and dunked it into the water.

"Your hands are bleeding and your nose is red as a poker!" His voice, angry at first, softened as he cleaned the streaks of dirt from her face. "What were you thinking of, working in the sun all day when you weren't used to it?"

He was doing it again, going from gruff to tender, keeping her off balance. "I was thinking of helping you plant the garden," she said, fighting the threat of tears.

"It's all right, Lily. Cry. I don't blame you."

"Damn you, Matthew Logan, what do you expect of me? I won't cry! A rancher's wife wouldn't cry." She swallowed hard. "She wouldn't! Like hell, she wouldn't," Lily said as she lost the battle and tears rolled down her cheeks.

"Stand still."

Matt rinsed his bandanna. Lily couldn't see the dirt on the bandanna as he submerged it in the water, but she could imagine what she looked like.

Matt studied her for a moment before shaking his head in mock dismay. "What you need is to stand under the water barrel and wash everything."

"In the daylight?" she gasped.

"Clothes and all," he replied. "Besides, the light is about gone. Nobody will see you. Come with me." He grabbed her hand.

"Ouch!"

He looked down at her cloth-wrapped palms and went silent. "Oh, Lily . . . Lily, I'm so sorry for letting you hurt yourself. I never meant for this to happen."

"It doesn't matter, Matt. Don't you see? I learned to plant . . . something. What were we planting anyway, besides corn?"

"We planted beans."

"Do the pigs get the beans, too?"

"Not if you want them. The pigs can eat roots."

Tenderly he lifted her hand and peeled off the wet wrapping as she gritted her teeth. Her palms and fingers were a bloody mess where blisters had formed, burst, and left raw spots.

"Come into the barn," he said, "while I get something to treat these."

"I have to see about Jim and supper," she argued wearily. "Are the children back yet?"

"They'll be home soon. Kitty will look after them. I have to do something about you."

"Don't, Matt. I'll take care of me," she said, making a move toward the house.

"How? With what? You'll just make Jim feel like this was his fault instead of mine. For once, Lily, let me make amends." But he didn't wait for her to comply. Instead he picked her up, striding into the cool, dark barn as if charging General Lee's line at the second Battle of Bull Run. He deposited her on the pile of hay and pivoted around. "Stay there. And don't get any hay in your hair, or Jim will send for the preacher."

She stayed. Not because she was following orders but because she couldn't have stood if she wanted. Her hands were ruined. Her nose had to be as red as Matt's bandanna, and the rest of her was a mess. She didn't want the preacher or anyone else to see her looking like this. And the dance was only five days away.

Her whole plan to dance with Matt was in jeopardy. He certainly wouldn't want to take her to the celebration the way she looked. He wanted a western woman, but her effort to prove she could be one was a big failure. She'd made a better Comanche, she thought wryly.

Matt returned with Lily's nightgown, a drying towel, and soap. "The children are here. They're fine. Jim's fine. Kitty will feed them and put them to bed. He'll stay for the night and watch Jim so that I can take care of you."

"Take care of me? That isn't part of the bargain, is it?" She groaned, both from dismay and at the effort of bending her fingers.

Matt studied Lily for a moment. "Turnabout is fair play," he said.

He didn't seem angry. If she hadn't known he'd lost his sense of humor, she'd have thought this was the old Matt teasing her. "Turnabout? I don't understand."

"Remember what you said that first day, about watching Jim and me in the river without our britches?"

"Yes," she said, not yet sure where he was going with that remark, but beginning to get a bit worried.

"Well, now it's my turn." He leaned forward and began to unbutton the front of her dress. "The wind blew dirt all over you. We've got to get this off you before I can do anything to treat your blisters."

Lily tried to shimmy away. "What are you doing?"

"I'm taking off your dress."

"You're doing no such thing. It wouldn't be proper."

Matt took a step back. "Lily, there is nothing proper about anything that's happened here since you arrived. You thought I wanted a wife, and you came out here alone. That's not proper. You're an unmarried woman, living with two adult men in the wilderness . . . alone. That's not proper." He reached back and continued his unbuttoning. "And like I said before, you're wearing too many clothes!"

She might have stopped him if she'd been able to use her hands. She might have called for Jim if she hadn't been afraid of getting him involved and tiring him. She might even have insisted on helping him remove her clothes if she hadn't felt a weakness in her limbs that threatened her ability to do so.

He threaded her arms through the sleeves of her bodice and unhooked the waistband of her skirt, lifting her bottom from the straw so that he could slide it down over her petticoats. When he reached for her chemise, Lily let out the breath she'd been holding, and raised panic-stricken eyes.

"I think this is far enough, Matt," she whispered. "There's no dirt on my chemise."

"All right." He knelt down and unlaced her boots, taking an inordinate amount of time. When he finally finished rolling down her stockings and pulling them from her feet, he gave her an uncertain look and lifted her again, carrying her from the barn. Outside, he glanced at the house. Lily realized from his expression that he knew she had probably watched him make use of the shower in the past few days.

"Can you stand alone?" he asked.

When she nodded, he let her go, opened the back doors to the barn, and propped them so they shielded the water barrel from the house. "I'll release enough water for you to wet your face and arms, then we'll wash and rinse your hair."

"We?" she whispered.

"We," he said calmly, leaving no room for argument.

The water had been warmed by the sun and felt wonderful. Lily turned her face up to it, letting it sluice over her.

Matt hung his hat on a nail on the door. Then, heedless of his own clothing, he stepped beneath the dripping barrel and began to lather a bar of soap into her hair.

Lily closed her eyes to shut out her overwhelming awareness of his presence. His fingers massaged her scalp, then moved down the back of her neck and over her shoulder, soaping the rest of her. He rubbed the bar across her chemise, circling her breasts, touching her with the soap instead of his hands. Even if she'd wanted to, she couldn't have stopped. The sensation was too powerful.

She leaned back against Matt. The soap slid from his grasp. Matt had known Lily was beautiful, but he hadn't admitted that she was so irresistible.

His body, the part Jim had accused him of neglecting, responded shamelessly.

"Can you stand alone?" he asked, holding her arms as he stepped back.

"Of course I can. Why would you think I couldn't?"

He gave a tight laugh. "Because you're sprawled all over me."

With a gasp she forced herself upright once more. "How dare you—" She opened her eyes and let out a shriek.

"What's wrong?"

"Soap . . . in my eyes."

"Stand still. I'll pump more water." Matt applied himself to the hand pump, working it vigorously. Damn. He was so ready for her he'd be forced to climb into the barrel to cool his raging desire.

The water fell, washing away the soap. "I think that's enough, Matt." Lily's voice sounded as tight as his Levi's. "You're making a mudhole."

"Good. Maybe that old sow will come home and wallow in it."

Lily reached for the drying cloth, draped it around her shoulders, and moved back into the doorway of the barn. "What old sow?"

"Our best sow disappeared in the rain. We need the litter she's about to drop."

"What do you do with the pigs?" She'd seen no hog meat in their larder. The only signs there were pigs anywhere were the mud and the low, covered shelter next to the barn.

"We sell them. Our pigs are the only ones in west Texas. It was one of Jim's ideas. Pigs and chickens. Raising them turned out to be a little harder than we'd counted on. We have to fence up the chickens to keep them from getting eaten by wild animals, and the pigs eat food we ought to have. So I don't know how smart it is for us to keep on."

But you're bound to keep trying, for Jim's sake.

Lily looked down at her feet, then moved back toward the water trough. She tugged a pair of her drawers from the fence and dunked them in the water.

"You're not going to rewash your clothes now, are you?" Matt asked.

"No. I'm cleaning my feet."

"I'll do that." He lifted Lily to the side of the trough and submerged her feet. Once he'd cleaned them, he turned her around and dried them with the bottom of her drying towel. "Now let me get you back in the barn where I can get some of Kitty's ointment for those hands."

"Can't you do it out here?"

"I could, but that trough is going to cut a hole in your bottom before long. Hold on a minute."

Moments later he carried her back inside, depositing her on an old horse blanket he'd spread on the hay, then disappearing into the tack room. He returned with a clay pot filled with clear, fragrant ointment.

"I think there's just enough."

Taking one of her hands, he turned it palm up. As lightly as he could, he rubbed the salve across her blisters, up one finger and back down it again until he had coated all the raw area. Then he did the same to the other hand.

She didn't make a sound. She just watched him. But the pain she felt was reflected in her eyes. And he couldn't tell whether it was because of the blisters or because she was so open and vulnerable. All he wanted to do was wrap his arms around her and promise her that he'd never hurt her again.

But he couldn't do that. Even the promise was a commitment, one he wouldn't make. Still, he couldn't let her go without saying something that let her know his regret. The easiest thing was the truth. "I'm sorry, Lily. I've brought you so much distress. You don't deserve this."

"Matthew." Just his name was all she said, but she couldn't hide the shiver that followed.

"You're wet," he said huskily. "I think you'd better get into some dry clothes before you catch a cold."

"It's too hot to catch a cold."

"True, but some dry clothes might still be in order before we go inside. To keep down curious questions?"

Lily didn't look forward to going inside and explaining her situation to Kitty or Jim. Dry clothes would save questions, and although she had dry clothes, they were no longer clean. She looked down at her hands and grimaced. "I think you're going to have to bind my hands."

He studied her hands, then left the barn, returning with one of her dry petticoats from which he ripped one of its many ruffles. Moments later her hands were securely bandaged, the ends split and tied to hold the cotton strips in place.

Lily reached for the buttons on her wet undergarments, tried unsuccessfully to maneuver her bound fingers, and groaned in frustration.

"We should have changed your clothes first," Matt admitted. "Sorry, I'm not much good at this kind of thing."

"You'll have to take the bandages off," Lily said.

"No, the medication is almost gone. They have to stay on for now. I'll have to help you."

She was afraid he'd say that.

"At least close the barn door, Matt."

"Why?"

"So . . . so it will be dark."

He ought to just pick her up and take her into the house, let Jim or Kitty help her. But he couldn't bring himself to do that. He was responsible. He had to set the damage right. But, maybe darkness was better. He walked over to the doors and kicked the wooden block away. The heavy doors swung shut, closing out the fading light.

In the half-darkness he made his way back to Lily. Steeling himself against the reaction that was sure to come as soon as he touched her, he knelt down beside her and reached forward.

The tiny buttons were sheer torment. The garment, still wet, stuck to Lily's skin, avoiding total exposure of her breasts.

"Could you close your eyes?" she asked warily.

"I might miss my target. That would be worse."

"Then I'll close mine." Lily took a deep breath and

proceeded to do just that. "Hurry," she managed to say. "Before . . . before we both catch a cold."

Cold? There was nothing cold about the air around him. The temperature of the barn rose with every button. "I don't think that's going to happen. At least not to me."

One more button and he'd be finished. "I miss them, you know," he said softly.

"Miss what?"

"The freckles. They made you special."

Her eyes flew open. "I just traded them, Matt."

"For what?"

"For other things I thought you'd like better."

Suddenly it was ten years ago and her heart was once more in her face. Her loneliness. Her longing. He'd hurt her then. He'd refused her childish proposal and ridden away, telling himself he'd forget every painful thing in his past. Lily had been wrapped up and discarded along with all the other things in Tennessee. How could he have forgotten her? How could he hurt her again?

He got to the bottom of the buttons and untied the string that held the petticoat in place. "Lily. I know I'm going to regret asking this, but what did you trade your freckles for?"

"Nothing that seems very important anymore," she answered, thinking of how foolish all the etiquette lessons and the finishing school were now. She started to put her hands on his face, looked at the bandages, and touched him with her fingertips instead. "I think what you and Jim and the children are teaching me is so much more important."

She couldn't see him, but in her mind she looked past his eyes, into his soul. "I know you don't believe it, but I'm going to make you a good wife. Sooner or later, you're going to realize it, too."

Then before she knew it, their lips met and his arms were around her. Her breasts rubbed against his shirt, and her belly seemed to ignite. Kissing him felt so good, so right. He had to feel the same way she did. Finally, just as she thought she was going to burn up, he jerked away.

"No, Lily, this is wrong. We can't do this."

"Why is it wrong, Matt? Tell me. I need to understand why something so glorious is wrong."

The backs of her hands slid around his neck, and she held him firmly over her, unwilling to let him go.

"Because I can't make love to you."

"Don't you want to?"

"You have to know I want you." He rocked against her and felt her shiver. "Don't you feel that?"

She did. Obviously the last ten years had made some changes in Matt that she didn't know about.

"Wouldn't it be better if you unfastened your trousers?" she invited softly.

He groaned as he rolled away. "Lily, what am I going to do with you?"

No. She wasn't going to lose him now. She'd simply have to do something very forward and . . . outrageous. She reached out and touched him where he thrust against his trousers.

"Lily!"

"Maybe I'd understand if you demonstrated." Her fingertips danced lightly up and down his body.

"Don't do that."

His words said no, but she felt him moving to meet her touch. "Please love me, Matt. I told you in the beginning I wanted you to treat me as you would the woman you were going to marry. And I don't think you'd tell her no."

"You don't know what you're asking." Matt didn't know what he was doing either as his hands rose to fondle her breasts.

"Oh, Matt," she whispered, twisting her body free of her chemise so that his work-rough hands were touching bare skin. "Could you kiss me again?"

He rolled her over, took both her wrists in his hand, and held them over her head as he straddled her body with his legs. "Stop it, Lily, or I won't be able to."

"Please, Matt," she said, instinctively lifting herself against his hard body.

Matt groaned in frustration, fought his desire, lost the fight, and captured her lips once more. He kissed her mouth, invading it with his tongue, pulling away and moving slowly down her body to her breasts, then back again. Every move he made she followed. They were both on fire, and this time he couldn't stop.

His hands roamed across her body, touching, rubbing, falling back so that his lips could confirm what he'd known from the first. Lily was perfect. And she was as caught up in her need as he. He'd thought he was hard until he found the opening in her drawers and felt himself on the verge of exploding as he pressed against her. Hell, he'd been hard most of the time since she arrived; that's why he'd avoided the house, why he'd made himself stay angry. But nothing had prepared him for this tide of feeling.

He lifted himself against her and listened to her small sounds of welcome until he'd almost gone too far, then forced himself to pull back and take in a calming, steady breath. It didn't help. All it did was keep him from going over the edge. He turned to his side, pulling slightly away so that he could work his hand down to the vee between her thighs. As he pressed his hand lower he found her moisture. Then his pants and boots were gone and he was moving inside her, caught up in the fire that raged unchecked, until it consumed them both.

Lily had finally won.

He just couldn't be sure what.

Lying there, still joined, his chin in her glorious hair, the realization of what had happened hit him like ice water. He'd been her first. Lily had wanted this as much as he, and she'd given him the most precious thing she had to give—herself.

Then he realized what that meant.

"Damn it to hell, Lily. I didn't intend to do that."

"I know."

"I told myself that you really hadn't saved yourself for me. You lived through a war and a city being overrun by outsiders who thought they were entitled to the spoils, and you were still a virgin. What if Jim had never sent that letter?"

"I don't know. I guess what's meant to be will be. I was sure you'd come back for me."

"A man makes his own fate, Lily. Don't make me a better man than I am. If Jim hadn't written that letter, I wouldn't have."

"But he did. And we're here, together, just as I'd dreamed we would be."

Lily the dreamer. What had he done? He rolled away, not wanting to contemplate the wrong he'd just committed. Not wanting to, but facing the consequence. Now he had to do the right thing. He was an honorable man; he had no choice.

"You won, Lily. We'll be married as soon as possible."

Lily heard Matt's words. She'd won. He was going to marry her. She should have been filled with happiness, but he hadn't said the words she needed to hear. He didn't love her. He was just doing the honorable thing.

She sat up, crossing her arms over her chest as if they could protect her from the pain that overwhelmed her. Was that the kind of marriage she wanted? No. She'd lost her mother's love. Even though Aunt Dolly had taken her in and cared for her, she lived for most of her life in a home that wasn't really hers. Growing up, she'd known she never really belonged there. Now Matt was prepared to offer her the same thing. At least Aunt Dolly loved her.

Matt didn't.

She didn't know what she would do. For all her adult life she'd focused on her goal: marrying Matt Logan. Why did that suddenly feel wrong? She needed time to think.

Lily stood up and started pulling her clothes on. She managed to tie the strings on her petticoat. The chemise she just pulled together.

"What are you doing?" Matt asked.

"I'm going to the house."

"Lily, this must be new and strange, and God knows, I'm sorry it happened, but—"

"Don't worry, Matt," she said in a voice so tight that she could scarcely get the words out, "I'm going to let you out of our agreement. You don't have to marry me. I'll stay for a while, to look after the children, until Jim—until he's better."

"What are you saying? You're going to marry me, Lily."

"No, Matt. I'm not."

The next morning, Lily woke before the children. She lay there, thinking about what she'd done. She'd never love another man, but she couldn't deceive herself any longer. Her future with Matt had always been based on her belief that he'd love her. He didn't, and probably never would.

She didn't know what she'd do.

For now, she had to find a way to help Jim and the children. If that meant she would have to leave the Double L, she'd do it. She knew now that she could never live in the same house with Matt and not want him. And she could never conceal that want.

With a heavy heart, she dressed and climbed down the ladder, where she came face-to-face with Jim, who was sitting at the kitchen table.

"Lily, your hands."

"They're much better this morning," she said, unwinding the bandages to review blisters already healing.

"You were in the barn a long time last night. And you have hay in your hair again."

"Yes, I do," she answered softly, knowing even as she did that Jim knew. "Don't worry, Jim. I'll be fine. Matt won the bet. I'm going back to Tennessee."

"No, I won't let you. We need you here, Lily," he said with grim determination. "If Matt won't marry you, I will."

12

Lily smiled sadly at Jim. "Thank you, but I can't accept your proposal. I care about you. But I . . . I don't love you that way. It wouldn't be fair to you."

"It doesn't matter, Lily. I care about you, too, and I'll be good to you for whatever time I have left. Then, after I'm gone, half the ranch will be yours to keep for my children."

"Oh, Jim," she asked wistfully, "why doesn't Matt want me?"

Jim pulled her down beside him on the bench and put his arms around her. "I think he does, Lily. If he didn't, this would be so much easier. He could just look on marriage as a way to take care of the children after I go, but he's separated his feelings from his responsibility. He can't allow himself to want something just for himself."

"But this wouldn't be just for him; it's the right thing for everyone."

"I think he's afraid to take a chance. You know he didn't really want to go to war, but he believed in the Union. When he fought for the North it almost killed Papa. To make up for what he saw as Matt's betrayal, Papa joined the Tennessee Volunteers and was fatally wounded in his first battle.

"Matt always thought if he'd stayed home, Mama and my sister wouldn't have died, and the plantation wouldn't have been burned. Then when he couldn't find a way to save the land, everything just got buried inside him. He was afraid to love anything or anybody else. If he didn't, he wouldn't hurt so if he lost it."

Lily rested her head on Jim's chest. "But he loves you and the children."

"Yes, he does, even if he does try to hide it. But we're a built-in part of his life, a part in which he has no choice. He loves you, Lily, but that's personal, and to him, that's selfish. Loving you could bring you great harm."

"That doesn't make any sense. I'm the answer to his problem, and I am his problem?"

"Give him some time, Lily."

"So what am I supposed to do, Jim? I can't walk away from you and the children, and I can't live with a man who doesn't love me."

"I think what you need to do is nothing. Let Matt fight his own demons. Just don't make it easy on him by leaving. Sooner or later he's going to admit that he loves you, I'm sure of it."

He pulled his handkerchief from his pocket and handed it to her. "Now blow your nose, and we'll fix breakfast."

This morning, because her hands were still stiff and sore, she let Jim prepare the biscuits. But she put them in the oven while he sliced and fried the salt pork.

"I ought to tell you, Lily. We aren't quite as bad off as it looks. Until you came, Matt kept us supplied in beef. It's just been the extras we've eliminated. Matt thought if you saw we were bad off, you'd leave."

"Why, that hard-hearted rascal," she exclaimed,

"making the three of you suffer so that I'd think you were on the verge of starvation. And I believed him."

Jim laughed. "We may not set a table like you did back in Memphis, but we're better off than most. Will's just going through a growing streak and Emily, well, look at her. Does she really look starved?"

Lily thought about the round little body she'd bathed, and wanted to strangle Matthew Logan. "So he thought that would make me turn tail and run. Well, it didn't."

"Until now," Jim reminded her.

"You're right, Jim. I've waited too long for Matthew Logan to give up this easily."

Jim smiled. "He didn't win the bet. You've proved that you can be a rancher's wife. I don't know what else you have to do. And if he weren't so stubborn, he'd marry you."

Lily took up her slices of fried pork and placed them on a plate. "I ought not to tell you this, Jim, but Matt did agree to marry me."

The surprise on Jim's face was absolute. "Well, that's wonderful."

"No, it's not. I refused. He didn't ask me because he loves me or even because he wants me. It was just the . . . the right thing to do."

"I see."

"No, you don't," she said softly. "I guess I'm as stubborn as he. But I won't marry a man that won't love me." She leaned against the table and frowned thoughtfully. "About your proposal, Jim, I think it might be a good idea to let Matt think I'm considering it. At the proper time, of course."

Later that morning, Will left to pick up more swill from the hotel in Blue Station. The remaining pigs had to be fed, even if the sow was gone. Matt didn't come to the house for the midday meal, and Jim was left trying to make sense out of Lily's plan to consider his proposal, or at least make Matt think she was.

Jim couldn't be certain what had happened between Lily and Matt; he could only guess. It was probably just as well his thickheaded brother stayed away. Jim didn't know what he might do to Matt if he came in.

In spite of her hands, Lily threw herself into her chores with a fierce determination that reminded Jim of Matt's own determined attempt to save the ranch when their cotton crop had dried up and died. Though she hummed as she worked, he was worried. Jim had seen Matt grow more and more morose; he didn't want that to happen to Lily. He knew that Matt wasn't a man to change his mind, and this offer to marry Lily was out of character.

Emily stayed underfoot, clinging to Lily as if she knew something had changed. Finally, to occupy her while Lily managed to rewash the soiled clothing, Jim told her the story about the ant who stored up food for the winter while the grasshopper played. There was no one playing on the Double L, but Jim had the feeling that Lily had set herself some kind of new deadline, and he didn't want to see her fail.

And he didn't trust Matt.

Matt didn't show up for supper. Lily didn't even ask about him. Jim decided to keep quiet. When she put the children to bed in the loft, Jim couldn't help but hear her conversation with Emily.

"Something wrong, sugarplum?" Lily asked.

"Lily Angel, is Uncle Matt mad at you?"

There was a long pause before Lily answered. "Of course not. Why would you think that?"

Emily answered with childlike simplicity. "He didn't come to play with you today."

Leave it to a child, Jim thought, to go straight to the heart of the problem.

"Ah, Emmie," Will interrupted, "Uncle Matt and Lily don't play."

"Yes, they do. Daddy said so. He said that Uncle Matt and Lily were playing. That's why Lily had straw in her hair and how she losed her shoes. Uncle Matt got mad with me when I losed my shoes."

"Uncle Matt is just working very hard right now, Emmie," Lily explained.

"Why?" Emily demanded.

"So . . . so we can go to the picnic on Saturday," Lily replied.

"He won't go," Will said.

"Maybe he will," Lily suggested. "We have to believe in the things we want to happen. When I was a little girl I used to wish on a star. Let's each of us make a wish."

"I will," Emily said.

Will snorted. "Ah, I don't believe that stuff. Besides, you can't even see the stars through the roof."

"But you know they're there, don't you, Will? They don't disappear just because you can't see them, do they?"

"No."

"Then close your eyes and make a secret wish. Don't tell," she cautioned. "Just believe that it will come true. You, too, Jim," she called down.

Jim didn't answer. The silence that followed made him sad. Wishes ought to come true. But they seldom did. Still, it had been too long since the children had believed in anything. Not until Lily came. He had to find a way to make her stay. Though he'd thought Matt was the proper one to take a wife, it was beginning to appear that *his* marrying her could be a more reasonable solution.

"Now, Uncle Matt won't be mad anymore," Emily said with confidence.

"You're not supposed to tell," Will said in disgust.

"I didn't. Did you make a wish, Lily?" she asked.

"I did, and if mine comes true, Uncle Matt won't act like he's mad with me anymore."

"I know what you wished," Emily said. "Tomorrow I'll help you look for them."

"What?" Lily asked.

"We'll find your shoes," Emily answered, swallowing the end of the word in a yawn. "Then he won't be mad anymore."

Lily gave Jim a questioning look when she climbed back down the ladder. He didn't volunteer any response, so she simply bid him a pleasant good-night and pulled out the green-and-white-checked gingham fabric she'd bought to make Emily a dress.

Lily liked Jim's explanation about Matt liking to play in the hay with her, but she wasn't at all sure that Will had bought it. No matter. Lily knew she still wanted Matt. But she wouldn't lie with him again without marriage, and she wouldn't marry a man unless he loved her. She was afraid it would take more than finding her moccasins to get Matt to be honest. Either way, she intended to be there for Jim and the children.

If all else failed, she'd just have to find a way to get Jim and the children back to Memphis. Aunt Dolly would help her come up with a solution; she'd done it before.

In the meantime, her pride demanded that she continue to prove to Matt that she could be a rancher's wife, even if the bet was off. She didn't know any other way to win his love.

Lily laid out the gingham fabric. She had only three days before the picnic. She'd planned to make Emily a dress, and she refused to take the child to the picnic looking like some ragamuffin. Especially since Mrs. Wells had made such an issue of her need for a mother. The folks in town believed the Logan children were being neglected. That thinking had to stop.

Using an old apron for a pattern, Lily cut feverishly into the cloth, uttering a silent prayer that she wasn't making a mistake. Sewing was one of the few tasks Matt had outlined for her that she felt qualified to perform. Still, she wished she had one of those sewing machines made by Mr. Singer. She'd had one back in Tennessee, she should see about having Aunt Dolly send it.

Throughout most of the day and into the next, she stitched Emily's dress. Still she found time for Jim, preparing him special broths, mending his clothes. All the while, they talked, deepening a friendship that had been there from the first.

She'd draw up the rocking chair wherever he sat and ask him to keep her company as she sewed on new buttons. Rips were covered by patches held in place with neat little stitches. Mending was something she did know how to do. Her cooking was improving. And Jim was on her side.

"Have you ever thought about going back to Tennessee? Just for a visit?" she added when she saw the frown on Jim's face. "When you sell the cattle we could all go. You could even see a doctor while you're there. They have really good doctors back home, Jim."

"There isn't a doctor good enough to help me, Lily," he answered and changed the subject to a discussion of Matt and the children.

"There might be. Wouldn't it be reasonable to find out? I mean, think of Will and Emily."

"I am thinking of them," Jim argued. "I'm not wasting good money that could be better spent on their future."

Lily quickly settled into a routine, and Jim's routine was built around hers.

The few times Jim saw his brother, Matt was tense and short-tempered. His manner was becoming more demanding and less accepting.

In spite of what Lily said, Jim was worried.

Thank goodness for the Founders' Day Celebration. A trip to town was what everybody needed. He didn't want Lily to be disappointed. He felt sure she truly expected Matt to go.

Until she went back east or decided to forget about Matt and marry him, Jim intended to see that Matt treated her with respect, even if it killed him. There was always the possibility that Lily would do it for him. She was courting danger, and the outcome would either make things better or they'd have one hell of an explosion.

"Jim, I'm getting your suit ready for the picnic," Lily said at one point, holding up a vest that had been missing a button. "Do you think Matt's clothing needs any special attention?"

"No, but his manners do. And I don't think you can fix them."

"Don't be too sure about that," she said mysteriously.

Jim bit back a smile. On the other hand, maybe she had found a way to change Matt . . . to drive him crazy. He was certain if his stubborn brother let himself go, he'd figure out that playing in the straw with Lily was exactly what he wanted.

Unless—Jim thought back to the straw in Lily's hair and Matt's absence since—maybe Matt was only too aware of his feelings and had run scared. Maybe he just needed to find out that others were waiting for Lily if he didn't claim her quick.

Jim smiled. He hadn't planned to attend the celebration, forcing Matt to accompany Lily and the children. Now he changed his mind. The suit Lily had mended and brushed was his wedding suit, and it still fit. There was a time when he knew how to make a woman laugh.

The last time he'd courted a lady, he'd married her. He never expected to marry again, but he just might enjoy a bit of courting. He still believed Matt and Lily were perfect for each other. Matt just needed a nudge. And a dance was a good nudging place.

Lily continued to talk to Jim about seeing a doctor back east, but she couldn't tell whether she was making any headway. As worried as she was about him, she couldn't stop remembering what had happened in the barn. She wondered if Matt was as distracted as she.

Making love with Matt had been so much more than she'd ever imagined. She suspected that had a great deal to do with the man rather than the act. Though, she thought as a warm flush washed across her face, the act had been quite exceptional.

Touching her stomach, she gave thought to the one thing that could seal everyone's fate. Suppose she was with child. He would insist on marrying her then, and she'd have to accept.

But she didn't want that. She'd already turned down one offer made in guilt. She'd thought she was prepared to do anything to force Matt to marry her. Now that he had agreed, she couldn't accept. She wouldn't let Matt be shamed into doing the honorable thing. Holding a gun to his head was no longer an option.

The night before the picnic, Lily took Emily's dress and went to sit in the rocker by the fireplace. She was almost done with the first garment she'd planned to make for her new family. But if things went right, it wouldn't be the last. She still needed to make herself some work clothing. And, she thought with a smile, she still had the white muslin to make new drawers for the men.

That thought took her mind right back where it didn't belong: to Matt. To making love with Matt. One thing had changed: She didn't have to measure Matt's particulars. She knew what they were. His was a strong body, scarred but healthy. Somehow those scars were the measure of a man's efforts. Looking down at her healing fingers she knew, even if Matt didn't, that her own scars were a measure of her efforts as well.

She remembered how Matt had chastised her about her fair skin the day he picked her up from the train. He'd held his arm next to hers to show her what the elements did to skin. Examining her arm now she could see that the color had already changed. One day soon she'd look like Matt, at least the part of him that showed. She pulled up her skirt and drawers so that she could compare the areas protected from the sun with her arm. She'd learned another thing that night: Matt wasn't sun-bronzed all over.

She let out a satisfied sigh. She was beginning to look like Matt. Let the women back in Memphis protect their pale beauty with parasols and sunbonnets.

In the beginning, she'd had secret doubts. But now she knew that she was becoming a Texas woman and a rancher's wife. She just hoped it wasn't too late.

The fire burned down, and Lily's eyelids were heavy when she finally finished the hem on Emily's dress. Tomorrow she'd try it on the little girl and make certain it fit. She should have done it sooner, but she wanted it to be a surprise. She couldn't do anything about new shoes, but a bright green ribbon for Emily's hair could come from one of Lily's own dresses.

Lily glanced out the window toward the barn. Matt hadn't come home yet, but she expected him to spend another night sleeping in the tack room. Fine. He'd made his bed, as Aunt Dolly would say. Now let him lie in it. In truth, she didn't know what else he could do. She was reasonably sure that it was as hard on him as it was on her. Jim said that Matt didn't fool him with his standoffishness. The more he wanted to be with Lily, the more he stayed away.

It didn't take a smart woman to figure out that Matt didn't trust himself. Lily didn't pretend to be wise in the ways of love between a man and a woman, but she suspected that making love was a bit like eating taffy. Once you tasted its sweetness, you wanted more. She certainly had developed a yearning for it.

Eventually, if she worked hard, Matt would appreciate her. She looked down at her hands and remembered the bandages he'd wrapped around her bleeding fingers, the way he'd washed and dried her feet. He was already taking care of her. Eventually, he'd understand that responsibility meant love. All she had to do was wait.

Poor Emily. She and Will had spent all morning looking for her missing moccasins, without finding them. God only knew where they really were—somewhere between the reservation and the ranch. That afternoon, Emily had hugged Lily and renewed her offer to play in the hay with her if Uncle Matt wouldn't.

Lily put the dress away and changed into her nightgown by the fading light of the coals in the fireplace. Matt would play with Lily again. He'd have to dance with her tomorrow night. He'd have to touch her again. If not, she hoped the men in town filled her dance card. If they even had cards.

She filled the pot with water and coffee so it would be ready for the morning meal, then banked the coals in the stove.

Finally she unfastened her hair and began to brush it, thinking about what she'd accomplished in less than two weeks. Aunt Dolly wouldn't believe that she'd learned to feed the animals, do the family wash, and plant seeds in a garden. But she had. And she'd already learned to love Emily and Will.

As a child, no matter how tired she was, her mother had brushed Lily's hair every night. "Someday you'll be a fairy princess," she'd say, "who'll wear pearls and diamonds in her golden hair."

"Ah, Mama. I'll never have pearls and diamonds."

"Not if you don't believe," she'd say.

And with every stroke of the brush, she'd repeat the things she wanted for her child. Positive thoughts had become part of Lily's nightly routine, and for all the years that followed, Lily never forgot.

Stroke. *Emily will be beautiful in her new dress.*

Stroke. *Jim will get better.*

Stroke. *Matt will be proud of me.*

Stroke. *We'll attend the picnic and . . .*

Stroke. *Matt really will court me with the whole town watching.*

Stroke. *Matt and I will dance together.*

Stroke. *Matt will love me.*

She laid down her brush and began to plait her hair into a braid. There was no hay caught in the strands. But, with the right prompting, maybe she could convince Matt to play in the barn with her tomorrow night.

Later that night, Matt rode back toward the ranch. He'd spent twelve-hour days searching for any trace of the man who'd killed his cows, to no avail. Now Racer was showing signs of fatigue, and Matt let him fall into a walk. Until now, Matt had tried not to allow himself to think about Lily, about the golden-haired beauty who had proved she could do what he needed and more, but he caught himself thinking of her from the moment he woke up each morning.

Lily loved life, the children, and in spite of his attempts to dissuade her, she was beginning to love this harsh land. No matter how much he'd protested, he could see her goodness. By concentrating on the ranch he'd managed to close her out during the day. At night he pushed himself until neither he nor Racer could ride any farther. Then he'd fall into his bedroll and close his eyes in utter frustration and exhaustion.

Still he didn't sleep.

Dammit! He'd made love to her. He'd spoiled her for any of those fancy eastern men. When he'd realized what he'd done, he'd offered to marry her. But she'd turned him down. Turned down the Double L. Emily and Will. That was what he wanted, wasn't it? Why then did she fill his mind and his body with need?

But now he needed to go home and check on Jim. Matt wasn't fool enough to pretend anymore. Jim was going to die. What he'd done in sending for a bride had been a reasonable answer. Why had he been so stubborn? If his marrying Lily brought his brother peace of mind, why should he fight it?

Because long ago he'd disregarded his own wants and needs. He'd known he had to marry and he would. He had to hold on to what little sense he had left. The woman he married had to be a western woman who was strong enough to be a mother to Will and Emily, and a helpmate to him. Just because Lily was beautiful and loving didn't mean she had that kind of strength.

So why was he having such a hard time with her rejecting his offer of marriage?

Matt urged Racer forward, reining him in just beyond the barn, going the rest of the way on foot to avoid announcing his presence. He had some serious thinking to do.

The sow was still missing. When he searched for her he'd asked the other ranchers in the area if they'd had any cows butchered. No one had, and he was the only one who'd had cattle mutilated.

One decision had been made. He'd ride into Blue Station and call on the banker, Ambrose Wells. Matt had sworn never to borrow money again, but if Lily was going home, he was going to pay her way. He owed her that much. If it took borrowing money to take care of his family, he'd have to do it.

Matt walked Racer into the barn and removed his bridle and saddle. He gave the tired horse a quick rubdown and pitched hay into his stall. Moments later he stood beneath his homemade bath barrel, trying to clean away the grime from the long hours in the saddle. Inside the house was a family, his family, and he was separate from them. He had the ranch and the cattle and the responsibility for it all.

"You're wasting water." Jim's voice came from out of the darkness.

Matt let go of the rope that tilted the water bucket, and reached for the drying cloth he'd hung on a nail on the barn door.

"What are you doing up?" Matt asked.

"Waiting for you. I think we need to talk."

Matt turned around, though in the dark shadow of the barn he couldn't see more than his brother's outline. "Something wrong?"

"It's Lily."

"What's wrong with her?"

"Nothing yet. She's made up her mind that you don't want her."

"She told you that?"

"Yes," Jim said, adding casually, "she's making plans for the Founders' Day Celebration tomorrow. Emily has a new dress and I know she'll be disappointed if she doesn't get to wear it. Are you planning to take Lily?"

"I hadn't planned to, no."

"That's what I wanted to know."

Jim turned and started back.

"Wait," Matt called out. "Is that all you have to say?"

Jim turned around. "Well, no. I guess I ought to tell you that if you aren't going to take her, I am. Good night, Matt."

"Jim, you're in no condition to escort a woman to a dance."

Jim let out an impatient sigh. "I think we've had this conversation before, brother. I'm old enough to decide what I can and can't do. And I've decided. Of course," he added politely, "I would feel better if you came along, just to be there if . . . I need you. Besides," he added, realizing that Matt wouldn't know Lily had told him the bet was off, "you promised to court Lily."

Matt wrapped the cloth around his waist. He didn't like the idea of Jim taking Lily to the celebration. "Didn't she tell you? She's conceded that she's lost the bet."

"But you and I know that isn't true. I'm disappointed in you, Matt, and in me. You've spent ten years looking after my family. It's time for me to take some responsibility. This is one time I'm going to do what I think is right."

Matt bit back a sharp retort. His brother thought he was Sir Lancelot. "And what do you think is right?"

"Lily wants to be courted. I'm going to do it."

Matt swore. "That's the most foolish thing I ever heard of."

"Maybe, but I sent for a mail-order bride so that my children would have a mother. I think Lily is perfect."

"Perfect? Lily Towns? She's stubborn, willful, and pig-headed. And she gambles. And if she has to go to the dance, I'll take her."

"I thought you would."

"But we're not going for the whole day, just the picnic," Matt protested, not yet ready to let Jim know that he'd already decided to go. He just hadn't been able to back down. As long as it was on his terms, he could use the event. Besides, it was the perfect opportunity to find out more about the Scotsman.

"Of course, Matt. The picnic and the dance. And you'll dance with Lily?"

"If I have to," Matt agreed with a touch of reluctance. It wouldn't do for Jim to change his mind. It wouldn't do to let his brother know that he was looking forward to having Lily in his arms. The very idea of Jim and Lily. Suppose Jim actually married her? That thought sobered him. He'd have to live in the same house with Lily . . . and Jim. He couldn't let that happen.

If anybody married Lily, it definitely had to be him.

He let his mind run with that thought for a minute. It could work. She'd turned him down, but suppose he changed her mind and married her? For Jim's sake, of course. Nothing had to change. And he'd be in control. By the time Lily decided she couldn't take living out here, he'd be in a better position to send her back without having to borrow money. In the meantime, providing a woman to look after Emily and Will might be the last thing he would ever do for his brother. He owed it to Jim.

But first he'd have to change Lily's mind. He smiled. That shouldn't be too hard to do if he set his mind to it. He already knew she was a sensual woman who responded to his kisses . . . and more.

"You're sure she still wants to go to the dance, Jim?" He couldn't be too transparent, or Jim would intervene to protect Lily.

"All I know is that for most of the afternoon she's gone around humming and smiling. She even tried to teach Will how to do the Virginia reel."

"Good. That's very good."

Jim studied Matt and frowned. "I'm not sure I like that look. What are you planning?"

"I'm simply planning to court my fiancée. That's what everybody wanted, isn't it?"

"Don't hurt Lily, Matt. I won't let you do that. And don't punish the rest of us for your own stubbornness. Will and Emily are too important for that."

That stung. It was Will and Emily's future Matt was securing. And he wasn't any more stubborn than Lily.

There was a long silence before Matt finally said, "You

aren't going to marry Lily, Jim. I am. Now don't ask me any questions and"—he raised his voice—"stay out of it."

Jim smothered a smile as he headed back to the house, managing to whistle a few bars of a waltz before his breath gave out.

In the house Lily smiled. She'd heard Matt when he returned, just as she'd heard him every night. Jim's visit to the barn was a surprise, but she'd surmised from Matt's warning that they'd been discussing her.

Good. That meant that Matt was agitated. She intended him to be very agitated by this time tomorrow night. She intended for him to think that since he didn't want her, she was going to look around. It wouldn't hurt Matt to think there were other fish in the sea. He thought she was still a little girl, following him around with her heart in her eyes. Well, she wasn't. Her heart might still be in her eyes, but it was a woman's heart, and it was determined to have Matt Logan.

Lily closed her eyes and imagined herself swaying to the strains of the music. Yep, starting with the dance. If Emily had been listening, Lily decided, she wouldn't have heard music, she'd have heard the sound of ruffled angels' wings.

The man in the black Stetson and shiny boots rode into Blue Station after midnight. He woke the hotel clerk and took the only room left, the establishment's best. He signed the register with a flourish—Luke Conner.

"Can you take care of my horse?" Luke asked, pulling a coin from his vest pocket and dropping it on the counter.

"Sure thing. How long will you be with us, Mr. Conner?" the clerk asked, trying to focus sleepy eyes on the stranger.

"A few days, maybe a week."

"Come for the big doings in town tomorrow?"

"What big doings?" Luke asked innocently as he took his key and threw his bedroll over his shoulder.

"Founders' Day Celebration. That means Ambrose Wells's day. He claims the title, though he weren't the founder. Butterfield Stage started the place."

Luke mounted the steps, stopped, and looked back. "You say everybody will be here? That means the local ranchers?"

"Bet your best ten-gallon hat, they will. Don't have much entertainment in Blue Station. Won't nobody miss this."

That was exactly what Luke Conner was counting on, that and the fact that his first trip through the Panhandle wearing a kilt had commanded such attention that nobody had paid much heed to the rest of him. Before a stop at the fort to introduce himself to the commander he had donned western clothes and a new name. That ought to be enough to disguise him.

It never failed to amaze him how a beard, long hair, and a kilt changed a man. Of course, boots, Levi's, and a Stetson changed a man too, and they were a lot more comfortable on a western prairie and at a dance.

He was going to like living in Texas, at least for a while.

13

Saturday morning dawned bright and clear. Lily dressed and stood for a moment on the porch, breathing in the fresh scent of early summer. Sunlight hit the dust particles in the air, turning them into a blowing mist of gold.

In spite of the threat of drought and the mutilated cattle, there was something reassuring about the sameness of the plains. She hated to think she might lose this feeling of belonging.

Jim came out behind her, stuffing his shirt inside his trousers. "It's beautiful, isn't it?"

"Yes. It is."

"Matt didn't believe anyone else would see beauty out here. I don't think Maria ever did, not like you. I'm glad you're here, Lily. I hope whatever you want works out."

Lily gave him a quick smile and a hug. "I hope so, too."

With a contentedness she couldn't express, Lily turned back to the kitchen where her chores for the day began. "What will we take to the picnic?"

"While you're preparing breakfast, I'm going to kill one of the chickens. We'll fry it."

She turned back to Jim. "Kill one of the chickens?"

"We'll soon have a new set of chicks. I think we can afford to lose one of the old birds."

Lily caught the hem of her apron and pleated it into a wrinkled accordion. "Jim . . . I don't know how to fry chicken. I mean I know how, but I've never done it."

"You just get the breakfast done. I'll show you."

Jim left, and Lily swallowed the lump in her throat. Fried chicken. That's what they'd eaten on her birthday all those years ago, the day she'd asked Matt to marry her. Somehow it completed the circle. She felt good. She started to the kitchen, stepped inside the door, and stopped.

In the center of the table was the basket of fresh eggs Will had gathered and a small pitcher holding two stems of bluebonnets. Lily took a moment to sniff the blossoms.

"They don't have no smell," Will said.

"They don't have *any*, and they don't need one," Lily answered. "Their beauty is enough. Thank you, Will. For thinking of me."

"You're welcome. I found them in the pasture."

"Do you think we could transplant them here, to the house?" she asked. "Your daddy said your mother always wanted flowers."

Will nodded, pressing his lips firmly together to hide an obvious tremble. "I'll dig some up," he said.

She gave him a quick hug and moved around him to the pantry so he wouldn't know she'd seen the tears in his eyes.

It took her a minute to focus on the contents. There was little there she would have taken to a picnic back in Tennessee, but she'd saved the last two cans of peaches and some potatoes. She'd put some beans on to cook right away. The chicken and some gravy would complete their feast.

But for breakfast, she'd make a large batch of biscuits—extra for the meal later—and fry some slices of salt pork that had appeared mysteriously on the counter sometime after she went to bed. She assumed Matt had brought it, but she never heard him enter the house.

Soon the meat was browning in the skillet.

Lily used her apron to protect her hand as she opened the door to the oven. The biscuits had browned nicely. She pulled the pan from the oven and turned it over, dumping them in the breadbasket. Will brought the honey and poured it over one of the biscuits he'd split and laid out on his plate.

As Lily placed a biscuit on Emily's plate, Jim came in the back door holding the hen by its feet.

"It has feathers," Lily said in dismay. Aunt Dolly's chicken had probably had feathers too, but she hadn't remembered that.

"For now, but as soon as I've eaten we'll dunk this bird in some hot water and pluck it."

Lily nodded hesitantly. She filled Jim's cup and her own with coffee and sat down, wondering what made her think she could do this.

Emily crumbled her biscuit, then admonished by her father not to be wasteful, mashed the crumbs back into little balls that she could pop into her mouth.

"What will we do at the picnic, Lily?" Will asked.

"Oh, we'll visit. Eat. I don't know what they do at a Texas picnic. Back in Tennessee there'd be singing, maybe games for the children."

Will perked up at the last statement. "What kind of games will they have, Pa?" he asked.

"I don't know. Sack races, probably. Maybe rock throwing. We'll have to wait and see."

Lily ate quickly, swallowing the last of her breakfast as she folded the extra biscuits in a cloth and placed them in the basket. Then she reached for the straw broom and swept up Emily's biscuit crumbs.

"I'll help you pluck the chicken in a minute, Jim. Right now, Will, I'd like you to clear the table while Emmie and I take care of some special woman business." Emily slid from her bench and followed Lily into the parlor.

"Is it my dress? Is it done?" she asked excitedly.

"It's done. We'll try it on to make sure it fits, then you can play while I prepare our food for the picnic. Before we go you'll have a bath and a nap."

The fit was perfect, even better than Lily had hoped. Once on, Emily wanted no part in taking it off until she'd shown it to "Papa, Willie, and Uncle Matt."

"Oh no." Lily shook her head. "We're going to surprise our men. They can't see us until we're ready to go. It will be our secret."

"You has a new dress, too?"

"A brand-new dress," Lily nodded, "green like yours. I brought it all the way from Tennessee. Now take yours off so it won't get dirty."

"But I want to wear it," Emily whined.

"Later," Lily promised. "Right now you have to teach me to fry chicken. You like fried chicken, don't you?"

The child tilted her head in question. "Fyed chicken? Don't know about fyed chicken."

Lily dropped to her knees in front of Emily. The little girl had never eaten fried chicken. She'd been too young before Maria died, and they'd kept the chickens for eggs ever since. Lily caught Emily in her arms and hugged her, breathing in her sweet-child smell as she held her close.

An unexpected wave of longing swept over her. She could understand Jim's fierce determination to protect these children. They were so vulnerable, so eager to love and be loved. Emily saw her as an angel. Even Will, who tried to be so grown-up, had brought her wildflowers.

Lily's throat tightened. She turned Emily around and unbuttoned her dress, replacing it with the apron long outgrown.

All she'd thought about on her way west was that she would be a bride, that she'd marry the man she'd dreamed of for most of her life. She'd never expected to fall in love with two motherless children. But she had, and she refused to give up.

So, the picnic wasn't turning out like she'd expected. She'd just have to find another way to reach Matt. As Aunt Dolly would say, "There's no use crying over spilled milk. Let's call the cats." Right now, Matt was feeling guilt, not love. A little guilt wasn't a bad thing. She just had to find a way to change it into something stronger.

As she headed back to the kitchen she caught sight of a sliver of straw that had fallen from the broom. Leaning over, she picked it up, smiled, and stuck it in her braid.

It was Sergeant Major Rakestraw who finally found Matt's missing crooked-tailed sow. She lay near a pile of rocks several hours' ride due west of Matt's ranch.

What was left of her.

There was no question that she, too, had been intentionally mutilated. The litter of pigs had been cut out. The rest of her carcass had been eaten by buzzards and other wild animals; the remainder was covered with flies.

"Who'd do such a thing?" one of the enlisted men asked, tying his handkerchief over his nose.

"A crazy person," another commented.

"You reckon some medicine man was doing a special spirit dance here?" asked a third.

The final comment—"Looks like one of them slave voodoo things to me"—was the most ominous.

"Dig a hole and bury it," the sergeant barked.

The soldier with the bandanna lowered it. "Don't you think Logan'll want to see it?"

"Write up a full report, Billy. I'll need to send one to Washington, too." Sergeant Rakestraw straightened his back even more rigidly. "Now climb off those horses and bury the pig. I have a celebration to get to."

The chicken got fried, but Lily was glad she was packing the lunch just for her family. She wouldn't have wanted anyone else to see her first attempt. The outside of the chicken was browned to a crisp, while the pieces seeped pink juice that suggested the meat might not be completely done on the inside.

Nevertheless, by midday, the meal was packed and ready.

"Can we go now?" Emily asked, tugging on Lily's apron.

"Not until we get cleaned up and put on our best bib and tucker."

A worried frown creased the little girl's forehead. "I don't got a bib and tucker."

Lily stopped and gave her a hug. "That means your new dress," she explained.

Jim heated a kettle of water. When it began to boil he picked it up and headed for the barn. "Just going to shave," he said. "Will and I have already taken our clothes out there. We'll let you ladies have the whole house to get ready."

"You don't have to do that, Jim. Emily and I will use the kitchen."

"Maria never liked us being underfoot when she was dressing. Besides," he explained, "we want to surprise you with our good looks."

"What about Matt?" she asked. "Is he getting dressed?"

"I don't know," Jim lied valiantly. "But if not, I'm your date, aren't I?"

Lily didn't argue. But she'd seen Jim send Will to the barn with an armload of clothes earlier, too many clothes for just one man and a boy. She refused to speculate. It was imperative that Matt accompany them. Otherwise how could she make him jealous? If he didn't, she'd figure another way to reach him.

Today Matt would start to court her, and he'd learn to love her. She'd wished on her star. It didn't matter that she couldn't see the star.

Once the men were gone, Lily bathed herself and Emily. Not in the tub, that would take too long, but it was a bath all the same. The water was hot and sweet-scented from a drop of rosewater she'd added. Once the chicken flour was gone from her face and hair, she turned to Emily, who was a more intensive job.

Finally, the child was clean, her hair brushed and combed into a mass of ringlets. Lily frowned over Emily's too-small pantalet and chemise, but there was nothing she could do about those now. At least nobody would see them beneath the new gingham dress.

"Now, you sit down at the table and don't move while I dress."

Squirming in her excitement, Emily complied. "When do we go?"

"Soon."

"Will Uncle Matt be there?"

"I'm not sure."

"Mr. Kilgore's coming?"

"That's what your daddy said."

"And Kianceta?"

Lily pulled on her white lace stockings and slid her feet into a pair of white leather shoes with little bows.

"Yes, Kianceta is coming, too."

"I like Kianceta," Emily announced. "She used to come to play with me, before Mama sent you."

Lily, in the process of fastening her bustle, paused. Emily tended to see things the way she wanted them to be. Maybe that was the way to do it, Lily thought as she pulled the long-trained skirt over her head and arranged it so that its front fell into the pleated drapes that wrapped around and were caught up in a cascade down the back. Her corset pushed her breasts up so that she'd have to wear a chemisette, a chemise with extra ruffles, to cover them.

Lily smiled. It would do Matt good to be reminded that she'd wear dresses like this every night if she went to Paris.

"What do you think?" she asked the child, lifting her skirt as she whirled around, then tilted her head and assumed a flirty pose. "The dressmaker said it matches my eyes."

The answer she got was gruff and immediate, and not from Emily. "What there is of it matches your eyes all right, but where is the top of it?" Matt stood glowering in the doorway.

A different Matt.

A clean-shaven Matt, wickedly elegant in a black frock coat and trousers that clung to his thighs like a second skin. No question about his drawers tonight. He couldn't be wearing any.

"Don't you have something that doesn't expose quite so much of you?" he asked.

"The same could be said for you, Matt," she whispered, deliberately refraining from telling him that she hadn't yet donned the jacket.

"A shawl—no, make that a blanket." He pushed past her and ripped the quilt from Jim's bed, draping it around her shoulders and gathering it up around her neck.

"Don't you think I'm going to look a little odd?" she managed seriously.

"There's no way in hell you could ever look odd," he answered, his hands hanging on to the edges of the quilt, and resting on her chest. "You know I'll have to take on every man in Blue Station who has too much to drink."

"You will?" She sounded wistful, bemused. That surprised him. When her hands lifted up the quilt and settled on top of his, the heat seared the hair on his fingers.

"Emily," Lily managed to say in a reasonably even voice, "go show your daddy your new dress."

" 'Kay." She slid from the bench and ran for the barn, calling, "Daddy, Daddy, look at me."

If Jim answered, Matt didn't hear him. He'd come inside to give Lily a warning about what she could expect in town. But when he caught sight of her, still in her chemise and drawers, he'd been struck by the explosion of desire he'd barely kept under control for the past three nights.

Then she'd slipped into her skirt, and he'd seen the creamy white half-moons of her breasts winking at him above her corset. He'd gone into an emotional stampede. Now she was staring up at him, her green eyes alive with mischief, and he knew he was lost. The best he could hope for was that Jim would not be as mesmerized by Lily as he. Jim seemed serious in his desire to court Lily, and Matt didn't want to have to fight off his brother along with the rest of the men at the picnic.

She licked her lips. "Matt, you're—you're looking very handsome. Am I to assume that you're coming with us to the celebration?"

"You're damned right!" He showed his anger before realizing it probably wasn't the best way to begin his courtship. He tried to control himself. Tried and failed as he said, "I hope there's a top to that dress."

She dropped the quilt onto the bed, tucked one finger under the strap of her chemise, and smiled. "There is, but it's long-sleeved and as you said before, there's probably too much of it."

He moved closer, took a deep breath, and hoped he wasn't making a colossal mistake. "Lily, I want you to know that I intend to carry out my part of the bargain."

"You don't have to do that. We've already decided that all bets are off."

"Yes, I do. The town believes that we're going to be married, Lily. I intend to keep my part of the bargain, and I expect you to do the same."

Lily seemed to be more interested in her skirt than in what he was saying. She leaned forward, arranging the folds in the front of her skirt, then turned around, looking over her bare shoulder. "All right. I suppose I could go along for one more night."

"Good, then it's settled." He didn't know why her decision didn't make him feel better, but it didn't.

"I don't think the bows in the back are straight, Matt. Would you make sure they're lined up just right?"

She wasn't paying him any attention. She didn't seem to care about anything but her clothing. Matt hadn't expected that. He looked down at the skirt and swallowed hard. "Lily, I don't know anything about women's clothes."

"Somehow I don't believe that." She gave a shake to her lower body and struggled to see behind her. "Just make sure the ends of the bows aren't poking out in different directions."

Matt couldn't tell that anything was poking anywhere, except her bottom and her breasts. At least her bottom was covered. He moved closer. Just as he reached out to unfurl one of the bow's ends, Lily turned suddenly.

"Oh, Matt. Your chin. You cut yourself shaving." She caught his chin, lifting his face to be examined, lifting his gaze from her exposed breasts to a spot only inches from her face.

From her lips.

He opened his mouth to protest. Yes, he'd cut himself shaving. He'd stood in front of the mirror, practicing what he'd say and do in his courtship to the point that he'd been lucky he hadn't amputated his nose.

Now all that planning went right out of his mind. All he could think about were lips, pink lips parted slightly, asking to be kissed.

"Does it hurt?" she asked in a throaty voice.

"Dammit, Lily, you're teasing me."

"You certainly curse a lot. Why is that, Matt?"

"Because you're a witch. You don't have any idea what you're doing, do you? What you make a man want?"

"Other men. Not you, Matt. You made it clear that you don't want me. That's all right. I'm not going to bother you anymore. So why don't you just forget about the dance? Really, Jim will take me. I don't want you to do anything you'd rather not do."

"Rather not do? Lily, you've got me so riled up that all I want is . . . this."

Then his hands were around her waist, holding her against him. Something wild flared in her eyes and tore away the last of his restraint. His lips touched hers, lightly he told himself. He had to win her over, court her. But his mouth fastened on hers in a full assault.

She struggled for a moment, then rocked against him, making little sounds as her fingers slid underneath his coat and began kneading his back.

His hands drifted lower, aiming for her bottom.

Then his fingers reached that round little fashion piece formed of horsehair and stays.

He jerked his mouth away. "What in the hell?"

She blinked, so caught up in the moment that she forget her plan to push him away. Then he pressed the bands of her bustle into her skin.

"If you're concerned about too many clothes, why are you wearing this torture rack?"

"So take it off," she quipped, unable to stop teasing him one last time.

"I'll take it off all right and turn it into an egg basket. It and every other one you own."

He rammed his hands beneath her skirt, ripped the bustle away, stepped back, and planted a booted foot in the middle of it.

"Is it dead?" Jim's amused voice came through the parlor doorway where he stood, the expression on his face a valiant attempt to control his laughter.

"Get in the wagon." Matt whirled and pushed Jim ahead and out of the kitchen. "Don't say a word, Jim," he said. "Not a single, solitary word."

"I won't," Jim agreed piously.

Matt stopped on the porch, as stiff as a starched shirt. This wasn't what he'd planned. He'd intended to seduce Lily. The opposite was happening, and Lily seemed to be playing with him. "Jim—"

"If I were you," Jim went on, "I'd carry my hat somewhere besides on my head."

Matt felt his face burning. He let out an oath, ripped off his Stetson, and walked off toward the barn.

At that moment a buggy carrying Allen Kilgore and Kianceta pulled into the yard. Jim smiled at Lily and turned to greet the couple.

Lily, riding high on confidence, felt her spirits plummet as Jim grabbed the post for momentary support, then walked slowly down the two steps onto the hard-packed earth beyond.

"Fine day for a celebration," Allen said. "Something wrong with Matthew?"

"Nothing that a good wife couldn't fix," Jim said softly.

"Little tiff between the future bride and groom?"

"More of a heated powwow," Jim answered. "You know, Matt always gets angry when he feels like he's lost control. He's having a hard time learning that sometimes it takes a bit of negotiating to reach a settlement."

"Matt's face looked more like he was getting ready for a war dance than a truce," Kianceta observed.

"I'd say that was a fair observation," Jim said. "Too bad we don't have some of Rides Fast's elixir. He could use a little something to settle him."

The Logan wagon, being pulled by a skittish Racer, burst through the barn door and stopped behind the Indian agent's buggy. Matt was driving. Emily and Will were already seated in the rear.

"Why don't you ride in with us, Jim?" Allen asked. "It will be easier than getting up in that wagon."

Jim glanced back over his shoulder at Lily as she slid her arms into her jacket. She pinned on a jaunty straw hat adorned with green ribbons and yellow daisies, then stepped onto the porch, pulling on long yellow gloves.

"Good idea," Matt said. "You lead the way."

Jim gave his brother a quick frown, as if he were about to argue, then climbed into the buggy. Allen applied a flick of the reins to his horse, and the wagon moved off.

"What about it, Lily?" Matt called out. "Are you ready?"

"I'm coming," Lily answered, the picnic basket in hand.

Matt could only stare at her. She'd added a long-sleeved jacket covering up the breasts. But he would know, all night he would know what was concealed beneath. Without her bustle, the long train of her skirt caught in a splinter on the rough boards on the porch.

She tottered for a moment, almost dropping the heavy basket.

"I'll help her, Uncle Matt," Will was quick to offer.

"No. Stay in the wagon. The basket is too heavy for either of you."

He slapped his Stetson on his head and slid his feet from the buckboard to the ground. He took two giant steps to the porch and took the basket from Lily's grasp. After placing it in the wagon, Matt climbed back to his seat.

"Uncle Matt, a gentleman is supposed to help a lady into the wagon," Will said. "Mama told me."

"Never mind, Will," Lily said airily. "I'll manage." She pulled up her skirt, giving the startled man a clear view of her drawers, and swung herself up beside him. Settling her skirts, Lily smiled and opened her parasol.

Matt groaned. "At least you're back to normal."

"You mean this?" She twirled the lacy appendage before her face, then lifted it once more to shield herself from the sun. "I don't have to keep to my original plan anymore."

He didn't look at her. "What plan?"

"To have my skin match yours. Look."

She held her arm out next to his, pulling up the cuff of his sleeve. "The other parts of me are pale. But my arms and face have already turned quite brown."

Matt sighed. If it weren't for Will and Emily, he'd turn the wagon around and go back to the ranch. That was where he belonged. That was where Lily belonged as well. *Remember, you fool, you're supposed to be courting her.*

For just a moment he seriously toyed with the idea of wasting money on a ticket to send Lily back to Tennessee. He'd come up with the thousand dollars to honor Jim's agreement, and he'd find another way to provide a mother for the children.

Sure, and the well wouldn't go dry and the creek would run through the summer. No, he'd already been down all those roads and they led nowhere. He had to convince Lily to marry him. It was the only solution to the problems he and Jim faced, and it was the moral thing to do. It had nothing to do with his wanting her. It had nothing to do with kisses that made him think of having her in his bed every night.

But how in the hell was he going to court her without making his need for her obvious to the world? He didn't know yet. But he had to stay in control, otherwise she'd know the truth, and he couldn't open himself up to that. It was too late to worry about Lily's future; he'd already ruined it. And like Jim said, Lily was nothing like Maria.

Like hell she isn't. She's a woman who wants something

now. *Sooner or later reality will hit, and she'll be on the first stage back to Memphis.* He just had to find a way to keep her. Not because he wanted her, that wasn't the issue. Her staying would be for the children. Maybe later he'd send her back and let her take Emily and Will with her. As long as he went into the marriage with that knowledge, he'd find a way to deal with the situation when it came up.

Though Emily and Will kept up a steady stream of conversation, the silence between Matt and Lily spoke louder than words. The future bride and groom were about to become part of the Founders' Day Celebration. Matt knew that they would both be forced to play out their designated roles.

For different reasons.

14

At the end of Main Street, beneath the apron of the wash tent, the mayor was making a speech. Matt drove Racer up to the livery stable, came to a stop, and called out, "Hello!"

There was no answer.

"Can we get down, Uncle Matt?" Will was trying hard to control his excitement.

"Yes, but look after your sister. And don't go anywhere until we find your father. Hello, inside. Anybody there? I have a horse out here that needs stabling."

When there was no response from the livery operator, Matt climbed down and unhitched Racer. He led him into the stable and into one of the stalls. Apparently the stable was being operated on the honor system while the owner enjoyed the celebration. When Matt turned back to the wagon it was surrounded by men ready to assist Lily from her seat.

It was beginning already, the men swarming over Lily. He was supposed to be courting her. How could he do that with every man in Blue Station in the way?

By making it obvious that she was his, that's how.

Matt started forward. "Excuse me, gentlemen." He shoved through the crowd to Lily's side. "Are you ready, darling? I want to introduce you to the ladies."

He caught Lily around her waist and swung her to the ground, then took her hand and tucked it beneath his arm, half dragging her down the street to where the mayor was just finishing his speech.

"Slow down, Matt," Lily protested, "the children."

He glanced behind. "Stay with us, Will. Don't let Emily get lost."

"And in closing," the mayor was saying, until he looked up and caught sight of Lily, "in closing, I'm proud to be a citizen of Blue Station, the town ready to claim its place in the future of Texas."

A scattering of applause rippled through the listeners as the mayor left the platform and headed toward Lily. "Hello. I'm Ambrose Wells. I'm so happy to see you again, Miss Townsend."

Harriet Wells and Ora Manley rushed toward Lily from opposite directions, boxing her in. "Indeed, I'm glad you decided to accept my invitation to come to the celebration," Mrs. Wells said, loudly enough so that everyone would recognize her claim on Lily for the evening.

Harriet was wearing the dress she'd wrestled from Lily's hand at the trading post. That she'd had to add an entire panel down the front of the garment in no way diminished Harriet's claim to be the best-dressed woman in Blue Station.

"Your dress is lovely," Lily said, ready to be friendly to the overbearing woman.

"Why yes, it's the latest fashion back east. I'm sure you see now that it wouldn't have looked right on you."

Mrs. Manley leaned forward, speaking across Matt and Lily as if they weren't there. "Harriet, did you see Allen Kilgore? He actually brought that woman with him." She turned toward Lily. "She's a white woman who was captured by that Comanche chief."

The children caught sight of the Kilgores and their father, and ran toward them.

Lily felt Matt's grip on her arm tighten, making a motion to follow. But Lily stood firm. "You mean, Kianceta? I've met her."

Harriet's mouth fell open.

"Well, of course Kilgore is all right," the mayor said in a conciliatory voice. "But he's a Mormon, some kind of missionary. They have some peculiar ideas about equality."

"They both seem very nice," Lily said in a voice that was not quite so cordial.

Harriet started to speak, then hesitated. Finally she flipped open the small fan attached to her wrist by a ribbon and began to fan herself. "Well, of course, my dear, you wouldn't know, but we don't socialize with the Indians."

Matt's fingers dug into Lily's arm again. "Lily, we'd better—"

Lily cut him off. "Just a minute, Matt." She took a good look at Harriet Wells and Ora Manley and decided that if these two were examples of the leading citizens, Matt had good reason to avoid the people in Blue Station. "I want to hear exactly what is expected of a proper rancher's wife."

"Well, you're not going to hear it here," he muttered, making no attempt to keep his reaction to himself.

"Now, Matt," Ambrose began, "you know how the ladies are."

"Will you look at her, Harriet?" Ora rattled on, oblivious to the impending explosion. "She's wearing white woman's clothes."

"But she is white, isn't she?" Lily asked innocently.

Harriet scoffed. "Well, her skin is, but she's lived among those heathens so long that she's taken on all their ways."

Lily smiled. "Then I don't know why she'd choose to wear a white woman's clothes. The Indians' garments are certainly a lot more comfortable."

Ora Manley looked confused.

"And cooler," Lily added. "No petticoats. Matt's been telling me that I'm wearing too many clothes for this heat. I'd thought about having some skirts like the Spanish women, but after observing the Comanche women wearing tunics, I've decided their way is better, don't you think?"

Harriet and Ora looked stunned.

"Why, I certainly do not," Ora finally retorted tartly. "No self-respecting white woman would show her legs like that."

"I'm certain that Lily is just funning us," Ambrose said hastily. "She doesn't know how revealing those clothes are."

"But I do. Kianceta presented me with one when Matt and I went to the reservation for supper, didn't she, Matt?" She turned her gaze to Matt for confirmation.

"And you looked lovely wearing it," Matt answered with a big grin.

Lily waited to see how the hen court would react to that. She hadn't expected Matt to enjoy himself, but from the look on his face, he was.

"Of course you couldn't be rude," Harriet admitted hesitantly.

Ora nodded. "Yes. You wouldn't know our customs." She turned to Matt with a frown. "Shame on you, Matt, for not bringing your fiancée to visit us first."

"Men just don't know about polite society, Lily," Harriet confided. "But as a new bride and a member of our fine community, we'll help you learn. Now then, you're expected to join us for our picnic. We're spreading our food on a table beside the wash tent. The beef Ambrose is having barbecued smells heavenly, doesn't it?"

"It certainly does, and I thank you for the invitation to

join you," Lily replied politely, "but the Logans are sharing their meal with Mr. and Mrs. Kilgore."

"Mr. and Mrs. Kilgore?" Ora repeated with a gasp. "You're eating with them?"

"Yes. I find her story so admirable," Lily went on. "She could have returned to her people, but she stayed with her adoptive father. I'm not certain I could be that brave. Oh"—she looked up—"there they are now. I believe they're looking for us, Matt." Lily threaded her fingers through Matt's, turned, and dragged him through the crowd, mumbling under her breath as she walked.

"Old busybodies. How dare they? Who'd want to share what they brought anyway? It's probably full of prune juice and arsenic. If it isn't, it ought to be."

"Are you sure, Lily? By joining Allen and Kianceta you run the risk of being shunned. Living out here is hard enough without the companionship of other women."

Lily stopped. "Am I sure? You think I'd rather sit with those old hens than Allen and Kianceta? If that's the kind of companionship being offered, I can understand why Maria wanted to leave."

"That's what I've been trying to tell you," Matt said. "You wouldn't like it out here."

"I like it out here fine, Matthew Logan. I just have to do a little refining of 'polite' society, starting with letting those two harpies explain being rejected by us in front of the town."

Matt had been angry, then amused. Now he was thunderstruck. She was serious. Did she really understand what she was doing? Miss Lillian Townsend was announcing to the entire town that she preferred the company of an Indian agent and an adopted Indian over the mayor and the town merchants.

"Lily, you might want to think about this. I need to be honest with you. I avoid coming to town unless it's absolutely necessary. With a man, it's different. But you'll get pretty lonely if you cut yourself off. You don't understand how cruel those women can be."

"I understand. I just left a town full of women exactly like them. Now, unless you have some objection to eating more of my cooking, let's join our friends."

Still holding his big hand, Lily resumed her determined march toward Jim, Allen, and Kianceta.

"Hello, Mr. Kilgore," she said, then turned to Jim, concern on her face. "Are you all right?"

He took a deep breath. "I'm fine."

Then, with a smile to Kianceta, she said, "I didn't have a chance to speak to you before we left the house. Kianceta, I'm so glad the dress fit."

"It fits perfectly. Thank you. I'm honored to wear your dress."

Matt looked from Kianceta to Lily and back again, studying the fit and the flow of Kianceta's pink walking dress with the frilled cuffs.

"Your dress, Lily?" he asked.

"Not anymore."

Matt tightened his fingers around Lily's. "You loaned Kianceta a dress? How did you manage to do that?"

"Don't be rude, Matt. Kianceta gave me one of hers. I simply returned the courtesy."

"We taked it to her, Uncle Matt," Emily interrupted, unused to being ignored. "When we went to school, 'member?"

"Yes, you did," Lily said. "We wanted everyone to have a new dress, didn't we?"

"Yes, and we look boo-ti-ful, don't we, Uncle Matt?"

But Matt didn't answer. He was studying Lily.

"Papa! Papa!" Will, who'd wandered away, came to a skidding stop in front of the group. "They're going to have a sack race, just like you said, except without a sack. They tie two of our legs together, and we have to hop to the finish line. The winners get a prize. Can we enter?"

"I don't see why not," Jim agreed. "Go to it."

"No, you don't understand. Me and you. It's a father-and-son race."

A pained expression appeared on Jim's wan face. "I'm afraid not, son. I don't think I could manage even one hop. I'm sorry."

Disappointment brought Will's excitement to an end. He swallowed hard and went to stand by his father. "That's okay. I didn't really want to fall down and look silly anyway."

"I'll hop with you, Willie. See, I can hop good." Emily demonstrated, sending up a cloud of dust.

"It has to be two men, silly!" Will said.

Matt glanced down and realized that he was still holding Lily's hand. Hastily, he let it go. "Yes, it does. I'm not a father, but I'd like to enter the race with you, Will, if you'd have me as a substitute."

Will looked at his father, uncertain about his response. When Jim nodded, Will excitedly began to explain the mechanics of the event to his uncle. Lily felt her heart swell as she watched Matt place his hand on Will's shoulder and nod in response to Will's description.

"But I want to hop, too, Lily." Emily was ready to cry at being left out.

"If they have a race for women, we'll hop," Lily promised. "In the meantime, let's buy a piece of rock candy from Mr. Tolliver."

The proprietor was reluctant to leave his place in the window, but when Lily gave him her best smile, he found a sweet for the child and one for Lily as well. Emily's attention was quickly diverted when they rejoined her father and the others.

"I wouldn't have believed that," Allen was saying. "Matt in a sack race down Main Street."

"Matt is a good man," Lily said. "He'll make a fine father." And from the looks of the women who watched as he walked by, Lily knew he was the most handsome man there. But how Matt looked wouldn't have mattered. It was the spectacle he was prepared to make of himself for Will that made her heart swell with pride.

"You really care about him, don't you?" Jim said.

"Yes. I do. But as far as he's concerned, I'm going to consider all candidates, including you."

"I'm flattered," Jim said with a chuckle. "But somehow I don't think he would make a good brother-in-law for you."

Kianceta frowned. "Brother-in-law?"

"Yes. Matt thinks that Jim is courting me, too," Lily explained.

"Why would he think such a thing?" Allen asked, unable to conceal his amusement.

"Because I am," Jim answered. "Matt believes Lily has changed her mind about marrying him. I'm making sure he keeps on thinking that."

Kianceta gave Lily a stern look. "Have you?"

"Of course not," Lily said, "but he doesn't know it yet."

"I see," Kianceta said. "Well, you may be taking a big chance. All the women in town are giving him their best woman looks."

Allen laughed. "Woman looks? What's a 'woman look'?"

Lily didn't have to be shown. All she had to do was watch. But Matt seemed oblivious to them all . . . until he came to the woman standing in the door to the saloon. He stopped and exchanged some words of conversation with the dark-haired woman.

"Who is that?" Lily asked.

Jim leaned forward to see. "Oh, that's Lorna. She runs the saloon. She and Matt used to be . . . friends."

Lily didn't have to ask what that meant. The only

thing that saved the situation was Jim's use of the words "used to be."

This was a complication she hadn't expected.

When Jim had suggested that there were no women available for marriage, she'd believed him. What he'd meant was there were none he wanted to be the mother of his children. "They aren't friends anymore?"

"I don't think so. In the last year or so, Matt decided he didn't have time for a personal life. I was hoping you'd change all that."

"I intend to. You just keep courting me, and, Allen, I'd appreciate it if you'd pass the word to everyone that I really like to dance."

Allen smiled. "I will. This looks like it might turn out to be a very interesting evening. If we're going to see this race, we'd better find us a good watching spot. Come on, Emily, let's me and you commandeer the benches in front of the trading post."

With Emily dancing along beside him, Allen started into the crowd. "Excuse me. Move aside, please."

A path suddenly cleared. Lily felt as if she were following Moses as he parted the Red Sea.

However, the benches Allen mentioned were already claimed by onlookers who were not interested in giving them up. Lily couldn't decide whether it was because of Kianceta or her. By this time, Jim's face was ashen and his breath rough and strained. He held on to her arm as a brace rather than manners. Kianceta had moved to Jim's other side and was half supporting him. Glancing anxiously around, Lily noticed the balcony of the hotel. It formed a roof over the wooden sidewalk and was shaded by the building.

"Up there, Allen," she said, pointing. "Can we get Jim up there?"

"We certainly can."

Allen wasn't a big man, but after a word with Lorna, it

took only a dollar and a few minutes until he'd found one who was. They took Jim past the saloon and into the lobby of the hotel where Allen and the stranger made a seat from their arms and transported Jim up the stairs. He was able to step through the doorway and claim seats where he and Emily could watch the activities without being caught in the crowd below.

Making certain they were settled, Lily went back down the stairs and up the street to the race's finish line. She wanted to be there when Will and Matt crossed it.

Searching the throng of contestants gathered at the starting point, she had no trouble finding Matt. He stood half a head over the other contestants. As she watched, he turned his head, his gaze catching hers in a ray of heat as strong as if they stood directly opposite each other.

"Good to see Matt taking time with Will," a man Lily recognized as the station agent, Luther Frazier, said. "Soon, he'll be the only paw the boy has."

"Jim is going to be fine," Lily said tersely, turning back to check the hotel balcony. Allen was gone. Emily was sitting in Jim's lap, and Kianceta was beside him. Jim leaned forward and waved to Lily.

"Thought I'd better come down here and protect you from the witches," Allen said from behind her. "I usually have to guard Kianceta. But since you came to her defense, she's ready to take on the town women herself."

"I'm very fond of Kianceta, Mr. Kilgore. She is an unusual woman."

"You don't have to tell me. I know how special she is. I'm proud to have her as a wife."

The crowd suddenly started to yell. A gunshot was fired, and the racing teams started off with a rush. At the back of the pack, Matt and Will moved slowly but steadily along, passing the others who, in their haste, stumbled and fell or got out of step and fought against each other.

As they drew closer, Lily could read Matt's lips. "Steady, boy," he was saying. "I'll match your steps."

Only two teams made it to the end: a father and son, and Matt and Will.

"Hurry, Uncle Matt!"

"Hurry," Lily called out. "Winner gets the drumsticks."

Matt didn't look up, but he smiled and Lily knew he'd heard her. Then they were crossing the finish line, both teams, at the same time.

"We did it! We did it!" Will jumped up and down, screaming, "Papa! Look, Papa, we won!"

"Quiet! Quiet, please." The judges were trying unsuccessfully to capture the attention of the crowd. Finally the starting gun was fired again.

"Looks like we have a tie," he finally said. "So, our prize of twenty-five cents will have to be divided between the boys. We'll just make it fifteen cents' worth of candy each from Mr. Tolliver's store."

The ropes were untied, allowing Will and the other boy to charge through the crowd and into the store. Matt walked toward Lily. "Drumstick?" he asked.

"If you're brave enough. You do understand this was the first time I've ever fried chicken, Matt. You might want to eat barbecue instead and leave the drumstick for Jim."

"It's a hard decision," he said seriously, "whether to eat the Wells's barbecue, or barbecue the Wellses. Still, I don't know. The last time we ate fried chicken together I got birthday cake and a marriage proposal."

Lily gasped. She'd remembered, but she hadn't expected him to. "I have no cake to offer you today," she said quietly.

The rest of that day's menu lay unspoken between them. *Marriage proposal.*

"No matter. I'd be pleased to share fried chicken with you again, Lily."

• • •

From his hotel window, the man who now called himself Luke Conner watched the proceedings. The hotel clerk had pointed out the men he needed to know: Jim and Matt Logan and another rancher, a widower, with a houseful of children. The widower would be an easy target. But he'd been told that the Logan brothers were stubborn and standoffish. He'd been thinking about how he could convince them to sell. His original plan was still good, but now that he'd seen the younger brother, he could smell success.

Luke gave a final check to his appearance and nodded. He strapped on his gunbelt and inspected his revolver. Finally, the Stetson. Yep, he was a cattleman now, with money to spend and deals to make.

The dinner was about to be spread. According to plan, once the food was eaten, they'd pull out the piano from the saloon and dancing would begin. It was time for Luke to join the party. He'd seen the yellow-haired beauty who was to be Matthew Logan's wife. She looked a cut above these Texans. It wouldn't hurt to have the lady on his side. It wouldn't hurt to have her on her back either. Depending on the lady, that could come later.

When he'd completed his mission.

Lily sent Matt back to the wagon for their baskets while she went to check on Jim. After he delivered the picnic makings, Matt joined Luther Frazier in the saloon for a drink. He was standing at the bar when the stranger came through the door that led into the adjoining hotel.

Matt watched in the mirror as the man walked up beside him and propped one booted foot on the rail.

"Name's Luke Conner, Mr. Logan. If you'll excuse us, Mr. Frazier, I'd like to buy Mr. Logan a drink."

"Sure, Mr. Conner." Luther began to back away. "I'll see you later, Matt."

Matt continued to study the newcomer in the mirror without turning toward him. "That's an interesting accent for a cowboy."

"I'm not a cowboy."

Matt frowned. He was automatically suspicious of a stranger. But he ought to know who this was. There was something about him. Then he knew. "You're the man in the kilt—the Scotsman."

"I am from Scotland," he admitted. "But that was a long time ago. About that drink, what'll you have?"

"I'd rather have an explanation. Why would a stranger want to buy me a drink?"

"Because he'd like to talk a little business. Interested?"

"Not particularly."

"I think you will be, when you hear what I have to say."

"I doubt that, Conner. I have no intention of selling my land."

"Not even when I tell you that I'm already in possession of all the land around you, including the land between you and the river?"

Matt steeled himself to hide his surprise. "That's free range."

"Not anymore. By the first of the month, it will belong to me."

"How'd you pull that off?" Matt asked. "I've been trying to buy it for years."

"Let's just say I have a friend down in Austin who sees the value of bringing progress to Texas."

Matt glanced out the saloon window overlooking the street. The friend in Austin couldn't be the governor. But others might not feel as strongly about the wrong kind of outsiders moving in. Sergeant Rakestraw would be able to find out. Matt might just take a ride over to the fort tomorrow and chat with him.

"So what does this mean to me, Conner?"

"It means your cattle won't have water. My associates have instructed me to protect our water and grazing land."

"A fence?"

The Scotsman nodded.

Matt hadn't expected that. "You know my cattle aren't the only ones that come to the river. Goodnight and the travel drives may have something to say about a fence."

"Talk is cheap. Water isn't. Name your price, Logan."

"The Double L isn't for sale."

"It will be, and the longer you wait, the less I'll pay."

Matt took a swig of his whiskey and turned to Conner, giving him a look that made most men cower. "I don't like being threatened."

"No threat. The fence is fact."

"And how do you plan to accomplish that?"

"Barbed wire. I'm sure you've heard of it. There was a man in Austin last week taking orders. He gave us a demonstration. Once a cow touches the wire, it won't go near it again. Barbed wire will change Texas like nothing else ever has."

"Texans don't much like change; they've been known to resist," Matt observed. "Don't imagine your fence will be accepted without a lot of . . . discussion."

"Trust me, Mr. Logan. Change comes with money and power. And I have both. Do you?"

Matt had to hand it to the stranger. He didn't mince words. He made his threat and left it standing there, looking down your throat. "Trust you? Trust a man who butchers cows and wastes the meat?"

Conner didn't react to Matt's accusation immediately. He waited before he said, "Butchers cows? I don't know what you're talking about. I intend to drive our cows to the railroad and send them back east to a processing plant."

"You didn't kill three of my cows and leave them on the prairie for the buzzards to eat?"

"Why would I do that?"

"As a warning."

"I might have, if I had thought it would work. But you don't impress me as the kind of man who would take a warning lightly. So I'll just say it straight out. Name your price, Mr. Logan, while I still feel generous."

"Forget it, Conner. I'll do without your water, if I have to."

"Not for long, Logan. Not for long."

Luke Conner turned and walked out of the saloon, past the piano player and a fiddler who were setting up on the sidewalk. He caught Lorna by the hand and dragged her into the street where the citizens were lining up. "Walk with me, lassie, and tell me all Blue Station's secrets. I just might share some of my fortune with you."

Matt swallowed the last of his whiskey. He didn't doubt the man had a fortune to share, which was more than the Logan brothers had.

Later that afternoon Allen commandeered a table from inside one of the hotel rooms and dragged it to the roof.

By that time, the children were tired and hungry.

Matt watched Luke Conner join up with Ambrose Wells and move easily from one group of citizens to the other. He was a danger that Matt couldn't fight. With the banker in his pocket, the Scotsman was on his way to getting what he wanted. The friendship between Conner and Wells could also present problems for any of the smaller ranchers. Matt let out a deep sigh. Change was coming whether Matt wanted it or not.

"What's wrong, Matt?" Lily stopped unpacking her picnic basket and came toward him.

"Nothing. At least nothing I can do anything about. Where's Kilgore?"

"He went to get a pitcher of water and some of Mr. Wells's barbecue."

"I wish he hadn't done that. We'll eat what you prepared."

Jim agreed. "Of course we will. But if our banker wants to provide beef for the citizens, I think we ought to let him. That way we don't have to butcher one of ours. Look, Emily, there's your grandfather. I didn't expect to see him here."

Sergeant Rakestraw and his escort rode down the street, climbed from their horses, and tethered them to the rail outside the trading post.

Moments later Emily was flying into her grandfather's arms. Will came along more slowly, waiting until the officer lifted Emily into his arms before extending his hand to be shaken.

Kianceta and Lily moved toward the railing and watched as Sergeant Rakestraw proceeded through the crowd and disappeared beneath the balcony into the hotel.

Quickly, Lily laid out the contents of her picnic basket. "I hope we have enough food."

"We will," Kianceta assured her, and began to spread her contributions along with Lily's.

Matt didn't miss the stormy looks being sent toward the roof by the women of Blue Station. He wasn't certain whether the frowns were directed at him or the Kilgores.

"Matt, Jim, Mrs. Kilgore." Sergeant Rakestraw swung Emily to the floor and greeted everyone enthuastically, then turned to Lily. "And you must be Lily. Welcome. You've been sorely needed."

The gray-haired man took Lily's hand and gave her a quick, gallant kiss. Lily decided she liked him. His welcome was restrained, yet genuine, both to her and to Kianceta, who obviously knew the newcomer.

"I'm very glad to know you, Sergeant Rakestraw. I hope you'll join us for the celebration."

"Only for some of Wells's barbecue," he said in apology. "Have to get back to the fort." He stepped back and turned his attention to Matt. "Wonder if I could have a quick word with you before we eat, Matt."

Matt nodded and followed the sergeant back down the corridor and into the saloon. They found a table in the corner.

"Lily is a fine-looking woman, Matt. I'd say Jim did a right fair job of picking a woman for you."

"Lily is a fine-looking woman. But I'm having a little trouble tying her down, sir. She thinks she wants to do a bit more shopping around."

"Whiskey, barkeep," the sergeant called out. "I'm sure you can convince her. Just pull out some of that southern charm."

The old soldier scratched his chin thoughtfully. "I don't want to step out of line here, but I'm worried. I saw that Scotsman leaving as I arrived. You know he's after your land?"

"I know. He already offered. How'd you find out?"

"I heard about it. You refused?"

Matt nodded.

The old soldier let out a deep breath, then caught himself and took a sip of whiskey. "You know it might be the wise thing to do. Get Jim back to a doctor."

"He won't go. And I haven't insisted. Every doctor he's seen said there was nothing to be done."

"Have you considered sending the children back to a real school?"

It was hard for Matt to conceal his shock. "You're serious, aren't you? You're suggesting that I do what you never would?"

"The truth is, that's the last thing I want. I never should have sent Maria away. If she'd stayed here, she'd have been much happier. Things might have been very different."

"So what do you suggest I do about the Scotsman?"

"I've been working on that. Didn't want to alarm the ladies—or Jim—but we found your crooked-tailed sow, over toward the canyon. Pretty bad."

Matt's eyebrows shot up. "Found my sow? What do you mean, pretty bad?"

"She'd been ripped open. Whoever did it took the piglets and left her gutted."

Matt shook his head. "They didn't take any part of her for food?"

"Nope. Just mutilated her."

"She wasn't ready to drop the pigs. What would anybody do with them?"

Sergeant Rakestraw leaned back in his chair and grimaced. "Only thing I could figure is that somebody didn't want them born."

"You mean they want me to lose the income."

"Maybe. Maybe it's something else altogether."

Matt didn't drink his whiskey. He wanted to remain clearheaded. "How long ago you figure it was done?"

"I'd say it happened right after that storm. Had my men bury her. Couldn't see bringing the carcass home. Besides, I was headed here."

"Damn! I was counting on those pigs. I even planted extra corn to feed them. I thought it might be the Scotsman. Now I'm not so sure. You got any ideas?"

"Settlers, maybe. There've been some incidents over by the canyon and down the Rio Grande: fires and rustling. Don't know what to think. Makes no sense. All I can do is investigate. I'm sending a report to Washington. With any luck this will make them think twice about closing the fort."

"They're not serious about that, are they?" Matt asked.

"Well, since they've got the Comanche under control,

they think everything will be all right. I'm having a hard time convincing them otherwise."

Matt glanced out the window, catching sight of Conner. He remembered the raids, the killing before Rakestraw got things under control. They'd been lucky. Rides Fast kept his Comanche in check, but the anger was just under the surface, and there were other tribes. "Wells and the Scotsman seem pretty close."

Rakestraw turned to look. "Figures. He needs a local money man. Haven't found out who the real backers are. Conner's just the front man."

"You met him?"

Rakestraw nodded. "He came by the fort yesterday to tell me he's taken an option on the acreage between your land and the reservation. I thought that was to be a free buffer."

"So did I. I'd hoped to buy it myself someday. Didn't know the plans had changed. Guess I waited too long. Did he tell you they're going to fence it?"

"Fence it? He didn't mention that part of his plan. A fence will stir things up. Goodnight will be driving his herd north any day now. He ain't gonna like that. Neither is Rides Fast."

Matt leaned forward. "Neither do I. If he puts up barbed wire, my cattle won't be able to get to the river."

Sergeant Rakestraw was surprised. "You mean he got hold of the land on the other side of yours, too?"

"So he says. What do you know about Conner?"

"Not enough," the old man said, coming to a standing position. "I think I need to know more. Give my regrets to your family, Matt. I believe I'll skip the festivities and get back to the fort so I can start checking out our new neighbor. Bring the children when you can, Matt. And—" he stopped and turned back—"marry that girl. Your brother is a lot wiser than you think."

Marrying Lily was his intention. Everybody except Lily seemed to agree that it was a smart move.

Matt watched the sergeant leave. He respected Maria's father, but there was no doubt that family festivities were something easy for him to walk away from. Matt doubted the officer's escorts would be as pleased to miss out on the picnic.

Moments later he saw the soldiers, their tin plates piled high with food, following Sergeant Rakestraw down the street toward their horses.

What Sergeant Rakestraw told him was another worry. Matt had fought in a war, fought the elements, public opinion, and fate. Suddenly there was a new conspiracy afoot, all man-made. He didn't know what to think. The news of his dead sow was a blow, but not nearly as much as the news that his ranch was about to be hemmed in by the Scot. No, Conner had said "we." Who was backing him?

With his emotions being shredded from all sides, Matt was ready to go home, regroup, rethink what the Logan brothers were going to do.

He hated even to give thought to Rakestraw's suggestion, but maybe he was right. He could sell the herd, lease the land to Conner, and take everybody back to Memphis. Aunt Dolly couldn't take them in, but with her connections, they could make a new start. God knows, he was tired of struggling against odds that he couldn't change.

Except for one. Marrying Lily.

It was time he started courting her.

15

Matt met Allen Kilgore as he was coming out of the saloon. He was headed up the stairs, carrying a pitcher and a platter of barbecue.

"Been gambling?" the Indian agent asked. "You look like you just lost your last dime."

"Not yet, but you might be more right than you know. Everything I've done since I got to Texas has been a gamble. So far I've lost more than I've won. I feel like I'm down to my last hand," Matt said wearily.

At the top of the steps, Kilgore stopped. "Is there anything I can do to help, Matt?"

"Thanks, but this is something I have to do myself." Matt sniffed the pungent sauce on the meat. "Let's eat. We have to show our ladies a good time," he said, and walked onto the roof. "If I still remember how it's done."

Kilgore handed Kianceta the plate of crispy chopped meat and set the pitcher on the table. "We're hungry, women."

They filled their plates with Lily and Kianceta's combined picnic. Matt gave Lily a smile, reaching for the drumstick.

Lily watched Matt's expression and cringed inwardly. Her cooking had come a long way, but she knew that the art of frying chicken was yet to be mastered.

Will took a bite of his piece. "Yuck, it's raw on the inside."

"Mine's burned," Emily whined.

Matt made a great show of tearing off a chunk of chicken and chewing valiantly. "Oh, I don't know. Tastes fine to me. I think the problem may be our lack of culture. We don't know anything about fine dining, and Miss Lily does."

Lily almost choked on her biscuit.

Matt waved the drumstick about as he talked. "I happen to know that this is the way the president likes his chicken. And that's good enough for me."

Emily's eyes grew large. "The pres'dent?"

"The president of the United States of America," Kilgore said as he picked up the pitcher. "I read in a newspaper about his fondness for lemonade and fried chicken."

"Lemonade?" both children asked. "What's that?"

"Lemons. That's a tart fruit. You squeeze some and mix the juice with water and sugar. Then you pour it over some of Ambrose Wells's imported ice. Perfect with our chicken. And I just happen to have some."

Will and Emily looked balefully at the pink-tinged juice oozing from Will's piece of chicken. Never having experienced either lemonade or fried chicken, they weren't ready to be convinced of either.

Lily studied the serious expressions on the adults' faces, then began to laugh. "Thank you, Matt. Mr. Kilgore. But even I know this chicken is pretty bad. And unless you have that lemonade laced with some of Rides Fast's elixir, I don't think anything will change it."

"I don't know," Kilgore said seriously, "it might."

Lily looked at Matt. "You really don't have to defend my cooking, Matt. Look, children, I'm not going to make you eat the chicken. Have some of Mr. Wells's barbecue. I'm sure it's better."

"I disagree." Matt stood and removed his hat, placing it solemnly over his heart. "That poor bird gave his life to come to this picnic. I refuse to let it go unrewarded."

"You're right, Matt," Kilgore said. He stood, bowed his head piously for a moment, then made a great show of pulling an imaginary bugle from his pocket and pretending to play as he whistled "Taps."

If possible, the expression on Matt's face became even more serious. He studied the chicken, then announced with sudden inspiration, "I have the answer. Here's what we'll do: You will eat the barbecue. I will eat the chicken."

"Oh no," Jim protested, catching the solemn spirit of the occasion, "I insist you share the bird with me. After all, I'm responsible for its sudden demise."

Lily gave Matt a veiled glance. "Don't be silly. Either of you. It will probably make you sick."

Matt took another big bite from his piece. "Then if you want to become a rich widow, we'd better find the preacher quick."

He was putting them all on. She could see the mischief in his eyes. The gentle Matt she knew. A serious Matt, an angry Matt and, she blushed as she remembered, a passionate Matt. But Matt with a twinkle in his eye was a stranger.

"Well, I'm going to give the lemonade a try before the ice melts," Kilgore said, and poured a small amount of the liquid along with a few shavings of ice into each glass.

After the chicken, the children weren't taking Allen's recommendation of the pale drink. But ice in a drink was a novelty that couldn't be ignored. They each took a tentative sip, swallowed, and smiled.

"Where did they get ice?" Will asked. "It isn't even winter."

It was Matt who answered. "The mayor had it packed

in sawdust and brought in by special railcars. Then he picked it up at the rail yard in Abilene." He took a long sip. "Yep, perfect with a picnic."

Just then the sun slid behind the roof of the hotel, and music started. Quickly, the hanging lanterns over the wooden sidewalks were lit. The constant breeze moved the lamps in the twilight. Lily had the notion that they were keeping time with the piano player.

Lily stole a look at Matt, wondering what to expect next. He was watching her. The mischief in his eyes turned into a flirty wink. She suddenly felt alive with anticipation.

"Finish your food, children," she urged. "The dancing will begin soon."

"Dancing. Now that sounds like a fine idea," Matt said.

"But I don't know how to dance," Emily whined.

"Neither do I," Will grumbled. "And I ain't gonna learn."

"Don't say 'ain't,' " Lily said automatically. "Besides, one day you'll want to know how and then I'll teach you."

"No, thank you, ma'am. I think I'll go watch them get the fireworks ready. When do they start, Papa?"

"Fireworks!" Jim said. "I'd forgotten about the fireworks. Now, that sounds interesting."

"Yes, fireworks," Kilgore confirmed. "And if we plan to eat those peaches before the entertainment begins, we'd better get started."

Jim, who seemed to be enjoying a rare evening of respite from his constant shortness of breath, smiled and said, "Maybe Kianceta will serve them. I believe Lily is still . . . paying homage to the chicken."

Kianceta, who had seemed content to let the others carry on the conversation, laughed out loud.

A fiddler joined the piano player in the street below. Harriet Wells and Ora Manley started the dancing by pulling their reluctant partners out into the hard-packed earthen street.

"Take your places," the fiddle player said, "for the grand march."

"Aren't you going to dance with your lady?" Allen Kilgore asked Matt.

"Of course," Matt replied, and held out his hand.

"But I have to put away the food," Lily protested, her heart already doing the grand march inside her chest.

"I'll take care of the food," Kianceta said. "Go and dance."

"But what about Emily and Will?"

"We'll make a pallet for Emily on the floor," Jim said. "Will can go down to where they're setting up the fireworks display, so long as he stays out of the way." Jim pulled his chair closer to the rail. "And I'm going to watch."

Lily took Matt's arm. This was what she'd wished for. Now she had to keep herself from appearing too eager. After all, he thought she'd turned him down. No point in letting him know what she was up to . . . not just yet.

The music started. The dancers made two lines, the women on one side and the men on the other. So that she could move without tripping, Lily fastened the train of her dress to the hook beneath one of the draped folds of her skirt. The intricate movements of the dance were no trouble for her; she'd practiced them for years. Her dress swished against her petticoats as she danced, and her apprehension melted away. From one partner to the next she moved, smiling at the men, who returned her smile, and the women, who didn't.

As she and Matt made an arch for the others to sashay through, she couldn't avoid looking up into his eyes, eyes flashing with emotion. Could he really be serious about courting her?

"Do you have to flirt with all the men?" he asked in a growl.

"I'm not flirting," she quipped. "I'm husband-shopping. Remember?"

"But what about . . . about Jim? He thinks he's courting you, too. Aren't you being unkind to tease him?"

She glanced up at the roof and gave Jim a wave. "He is courting me," Lily said smugly as they dropped their arms and joined the weaving circle again. "And I'm not teasing."

Both she and Matt were breathless as the dance came to a close. She leaned against him for a moment. "You're a very good dancer, Matt. Where'd you learn?"

"Jim's wife taught me. She used to like to dance. Who taught you?"

"Aunt Dolly, of course."

Matt was about to suggest they take a walk when Ambrose Wells suddenly appeared beside them.

"They're about to play the Virginia reel, Miss Townsend. Will you do me the honor of this dance?"

"No," Matt said, holding firm to Lily's arm.

"I'd be delighted, Mr. Wells," Lily answered, pinching Matt's hand to force him to let her go.

Matt retreated to the balcony, where Lily watched him alternately pace and scowl. Two hours later, when Matt had managed to claim her for only one more dance, she decided that maybe he'd suffered enough. She could no longer see him, and that bothered her. Maybe she'd better get back to being his fiancée before the citizens of Blue Station.

Excusing herself from Mr. Tolliver, her latest dance partner, she made her way back to the roof. So much for Matt's concern that she might be shunned. That hadn't happened, at least not by the men.

Emily was asleep on the pallet with her head in Kianceta's lap. The only other person there was a tired Jim.

Lily took one look at his pallor and felt guilty that she'd neglected him. "Where's Matt?"

Kianceta answered, "He and Allen went to hitch up the buggy. We're going to take Jim and the children home."

"I hope this wasn't too much exertion for you, Jim," Lily said.

"No, I wouldn't have missed it, but I am tired."

"Then we'll all go. I'll find Matt and tell him. I'm ready, too."

She turned and headed back down the stairs, worried that her foolishness had hurt Jim.

Lily skirted the watchers lined up along the street, and headed away from the dancers. Just as she was almost out of reach, she was caught by the hand and pulled back into the street.

"Howdy, ma'am."

The cowboy was big, blond, and beaming with pleasure. "Luke Conner," he said, lifting her hand to his lips.

"Thank you, Mr. Conner, but I'm not dancing just now."

"Of course you are, darling. With me."

"No. I'm looking for my fiancé."

"Fiancé? A pretty girl like you shouldn't already be promised when you haven't met me yet."

"I'm afraid I am. Now, if you'll let me go?"

She tried to pull her arm away, tried and failed. Behind the rascal's lighthearted exterior was a man with a grasp of pure iron. She couldn't budge.

"Just one dance," he cajoled. "They're about to play a waltz. Besides, I'm hoping you'll help me with a little problem I'm having with your fiancé."

"Problem with Matt?"

He swung her around, smiling as though they shared a secret. "Yes. He's going to have to listen to my offer to buy his land. Once I block off the river, his cattle won't be able to survive."

She tried unsuccessfully to stop their movement around the street. "I don't understand. What do you mean, block off the river?"

"I'm leasing all the land around the Double L."

"But Matt dug a well."

"Which won't provide enough water for a real herd, and he knows it. He'd be better off to sell out now, while I'm still feeling generous. If you have any influence on him, Miss Lily, you'd best make him see the truth."

Lily faked a stumble, forcing the cowboy to stop. She tried once more to jerk her hand away. "If Matt says he isn't interested in your offer, he isn't. Let me go, sir!"

"Do as the lady says." Matt's voice was deadly calm.

The cowboy let go, hands out in front of him, and stepped back. "Hey, whatever you say, Logan. It's your call."

Matt pulled Lily into his arms. "Let's dance." He looked down at Lily, daring her to argue.

She didn't. This time Matt's expression was neither warm nor wicked. His movements were graceful, but controlled. He held her entirely too close as he whirled her intensely around the street. She felt as if they were flying low, bending and weaving like butterflies dancing a mating game. There must have been others on the street, but Lily didn't see them. When the music finally came to an end, they had left the roped-off area and were past the wash tent, in the dark.

His feet stopped moving, but he continued to hold her.

"Are you all right, Matt?" she finally whispered.

"No, but you already know that, don't you? You see so much through those green eyes."

"I know something's wrong."

"You mean other than the fact that the woman who is

supposed to be my fiancée has spent half the night flirting with every man here?"

"But you and I know that our wedding is off," she protested, waiting for him to correct her.

"Not so far as I'm concerned."

"Oh? Why not?" She waited for the answer that she'd craved for most of her adult life. Kianceta was right about one thing: She'd seen the way he watched her. Down deep inside, he had to want her. What would she do if he didn't? For just a while tonight she'd seen him forget about the pain and smile. That smile had made her heart feel good. How could she give that up?

She took a deep, steadying breath, willing her legs to hold her so that she wouldn't collapse at his feet.

"You never wanted to marry me, Matt. I thought you'd be happy to be released from our agreement. Why has that changed?"

"Jim was right. We—I need a wife."

"You need a Texas woman. I'm not."

"You will be."

"My cooking still has a long way to go."

"Yes, it does."

"And I'm not ready yet to drive the mule and plant a garden without help."

"You'll learn."

"We both know that I have a mind of my own."

"You certainly do. So use it."

There was a moment of silence. She could hear the music behind them. She could hear Matt's breathing. What she couldn't hear was any more lies. "The children need a mother, Matt. And I really care about them. But I won't marry a man who doesn't love me."

The children. They were the reason he *had* to convince her to marry him. And Jim. And . . . he was lying to himself. Sometime, when he hadn't even realized it was happening, he'd fallen in love with Lily. Now his own need for her was as great as Emily's and Will's.

His need and his fear.

Selfish reasons for bringing a woman to the ranch. He didn't have to remind himself what marriage would mean to Lily. After a few years Texas would take her zest for life and leave her worn and disillusioned. They might have had a chance, but Conner had upped the stakes. Matt couldn't do that, not even for the children. Not even for himself. He had to reject her. Damn it to hell, he didn't have a choice.

"Tell me, Matt," she said softly, "what else do I have to do to be a rancher's wife? I mean, if I could manage to be what you need, what would our future depend on?"

Me, he almost said. *I don't know what to do about you. But most of all, I don't know what to do about me.* "Jim," he finally answered, "the children, and the ranch. There's more at stake than just us. I've been so determined that I've lost sight of them. Maybe the time has come to stop. Maybe I ought to give all this up."

"It's that man, isn't it, that cowboy? He said he's fencing off the river. What can we do to stop him?"

"There's no 'we,' Lily. You don't need to worry about that."

She could hear the tension in his voice, the pain. "He wants to buy the ranch. Why?"

"To raise cattle."

"But you aren't interested in selling?"

Matt cleared his throat. "I never thought so before. Now, I have to consider his offer."

"Why?" she asked.

"Because of Jim and the children. It's time I started being smart. There may be a better answer."

"I don't understand," she said.

"You and Jim could take the children and leave here."

Lily couldn't begin to comprehend what he'd just said,

but she could hear the tightness in his voice. "You mean go back to Tennessee?"

"Yes. I mean we could sell the ranch and go back."

Still locked in his arms, she searched his face. "You can't mean that. Give up all you've worked for?"

"If that's what it takes."

"Jim doesn't want to leave, Matt. He's convinced that nothing can be done about his heart, and he says he doesn't want to shorten what time he has left by undergoing a long journey. I really think he wants so badly to have something to leave Will and Emily, to justify his life. Losing the ranch could kill him. Have you really thought this through?"

Matt shook his head. He hadn't thought about anything else for the last two hours. He'd watched Jim pretend to be strong, listened to his plans to court Lily. He'd watched Emily sleeping peacefully and Will's impatience to see the fireworks. He'd watched Lily dance and thought about losing her.

For the last few days, Lily had been the first thing he thought about when he opened his eyes in the morning and the last thing he thought of before he slept at night. He'd tried every way he knew to force her to return to Tennessee. He hadn't allowed himself to want to touch her, to hold her in his arms, to kiss her.

But he hadn't been able to stop. Even now, when everything he'd fought for was in jeopardy, he wanted Lily. Not for the children. Not for Jim. Not for the ranch. For himself.

"I didn't mean to cause you more trouble, Matt. I told you, I'm not holding you to the contract."

"You don't understand, Lily. Someone is threatening us for reasons I don't understand. I can protect you from the Indians, the bandits, even the land itself. But this is something new, and I can't take a chance on what I can't see."

"Life and death aren't so different, Matt. They both take courage and purpose. You've never lacked for either. You want to take care of Jim and protect his children from whatever threatens them. I can help you do that, and I will. But I think you need me as much as they do. Just for tonight, couldn't you be honest? Tell me what you want."

"Don't ask me to be honest, Lily."

"But I am."

He couldn't deny her simple request. She deserved the truth. "You're going to regret this."

Slowly she let the air out of her lungs. "Maybe. But I can't think that the truth could be any worse than not knowing."

That was the trouble. He couldn't think either. Every time he came near Lily, his thoughts scattered. All he could think about was the woman in his arms, waiting to be kissed. He'd started out the evening with the intention to court her, to break through her wall of resistance. He'd been determined to win Lily. Had he?

Behind him the music turned lively, playing a fast tune that resulted in a lot of clapping and cowboy yells. Lily waited.

Matt could no more have stopped himself from kissing her than he could have stopped the hot summer wind. It felt right to join his mouth with hers.

Something went off inside him like fireworks. Hot and wild and demanding. He wanted her so bad that he was about to explode. The mad beat of his heart deafened him. They were caught now in a whirl of lights and sparkles overhead, as fireworks exploded above them. Matt let himself give in and pulled Lily even closer. He'd never thought to feel anything like this; he'd fought it, then under the guise of looking after his family, he reached out for it.

Lily's arms went around his neck, and for one moment, Matt felt as if they were surrounded by the bursting fire-storm of the celebration.

"Dammit, I love you!" he said and kissed her.

He shuddered at the pleasure of it, at the joy, at the melding of two people who couldn't get enough of touching each other. Then the explosion was over, and the dying sparks floated to earth. The display was complete. He felt Lily pull back and catch her breath.

"Let's go home, Matt," she said.

Matt released her, slid one arm around her waist, and started the walk back to get the others. Nothing had been decided, yet everything had changed. Both he and Lily were too caught up in what had happened to talk. He wouldn't have known what to say. She simply leaned her head against his shoulder.

The roof was empty. Allen and Kianceta were already in the buggy. Racer was hitched to the wagon where Jim, Will, and Emily were waiting.

"Since you're here," Allen said, "we'll say good night now."

"Did you see the fireworks?" Will asked. "They were swell."

"We saw fireworks," Matt said, assisting Lily into the wagon. "We definitely saw fireworks."

"Are you all right, Jim?" Lily asked anxiously.

Jim took a deep breath and managed a smile. "We're fine, Lily. Fine."

As the wagon left town, Lily noticed the light of someone's cigar in the shadows. The smoker stepped forward, just enough for the flickering lamplight to catch the pale color of his hair, then he tossed the burning ember into the street.

" 'Night, folks," he called out. "Be careful going home."

"Who was that?" Jim asked curiously.

"Just a Scotsman," Matt answered, "who thinks he's going to be a Texas rancher."

"And you don't think he'll make it?" his brother asked.

"I'm still deciding," was Matt's answer.

Lily woke early and, throwing on a wrapper, climbed down the ladder to start the day. Her heart still sang. Her lips still felt tender, and her body wanted to float off into a cloudless blue sky that went on forever.

She slipped out the door and walked lightly across the yard to the barn. But Matt was gone. In fact there was no evidence that he'd even slept there. In disappointment, Lily turned back to the porch and sat down on the steps. Why?

An hour later she still had no answers. The children, tired from their late night, were cranky, and Jim didn't even pretend to have enough energy to do more than get out of bed. Finally she stirred up a batch of pancakes, using the last of the milk in the cellar. The dough was still too thick. Since she didn't know how to milk a cow and Matt was gone, she had to make do. In the lean-to she found a bottle labeled *syrup*. She poured a generous dollop of liquid into the batter, then added another until it was finally of a consistency to cook.

A lot of good that did her. The children only picked at theirs and Jim didn't even try. After breakfast Emily and Will went to gather the eggs, and Lily cleaned up.

Lily couldn't keep from wondering where Matt was and why he'd left so early. Finally, she gathered up the rest of the pancakes and covered them with a cotton cloth. She'd take a walk, and if she ran into Matt, she'd feed him. If not, she'd feed the birds.

She needed to think about where she and Matt were headed. In her mind, there was no longer any question of their connection. He'd said he loved her. The only thing that remained to discuss was how their lives would change.

When she came west she'd come to Matt, the boy who'd made her believe in herself when she was a homeless girl with no future.

Through the years Matt had remained that boy, the one with the pain in his eyes, the boy who'd rejected her little-girl adoration and gone away. For all the time since, she'd made herself into the kind of woman she thought he'd be proud to marry. But more than that, she'd sworn that she'd heal his bad memories, that someday her future would be his.

Because she'd loved that Matt, she loved the new Matt and expected him to love her in return. But maybe love wasn't enough. He couldn't face her this morning. His absence spoke louder than words.

So be it. She wouldn't hold him to his promise anymore. Before she left she built up the fire. From the sewing box she took the contract drawn up by Aunt Dolly's lawyer and fed it into the flames. As it burned she picked up her food.

Matt couldn't sell out to the Scotsman. She had to take Jim and the children back east long enough for him to find a way to save the ranch. But how? They had no money to buy tickets and no money to live on once they returned. Unless Aunt Dolly could help.

If they were gone, Matt's burden would be lessened.

The horror of leaving Matt swirled around in her mind, carrying her farther and farther as she left the yard and walked in a new direction. She'd been east, toward the reservation, and she'd been to town. Now she walked west, past the barn and the well, in the direction of the creek. The afternoon sun, almost directly overhead, was warm. She quickly came to wish for Maria's hat.

She glanced behind her periodically, always keeping the barn at her back. There were no roads, no trees, no mountains to use as guideposts. Everything was the same, an unending carpet of range grass and bluebonnets ruffled by the wind. The murmuring made a soft music that rose and fell, broken only by the occasional cry of a bird. Though nothing like her Tennessee home, she felt a strange closeness to this land. Through drought and cold, the prairie struggled to survive, just as the people who lived on it. Leaving would be hard.

And then she topped a slight ridge and stood, overlooking the creek that snaked its way across the corner of the Double L, a sparkling ribbon of water. It would go dry in the summer, she'd been told, but now it twinkled merrily, adding a new sound to the melody of the plains.

Upstream a cow was drinking. No, not a cow, it was One-Eyed Jack, the bull. Proud and strong he stood, bending his massive neck to drink, wielding horns that, had they been pointed down instead of up, would have embedded themselves in the ground.

Caught up in the power of such a magnificent creature, Lily sank down to the ground to watch. In the distance beyond, six or seven cows were grazing contentedly, unaware they were being watched by a woman almost surrounded by clumps of tall grass.

The warm sun beat down on her. Butterflies danced across the prevailing wind like the bright petals of the summer wildflowers back home along the banks of the Mississippi. Overhead, big whipped-cream clouds moved across the sky, temporarily obstructing the sun. She understood Matt's fierce determination to stay here. It was more than just the Double L; there was a tie to the land that tugged at her sense of belonging.

Out here, all her worries seemed lighter. She lay back and closed her eyes.

16

It was late afternoon when Matt reined in Racer and realized how far he was from the ranch. For most of the night he'd been caught up in the memory of dancing with Lily, of kissing Lily, of touching her.

Finally, he'd saddled Racer and ridden out before he did something he might regret. He had to think about the Double L, not Lily.

Damn that Scot. Damn those outsiders who thought they could just come in and take over what others had sacrificed for. There had to be a way to stop them. The price they'd paid for the Double L was too great to give it up. But the price for staying could be greater.

Suppose he sent Jim and the children back. How could he afford to do that?

Finally it came to him. He was letting Conner's threat stop him. He should be using the Scotsman. He didn't have to sell; the land could be leased long enough to get Jim and the children settled.

And Lily.

Yes, it could work.

Convincing Jim wouldn't be easy, but maybe there was

a way they could all get what they wanted. The only way Jim would go was if leaving meant that the children's future was secure. Matt thought he saw a way.

Once they were back in Memphis, he'd get Aunt Dolly out of the hotel. He'd find a place for her, Jim, and the children. With a housekeeper and Lily to look after them, Will and Emily could go to school, and Jim could see a proper doctor.

This was the first week of June. He'd make the deal effective the first of July. That would give him a month to round up his cattle and fill his orders for the reservation and the fort.

The rest, he'd sell. Goodnight's herd would be moving north soon. For a fee, the rancher would let Matt's cattle join the drive.

Sergeant Rakestraw could advance him the money for the steers consigned to the army, and Matt could buy his family tickets back east. The temporary-lease money from the Scotsman would keep them going until he could find work as a cowboy for some other spread. Then later, when Jim was better, they'd come back and start over. The future of the Double L would be put on hold but not abandoned.

Yes, Jim and the children would go along with his plan, once they understood.

About Lily, he wasn't so sure.

Lily Towns made up her own mind. He could still see her standing up to those women in town, choosing to share her meal with Kianceta rather than the mayor. He'd been wrong about her learning to be a Texas woman. She'd done that and more. If he could choose a wife, it would be Lily.

He reached the creek and drew Racer to a stop so that he could drink.

Once Matt had a plan, everything fell into place. First he'd get back to the ranch and explain his solution to Jim. Then he'd talk to Lily. One way or another, it had to work. He'd make it work.

Matt was practicing his argument when he heard a shot. It came from upstream. Was the butcher at work again? This time he'd catch him. Then came a second shot, an animal's cry of pain, and a woman's scream.

He nudged Racer in the flanks, causing the big horse to rear and plunge forward. Someone was hurt. Moments later Matt could see two men on horseback. Soldiers, perhaps. The riders wore blue.

The first shot woke Lily and drew her to her feet. She didn't know who was the most surprised at her appearance, the bull or the soldier who was firing at the cows milling around. One cow fell, bellowing in pain.

One-Eyed Jack let out a cry of rage and charged. He missed the soldier doing the shooting and headed for the second man on horseback. Moments later his horn caught the horse in the chest, ripping it open.

The first soldier fired again.

Lily screamed.

Jack faltered.

The injured horse went down.

"Christ Almighty, Billy," one of the soldiers called out, "that devil's killed my horse. Shoot him!"

"I already shot him, Roe, and he's still coming."

The bull lunged past, made a wide circle, and started back.

"Shoot him again!"

"Shut up, you fool. There's somebody watching us. Climb on. Let's get out of here."

Billy pulled alongside and Roe climbed up behind his friend. "Tarnation! It's a woman," Roe said. "She's seen us. We'll have to get rid of her."

"I don't mind butchering a few cows, but I don't cotton to killing a woman, Roe. Let's just get out of here. We just wanted us some steak. What can she say different?"

"Don't matter. She knows we're soldiers, and now she knows our names, don't she? Rakestraw'll have us up on charges if we get caught. I ain't looking forward to spending the next year in the stockade."

One-Eyed Jack was walking slowly toward the soldiers, blood dripping down his hip as he stopped and pawed the earth in warning.

The men turned away.

Lily thought she was safe. Until she saw that they were simply circling the bull and heading toward her from a different direction. She couldn't run. She was on foot, and they'd catch her before she got ten feet. Jim had told her not to go off alone. Why hadn't she listened? Why hadn't she brought her shotgun?

Nobody knew where she was.

Then Jack turned and started toward her. The soldiers veered off, ready to let the bull take care of the woman for them. She was doomed. She had to face the soldiers or the bull. Either way, she didn't stand a chance.

Jack stepped up his pace. Just as he came even with her, she reached inside her pocket and pulled out pancakes wrapped in a napkin. She'd brought them to feed the birds and, in her musings, had completely forgotten about them. "Ho, Jack!" she said softly, and watched him come to a confused stop, his horns almost touching her skirt.

"Please, Jack," she whispered, unwrapping the cloth. "Look. I have pancakes with honey. Remember?" She broke off a piece and threw it to the ground in front of him.

The bull sniffed and picked it up.

He chewed the dough and stared at her with big dark eyes. For a moment she thought he might even be considering his next move. At least he wasn't charging . . . yet. "Now, Jack," she went on, "come along. You call your ladies, and we'll go to the barn. I'll make sure you get all the pancakes you can eat."

Lily turned slowly around and walked away, holding the rest of the crumbling pancake out behind her. Moments later Jack moved slowly forward, and the cows surrounded her. They started across the prairie.

The soldiers came after her. "We got to stop that bull, Roe. We can't let her get away."

"Not me. I'm not about to take that woman on. Anybody that can tame One-Eyed Jack has got to be in league with the devil. That bull's too close to her. He done killed my horse. Let's head for the fort."

"What about her?"

"Let her talk. By the time she does, we'll be long gone. All we have to do is pick up our money and head for Kansas."

"But we ain't going to Kansas," Billy said, "are we? I thought—"

"Shut up, you fool." Roe turned his horse and rode in the opposite direction.

In the vast openness of the plains their voices carried as if they were standing beside Lily. But she didn't turn back to see what they were doing. She was afraid to do anything other than walk carefully back toward the ranch. The bull seemed peaceful enough now, but she didn't want to think about what he might do if he got spooked. He took a turn to the left and began a slow pace behind her. She kept on walking.

At least ten minutes passed with Lily dropping more pancakes behind her when she heard more gunshots. Several shots, then silence, and one final shot. Had those men turned on each other? She only hoped they hadn't encountered any more of Matt's steers.

Then she heard hoofbeats. Rapid hoofbeats. A single horse.

"Hurry, Jack," she said.

"Lily? Is that you?"

The cattle scattered. Jack let out a bellow and ran away, the cows falling in behind. Lily turned around.

"Matt?"

He swung down from his horse and caught her in his arms just as her legs gave way.

"What in the hell are you doing out here?" he asked.

"You were gone when I got up, and I—I just went for a walk," she said, shaken. "And then I fell asleep. When I woke up, those awful men were shooting your cows."

"You saw them?"

"Yes. They were dressed like soldiers. They said they wanted some beef, but I don't think that's what they were really doing."

He held her close, tightening his grip when he realized she was shaking uncontrollably. "I know. We crossed paths a ways back."

"Those shots? Are you all right?"

"I'm fine. Ah, Lily, I know what I just saw, but I still don't believe it. What were you doing with that bull?"

"Jack saved my life. Those men were going to kill me. We've got to go after him. He's wounded."

"And you think he'll just let you walk up to him and examine his wound?" he asked incredulously.

The thought of the wounded bull took away the fear that had cowered Lily. Jack had saved her, and she owed it to him to do the same.

"Yes, I do, Matt. Let's check on your cows, and then I want to find Jack."

It was too late for Matt's cow, though he was convinced that if it had meant hauling the injured animal back to the ranch, Lily would have insisted.

"Hurry, Matt, please."

Matt lifted Lily onto Racer's back and climbed up behind her. "What's that?" he asked, looking at the napkin still half-full of pancakes.

"Breakfast."

"Looks like you lost most of it."

"I fed it to Jack. He likes pancakes and honey."

Matt shook his head. "I can't believe I'm doing this," he said, directing Racer along the path of flattened grass left by Jack and the cows.

"Stop," Lily called out suddenly. "See, there? It's blood. Jack is hurt. We've got to help him."

With an uneasy feeling, Matt glanced around. The shooters had disappeared, but what was to keep them from returning?

"Lily, this isn't a good idea," Matt began. "Jack's heading toward an area thick with mesquite trees and briars."

"Then let's hurry. Maybe we can head him off."

"That's not all. Look at the sun. It's going to be setting soon, and then the wind turns cold. You aren't even wearing a shawl."

"Like you told me once," she said lightly, "I wear too damned many clothes."

"Be serious. Let's head back. Tomorrow, when it's light, we'll come back and find Jack."

"You go back, Matt. Just let me off. I can walk. Bring your medical box when you come."

"Don't be foolish. I'm not leaving you out here."

"Well, I'd go back and let you find Jack, but I don't think he likes you."

Lily knew that if Matt made up his mind to force her to return, she wouldn't be able to stop him. Irrational as it seemed, she couldn't turn her back on Jack. Matt must think she was behaving like some silly child. So be it.

"What were you doing out here, Matt?"

"Thinking."

"About what?"

"That it's a good idea to leave Texas. Now I'm sure of it."

"Because of those two men?"

"Partly. And because . . . well because it's the smartest thing to do."

That statement was so extraordinary that she couldn't even argue. Instead, she went back to something more tangible. "Matt, someone told those men to shoot your cows. One of them had a knife. I think he was going to butcher them. Do you think it was the same ones who killed the cow near the reservation?"

"I do."

"Why?"

Matt thought about his answer. So far he had kept the implied threat to himself. But Lily had asked him to be honest. It was time he was. "That wasn't the first time," he said.

"What do you mean?"

"Somebody killed two more cows, before. Just killed them, not even for food. Then they butchered the sow."

"Why?"

"Sergeant Rakestraw thinks it might be a warning."

"Do you think these men work for that Scotsman who wants to buy the ranch?"

"I don't know. If he is responsible, he wasted the effort. I'm considering letting him have the Double L."

Lily gasped. "Sell your land?"

"Not sell, lease. He's going to try to fence off the river. All hell is going to break loose when he does that, and I don't want you in danger."

"We'll manage," Lily said, reassuring Matt when she had no idea how.

"Not this time. Without water, we can't make it. Leasing the land is the best way. I'll sell the herd and see that Jim, you, and the children get back to Memphis."

"Why on earth would you think we'd go?"

"Because it's the only thing that makes sense. We've been chasing a dream that's never going to come true. It's time we stopped."

"I see. And what do you plan to do once you get us back there?"

"I'll sign on with Goodnight. That way I can keep an eye on our land while I save up enough money to buy the section between ours and the river. I may have to go downstream some, but it will work. Don't worry, the lease money will keep you and Jim and the children."

Lily felt as if the night wind had blown through her. It didn't matter if he loved her, they were going to be separated again. All her dreams for a life with Matt were shriveling up and dying in this barren Texas prairie. He'd made up his mind, and deep inside, she knew there was nothing she could do to change it.

"Jim and I?"

"Jim and you. I want you to marry him, Lily. Taking care of Jim and the children is the most important thing either of us can ever do."

Lily stiffened, pulling away from Matt. He was sending her away. She'd spent ten years dreaming about a life that was never more than a foolish dream.

Her eyes blurred with tears. She almost didn't see Jack until she heard his low moaning bellow. "It's Jack, Matt. In that brush. Let me down."

Before he could stop her, Lily slipped off Racer and walked carefully toward a sparse thicket under the overhang of a big rock. "Jack," she said calmly. "Jack, it's me and I'm going to look at your wound."

Behind her, Matt slid to the ground, dropped Racer's reins, and started forward.

"No, stay where you are, Matt. He won't hurt me, but I don't know what he might do to you."

"You don't know that he won't hurt you, either."

"He won't. Do you have a knife?"

"I do. But I don't think it would make a very good weapon."

"Gather some limbs and build a fire," she said. "I may need to cauterize his wound."

"What do you know about cauterizing a wound?" Matt asked.

"During the war everybody learned. Aunt Dolly never turned away anyone who needed help."

By this time she was too close to the big bull for Matt to take a chance on spooking him. So far, the animal seemed to be more interested in fighting sleep than what Lily was doing. Still, Matt drew his revolver.

"Put the gun away, please. Just build the fire."

In years to come, if they survived Lily's doctoring a wild bull, Matt still wouldn't be able to explain why he reholstered his gun and started the fire. But he did.

Jack was standing, though Lily could tell that his weight wasn't evenly distributed. He was definitely hurt.

First she held out more of the pancakes, soggy with honey and the flavoring she'd found in the pantry. In spite of her bravado, she knew she was taking her life in her hands when she rose and walked slowly around Jack, looking for evidence of a wound. She found it, a dried smear of blood across his left haunch.

"I'm going to have to touch you, Jack," she said, kneeling slowly beside him. "It may hurt just a little, but I promise I'll be as gentle as I can."

The bull didn't move.

Lily took a deep breath and let it out. All he had to do was turn his head, and the tip of his horn would be in striking distance of her shoulder. She held out her free hand and moved it slowly toward him until her fingertips brushed the short, coarse hair on his hip.

The skin beneath rippled, but Lily didn't withdraw. "It's all right, Jack. We're friends, remember?"

She held out the pancakes once more and let him have a good whiff. She wasn't sure Jack understood friendship, but maybe he was open to a bribe. For a long moment she didn't move. Then slowly she slid her hand underneath and around his hip. There was no evidence of a wound there.

Good. "From what I can tell the bullet just grazed him."

"Fine," Matt said, dropping the limbs he'd gathered. "Let's go home."

"Not without Jack. He's lost some blood. I want to give him the night to rest. Then we'll take him home in the morning."

"And you think he's going to come meekly along? You always were a dreamer."

Lily lifted her chin, catching a curious, sad look in Matt's eyes. "You're right. I guess I was," she said softly.

"You and Jim."

"Well, I'm through dreaming, Matt." She turned her attention back to the bull. "I don't have any medicine out here, Jack, but I'd like you to lie down under the rock, so you'll be protected. Tomorrow I'll take you home with me, and we'll get you all fixed up."

"And you expect him to follow orders?" Matt commented skeptically.

"Come on, Jack, lie down and eat your pancakes." She laid the food on the ground.

The bull sniffed, then gobbled up the remaining crumbs.

Matt started to laugh. "Guess I've been using the wrong cattle feed. What did you put in those pancakes?"

"Well, I ran out of milk and had to add some water, and I used that special flavoring in the lean-to."

"Special flavoring?"

"In the brown bottle."

This time Matt laughed out loud. "That was some of Rides Fast's elixir. No wonder Jack is following you around. He's drunk."

"Oh, I didn't know. I thought it was vanilla."

"I hope you didn't give it to Jim and the children."

"They didn't eat them," she said, with a smile.

Jack ignored Matt and settled down exactly where Lily had told him. Matt would bet his last silver dollar that there wasn't a rancher's wife in the entire state of Texas who could do what Lily had just done. He'd better check his rope. Come morning he'd likely be leading a bull.

"You know Jim's probably sent for the army by now," Matt said as he struck a sulfur match against his boot and touched it to the dry limbs he'd gathered. They caught fire and sent an instant trail of smoke upward. A gust of wind swept in, scattered the smoke, and blew it away.

A blanket of dark clouds slid across the horizon, but there was no smell of rain in the air.

"If you're determined to stay out here, I'd better get us some food," Matt said, resigned.

Lily didn't stop him. She knew Jim would be worried, but she couldn't think of anything she could do about it. He couldn't leave the children, but worrying him wouldn't be good for his heart condition. Between clouds, she found an early rising star and closed her eyes. The last time she wished on a star, she'd asked for the impossible: that Matt would want her for his wife. Now he did and she didn't know what to say.

"I wish for . . . for . . ." But this time she couldn't reduce her wish to a single request. She wished that she was a child again, that Matt and Jim were young and strong. That Aunt Dolly's hotel and a life with Matt were still in her future.

Then she opened her eyes and looked out at the Texas twilight and breathed in the sweetness of the hypnotic land, and she knew that this was her future, the only one she'd ever wanted. Her only wish was that she could stay.

•   •   •

Matt hadn't admitted it to Lily, but they were closer to the ranch than she knew. Apparently her wandering had taken her in a circular pattern. In the time it would take him to find food, he rode back to the house. On the way back, he'd cut some beef from the cow that had been shot.

Jim was on the porch, waiting.

"Thank God you're here," he said. "Lily is missing."

"I found her. She's back there by the stream, with Jack. He's been wounded."

Jim came to his feet. "The bull? What happened?"

"It's too complicated to explain now, Jim. You probably wouldn't believe it anyway. I just wanted you to know that she's safe. I—we'll be home in the morning."

"In the morning? Are you sure you know what you're doing, Matt?"

"No, I'm not at all sure. Decisions have to be made, Jim. It's time you and I talked about the future, but we'll do it when I get back. I can't leave Lily out there alone. And she won't come without Jack."

Jim nodded. "Just don't throw away the present, Matt. Sometimes the future isn't what we think it is."

Matt had left his bedroll beside the fire. Lily untied it and spread the blanket on the ground. She couldn't do anything for Jack out here. The small herd seemed to know that, for they all lay down around him, as if they were protecting him.

Lily made her way to the stream and knelt beside it. With a cupped hand she brought water to her lips, satisfying her thirst if not her growing hunger. Her long walk and nap had left her hot and sticky. She slipped out of her petticoat and wet it, wiping the salty perspiration from her face. That wasn't enough. Darkness might bring cooler temperatures, but not yet.

With a quick glance around her, Lily unbuttoned her

dress and shimmied out of it, then waded into the creek. Any thought of submerging herself disappeared as she realized the water came only to her knees.

But it was deliciously cool, enticing enough that she lowered herself into the current, testing the bottom until she found a sandy surface. Stretching her hands behind her she leaned back, allowing her hair to float about her face in the water.

She could still hear the piano and the fiddle playing a waltz. She could feel Matt's arms around her and see his teasing smile. *"Dammit, I love you."* He hadn't wanted to admit it, but he did. Last night he'd fulfilled every condition of their agreement: He'd introduced her as his fiancée, he'd courted her, and he'd made her heart fill to near bursting.

Then this morning, he'd been gone. Why? Did he regret his actions? Had she forced him into admitting something he never wanted?

No, he wanted her. Even if he hadn't said the words, she would have known. Ever since the ceremony at the reservation, she'd known. It had just taken Matt a little longer to accept the truth.

The water made music in the silence. It flowed over her, driving away all the worry and fear she carried with her, replacing it with the whisper of excitement. Though she was alone in the growing shadows of the Texas twilight, she wasn't afraid. Instead, she felt curiously alive, as though her skin was absorbing the energy of the night.

She didn't know how long she lay half-submerged in the stream before she became aware that she was being watched, animal or human, from somewhere behind her. Slowly she raised her head and looked down at herself.

Her wet chemise was stuck to her, revealing every inch of her body to the watcher, just as it had the night Matt bathed her and treated her blisters. She could almost feel his hands on her skin.

What should she do? There was no hiding in darkness, for the sky was still colored purple and crimson from the rays of the setting sun. Sometime, while she'd been lost in her thoughts, the dark clouds had been swept away and the eastern sky was splattered with starlight.

A horse nickered softly.

And footsteps approached.

"Matt," she said and turned.

"Suppose it hadn't been me?" he asked, his voice thick with tension.

"Jack would have warned me."

"Jack's passed out," he said, then finished with "Suppose he hadn't. What are you thinking, lying in the water?"

His face was stern, his mouth drawn into a thin line. He'd removed his Stetson and stood, raking his long strong fingers through his hair.

"I was thinking about your hands, Matt, about how they feel touching my skin. My skin is on fire with the memory."

He growled low in his throat as he stepped into the water and jerked her into his arms. His kiss was restrained, an obvious attempt to control his passion. His body was still, his lips firm, too firm, too wooden.

She pulled away and looked up at him, creating enough space between them so that she could unbutton her chemise. She never took her eyes from his, as if the connection between them would hold him.

Finally the garment was open, and with a shake of her shoulders it was behind her and caught by the water, quickly disappearing from sight.

"You'll be chilled," he said.

"Then keep me warm."

He stepped back to the bank and pulled her up behind him. With a protest on his lips, he turned back to her and swallowed any words he might have said. Her drawers were gone now. Lily Towns stood in the lingering light like a siren, caught up in a spell that enveloped them both.

"Ah, Lily, don't do this."

She reached up and began to unfasten his shirt. "You can't stop me, Matt. I wished for another chance to love you. I've burned the agreement you signed. I release you from all blame. This time I'm not a child and you aren't legally or morally obligated to marry me."

"What are you asking, Lily?"

The shirt was gone. Her fingertips moved down to the trousers, playing for a moment across the bulge beneath.

"I want you, Matt. I want you to love me this night. Out here, under the stars, I want you to be honest with me. I want your love. If I can't have it forever, I want it tonight."

He lost the battle.

Moments later his clothes were gone and he was striding back to his bedroll beside the fire with Lily in his arms. Maybe it was the way she whispered his name over and over. Maybe it was the way her bare bottom curved beneath his hands. Maybe it was because he couldn't lie to himself or her, not anymore.

"I want you, too," he said. "Forever may have to wait. Tonight is now."

He knelt, laying her down on the bedroll, then pulled back and looked at her. "You are so beautiful."

She reached up and touched his lips with her fingertip. "So are you."

"I haven't shaved, and my face is lined and rough," he said.

"So are my hands." She rubbed her calloused fingertips across his cheeks and down his neck, rimming his nipples and rib cage. "Once they were the hands of a lady. Now they belong to a Texas woman."

"You know this is wrong." His voice was taut.

"I know this is right," she argued, arching her body so that she could nip at his chin.

He kissed her then, giving her everything she wanted and taking even more. His tongue delved sweetly into her mouth, his hands slid over her body, accompanied by Lily's exquisite murmurs and moans. He pulled away, covering her face and shoulders with kisses, capturing her breasts in a sensation so powerful that she lost her breath for a moment, then gasped to fill empty lungs.

His lower body had begun to move, as he pressed against her in a quickening rhythm that gathered urgency as the sounds of their responses grew more frantic.

And then he was inside her, joining them in a shower of sensation that began the moment he entered her and culminated in an explosion of fire and heat. Matt forced himself to stop, wait, make certain that she was with him but she refused.

"Oh Matt, Matt," she murmured, thrashing recklessly beneath him. "I love you."

Moments later he fell across her, their bodies still connected, his chin against her cheek. He was completely spent, sated with the fullness of what they'd shared.

The night air caressed his back, reminding him they were exposed to the elements, to the darkness that would bring a chill.

But not yet. Perspiration dampened their skin, leaving them slick with moisture from their lovemaking. Then Matt noticed that Lily was suddenly too still.

"What's wrong, Lily?"

"Wrong? Nothing is wrong, Matt. It's just that I never knew love could be like this." She sniffed.

"Are you crying?"

"Yes, I guess I am."

He tried to lift himself. "I'm sorry. I didn't mean to hurt you."

"Don't you dare move, Matt Logan. I like the way you

feel inside me. It makes me want to—" she began to move as he had done, slowly pressing herself against him—"to do this. Is it too soon? I don't know how or what a woman is supposed to do." Matt had no trouble showing her.

The next morning came too soon.

"Lily," Matt whispered in her ear. "We have to get back. There are decisions to be made."

She stretched and rolled over on top of him, looping her arms around his neck. "Just so long as you know this is already decided."

"*This* is part of what we have to talk about. We have to be practical."

Lily laughed. "I never thought you and Ora Manley were much alike. I guess I was wrong."

"What do Ora Manley and I have in common?"

"You both talk too much."

This time, she kissed him. And this time it was Matt who forgot about being practical. It was nearly lunchtime when they washed each other off in the stream and dried off with Lily's petticoat. Then they started searching for their clothes.

Lily's chemise and drawers were nowhere to be found. She finally pulled on her dress, wrinkled but still intact. Matt swore he liked her dress much better with nothing but her petticoat beneath.

While Matt saddled Racer, Lily called out to Jack. "Come on, boy," she said coaxingly, "let's go home so I can look after you."

He only stared at her. The cows around him mooed quietly.

"I'll make pancakes," she promised.

Finally, to Matt's surprise, the bull rose and, after steadying himself, moved at least two steps toward Lily, then stopped.

Matt climbed on the big horse and reached down to
pull Lily up. The night was over. They were staring the
future in the face, and neither seemed eager to talk about
it.

"Jim knows," Matt finally said. "We're closer to the
ranch than you knew."

"I knew," she whispered, and leaned against him, sigh-
ing as he slid his free arm around her waist.

"You have grass in your hair. And there is a red mark
on your neck."

"Where?"

He kissed it gently, then let out a deep sigh.

"It will all work out, Matt. Don't worry."

"How can you be sure?"

"Because I wished on a star."

He drew in a deep breath, capturing the womanly
scent of her. "You think you can make dreams come true?"

Jack bellowed behind, as if he were impatient with the
slow progress they were making.

"Oh yes, Matt. I can."

"And how can you be sure?"

"I own a shotgun, remember?"

Matt and Lily rode in, with Jack and the cows trailing
along behind. Matt opened the corral, and the strange en-
tourage moved inside. Jim rose from his chair on the porch
and watched in amazement.

Lily slid down and started toward the house. "Where
are the children?"

"They're inside. Are you okay?" He lifted a straw from
her hair and studied her seriously.

"I'm more all right than I've ever been," she answered
honestly and went inside.

Matt fastened the gate and headed toward the house.

"How'd you do that?" Jim asked. "Get that bull back here? Never saw anything like it."

Matt gave a dry laugh. "Guess you never thought Lily's pancakes could tame a savage beast, did you?"

"Lily's pancakes?" Jim smiled.

"Or maybe we should give credit to Rides Fast's elixir. She used it to mix up the pancakes when she ran out of milk, thought it was flavoring."

"Jack knows a good thing," Jim said as he walked toward the kitchen. Moments later he returned with the brown bottle. "I say we ought to follow his lead." Jim opened the bottle and took a sip, then handed it to Matt.

Matt looked at the nearly empty bottle. "Jack deserves the whole thing. He saved Lily's life."

"That's what she said. When were you going to tell me about the cattle?" Jim asked.

"We have a lot to decide, Jim. I'm sorry I haven't talked things out with you before now." He sat down on the step, resting his elbows on his knees.

"I guess I ought not tell you, but Lily went out the back door. She's gone to treat Jack's wound."

"Damn! What is she going to do next?" Matt sprang to his feet and moved toward the barn. "Lily!" he called as he entered the dimly lit building.

"Don't spook him." Lily crooned as she knelt beside the bull, "It's okay, Jack. Matt isn't going to hurt you. He just likes to pretend he's in charge."

"As of now, I am in charge, Lily," Matt said, dropping his voice, but refusing to talk baby talk to the quivering animal. "And in spite of what happened last night, I have a few orders for you."

"Orders?" Lily said lightly. "You're not really giving me an order, are you?"

"That's what I said."

Lily continued to sit beside the bull. As if she were soothing a baby, she touched Jack while she continued to talk to Matt in a voice that was oversweet. "It's like this, Matt. Men don't give women orders unless they're fathers or husbands, and you're neither, at least not until Sunday."

"And what happens Sunday?"

Jack snorted and turned his head toward Matt.

"Didn't I tell you? I'm sorry, but then we never did get around to discussing the situation, did we? That's okay. Sunday you're going to be my groom."

Matt let out a deep sigh. "Are you sure, Lily? I don't know what kind of life I can offer you."

"Just love me, Matt, the way I've always loved you. The rest doesn't matter. We'll take it one step at a time, starting with you being a husband. The father part comes later, doesn't it, Jack?"

Matt let out an oath. "You're asking a bull about me being a father?"

Lily gave the bull a pat and stood. "Well, I figure he's had a lot more experience at it than you. I love you, Matt, and we're getting married on Sunday. Remember, I do know how to use that shotgun."

17

Matt rode toward the fort, his mission hanging heavily over him. What Lily didn't know was that after he'd gotten the drop on the soldiers, they were more than willing to name the person who'd hired them to kill the cattle.

Now it was Matt's painful duty to reveal the truth and discuss retribution.

The gates were open, so he rode directly inside and up to Sergeant Rakestraw's quarters. When he knocked, the door was immediately opened by an orderly who saluted, then left the office.

"Matt, come in. What brings you to the fort?"

"I don't quite know how to say this, sergeant. I guess I just have to tell you what I know."

"About what?"

"I found the men who killed my cattle and probably my sow. They tried to kill Lily."

The sergeant looked shocked. "Tried to kill Lily? Whatever for?"

"Because she saw what they were doing. If Jack hadn't come along, she might be dead now."

He looked confused. "Jack?"

"One-Eyed Jack, the bull. He didn't take kindly to someone rustling his herd, and he's taken a fancy to Lily."

"I see. What happened?"

"One of the outlaws and the bull were wounded."

The sergeant picked up his pipe and dipped it into his packet of tobacco. "And the butchers?"

"On their way to Kansas. Or so they said."

"You let them go?"

Matt hesitated. "It seemed the right thing to do."

"Then I guess you know who paid them."

"I know. I don't understand why you did it, sir, but I don't want Jim and the children mixed up in all this. I think it's time for them to leave."

"Leave?"

"I can't protect them out here, and they need a stable life."

There was a long silence while the officer lit his pipe and drew on it. "What do you want me to do, Matt?"

"Tell me why. Why did you do it? Why would you sabotage your own grandchildren's future?"

"You don't understand. It was the only way I could help them. I didn't expect anybody to get hurt."

Matt felt as if they were carrying on two conversations. Nothing seemed to fit. "I was ready to blame the Scotsman or incoming settlers. But I never even considered you. Why?"

"I'm getting old, Matt. Texas is the closest thing to a home I have ever had. My wife lived here. Our daughter gave me two grandchildren here."

"That still doesn't explain why you had my cows and the sow killed. Why did you think that would solve anything? I just don't understand."

"No, I don't suppose you do. You remember I told you that there was talk about closing the fort. I couldn't let that happen. I'm too old to make a new life for myself. I've never been anything but a soldier."

Matt found himself defending the man who had almost cost Lily her life, the man who'd become one of the criminals he'd fought. "Sergeant Rakestraw, you won't be furloughed, you're too valuable. You'll always have a home with the army."

He shook his head. "No. My value to the army was as a fighter. I fought the Mexicans for the independence of Texas. I fought the Indians. And I fought my own countrymen to keep this country united. There will be no more wars for me," he sighed heavily. "I'm sorry about Lily. I never dreamed she'd get mixed up in all this."

"I'm sorry, too. If Lily had been killed, you could have started a range war. But I guess"—he paused—"I guess that's what you planned, isn't it?"

The old man turned around, his eyes suspiciously moist. "Hellfire, no, Matt! They were just supposed to kill a few cows so that I could claim some kind of uprising. That way the army would close some other fort and leave this one alone. I'd blame the trouble on the Scotsman and get rid of him before he took the river land. I never expected anyone to get hurt!"

"You'd set up a man, send him to jail, or get him hanged?"

"I wouldn't have let it go that far, just far enough to force him into leaving."

"Why?"

"For Will and Emily, to make certain you didn't lose the ranch. If I'm transferred, you'll be left out here with no one to help you keep them safe. And sooner or later, the Indians will get tired of being treated worse than slaves. They may die in the uprising, but there will be one."

"You really believe that, don't you?" Matt asked. "And for that, you'd put the blame on an innocent man."

Sergeant Rakestraw cleared his throat. "I would have let Conner go, Matt. I'd make sure there was no evidence to convict him, but the charges would serve notice to his stockholders that they should invest their money somewhere else."

"You know it wouldn't have worked," Matt said quietly.

"I guess not. But I was desperate. And I couldn't see any other way. I'll resign and I'll pay for your cattle."

He suddenly looked old, as if he'd wilted. Matt watched him take his seat behind his desk and rest his pipe in the battered tin tray in which he emptied his spent ashes.

Sergeant Rakestraw had never made any obvious attempt to involve himself in the ranch. He'd stopped by to chat from time to time when Maria and Jim had first married. When the cotton crops failed, he'd arranged for the Double L to supply both the fort and the reservation with cattle, but he'd still kept a distance between himself and his daughter's new family.

Then when Maria became ill, he'd sent the fort doctor to keep a watch on her, and later, Jim. But it had been Jim who insisted that the children visit their grandfather occasionally, and Jim who issued invitations to the old man for Sunday dinner. He rarely came, but apparently he'd been more concerned than he let on.

"I don't expect you to understand, Matt," he finally added.

"But I do," Matt answered. "I understand about family, land, a home. Texas has given and it has taken away. And it has claimed a part of you that you will do anything to keep."

The old man lifted his gaze to meet Matt's. "Yes."

"Then you'll keep it. Don't resign, Sergeant Rakestraw. We need you here."

"But those men. I paid them to break the law."

"Nobody got hurt. You just paid them to butcher three cows and a pig. They were family cows, and the pig belonged to me. A man can't be prosecuted for butchering his own animals."

"So, what about the Scotsman? He's leased the land. Your cattle will have no water."

"Don't worry," Matt said. "I have another idea. If it works, we'll just forget about all this."

The following Sunday morning dawned bright and clear. Matt, who'd been absent the previous three days, appeared promptly for breakfast. Afterward, he announced that they would be going into Blue Station for Sunday services.

"We're going to do what?" Jim asked in amazement.

"We're going to church," Matt said. "Sergeant Rakestraw will be joining us. I'll hitch up the wagon and we'll leave in an hour."

Lily felt her heart leap. She'd told Matt that they'd be married on Sunday, and he hadn't refused. But he hadn't agreed either. She'd been afraid to tell Jim, so she'd kept quiet. She'd started to think she imagined his declaration of love. Now, Matt was taking them to church?

"What about it, Lily?" Matt asked. "Are you still willing to have me?"

Jim turned his attention to Matt, his eyes disbelieving, as he said, "What are you saying, big brother?"

"I'm saying that Lily and I are getting married, little brother. Just like you planned."

"Well, I'll be damned. It's about time."

"Papa's cussing," Emily said.

"No, they're discussing," Will corrected.

"No," Lily interjected, "we're not discussing and I'm not taking orders, Matthew Logan. If you want to marry me, I expect a proper proposal."

"Ah, Lily, come on. You won the bet, fair and square."

"Bet? There was no bet. You set up conditions you

thought I couldn't meet. You thought I wasn't good enough to be a Texas woman."

"No," he said seriously, "I set the conditions because I was afraid you were, Lily."

"You certainly didn't act that way."

"Are they still dis-cussing?" Emily asked with a worried frown.

"No, Uncle Matt is going to propose."

"That he is," Lily agreed, trying hard to keep a straight face. "A proper proposal or no wedding."

Matt smiled. The little witch. She was serious. If he didn't get down on one knee and officially propose, she wasn't going to marry him.

"Do it quick, Uncle Matt," Emily said. "Mama sent Lily and she'll cause a fox to bite you if you send her away."

"A fox to bite you? Where'd you hear that?" Will asked.

"I heard Daddy say, 'A fox on Uncle Matt' if he didn't marry Lily."

Jim laughed. He stood and held out his hand. "Come, Emily, Will, let's go wash up and get ready for church. It isn't every day we get to go to a wedding."

Reluctantly, the children allowed Jim to push them outside, leaving Matt and Lily alone. Lily busied herself in clearing the table, while Matt sat watching her move deftly around the kitchen. He'd spend the rest of his life watching this woman take care of his family. How could he have ever thought she wasn't tough enough to be a Texas wife?

She'd done more. She'd filled up his heart and claimed his soul. It was time he put his need into words. Matt stood.

Lily turned around, untied her apron, and raised her gaze to meet his. "Matt, you don't have to propose. I don't need that to know that you love me. You've always defended and protected those you love with your actions. I don't need to hear the words. But you need to hear mine."

"Yours?"

"I love you, Matthew Logan. I always have and I always will. But you don't have to marry me. I'll stay and take care of Jim and his children as long as you need me."

Matt couldn't hold back a laugh.

"And we'll live in sin, will we? No, I won't have it. What kind of example will that be to Emmie and Will?" He started toward her.

"I don't know. I hadn't thought about anything but . . ."

"Loving me? And me loving you?" He took her hands and smiled, going down on one knee. "Miss Lillian Townsend, will you do me the very great honor of becoming my wife on this fine Sunday morning?"

"Are you sure, Matt?"

She couldn't mistake the love in his eyes.

"I'm sure."

"You don't want to wait a while?"

"Absolutely not." He kissed her hand. "I'm waiting for your answer, Miss Townsend."

"Mr. Logan, I'm just plain Lily Towns, and I'd be honored."

"There's nothing plain about you, Lily." He stood and kissed her, his gentle touch promising her a lifetime of loving.

Jack munched hay contentedly in the corral. The sun was bright, the sky a turquoise blue that matched the stones in Lily's necklace from Little Hen. The bluebells were in full bloom. The world was good.

Matt drove the wagon, filled with the people he cared about. Halfway to Blue Station, Sergeant Rakestraw, in full-dress uniform, joined the procession.

"Morning, Matt, Jim. Miss Lily. Children," he said with a twinkle in his eye. "Fine day for a wedding."

Lily looked over at Matt suspiciously. "Everyone knew about the wedding, but you didn't get around to telling me until this morning? Suppose I'd said no?"

"You didn't," Matt said.

"Well, just so you know, I like to be in on any plans made for me. I might not have been ready. Next time, give me the particulars."

The sergeant chuckled. "Uh-oh! Sounds like you're in trouble, boy."

"Sounds like it," Matt agreed.

Racer snorted.

"Daddy has particulars. Lily gets particulars," Emily went on with a pout. "When does I get particulars?"

Will grunted in disgust. "Emily, you don't even know what particulars are."

"Neither do you, smarty," she responded. "What are particulars, Lily?"

Lily laughed. "Sugarplum, particulars and what you do with them are something you'll understand when you're ready."

"And," Matt added, "sometimes, when you aren't."

"Where is the church?" Lily asked as they drove into town. "I don't remember seeing one."

"There isn't one yet," Jim explained. "We use the saloon for now."

Lily burst out laughing. "We're getting married in the saloon?"

"Well," Matt said with a grin, "we could just jump over the broom."

"Not on your life," Jim said. "This is an official event of the highest order. If what I see is what I think, you're even going to have a proper minister."

"Who?" Lily turned and glanced behind them. Allen

and Kianceta, Rides Fast, Kitty and Little Hen, were all leading what looked like the entire Comanche tribe.

"Allen Kilgore," Jim answered. "He's as official as it gets in this part of the state, unless you'd like Rides Fast to perform one of his special ceremonies."

"No, thank you," Lily said. "I've already been through one of Rides Fast's special ceremonies. I'm not sure I'd survive another."

Kitty rode up beside Lily. "Have brought gift, special elixir for celebration after important occasion of Matthew Logan's joining."

"Important occasion." Sergeant Rakestraw shook his head. "I don't know how that Indian always knows when something important is happening, but maybe it will be easier for me to leave knowing that he's watching over you."

Jim looked surprised. "Leave? Where are you going?"

"You didn't tell him, Matt?"

Matt shook his head. "Sorry, Jim. I know I told you we had things to discuss, but I was afraid my plans might get changed if I announced them too soon. It's like this: You and the children are going to take my honeymoon."

Jim shook his head. "What does that mean?"

"Sergeant Rakestraw is going to accompany you and the children back east for a visit. You'll see the best heart specialist in Philadelphia, and later, when you're well enough, you're going to fetch Aunt Dolly and bring everybody back here."

"You're not going to lease our land to the Scotsman, Matt?" Lily asked.

"No way. I'm selling some cows, but I'm not letting anybody use our land," was his firm answer.

"I don't understand," Jim said. "What about water for the cattle? If the Scotsman has leased the land between us and the river, how will the cattle survive?"

"I think there is a very good possibility that those

plans will change. Sergeant Rakestraw and I are working on that, Jim. Trust me."

"I trust you, Matt. I always have, but leaving you here alone, I don't know. Maybe you'd better come, too."

"It was your idea to come to Texas, Jim, and build a new life. We have. Texas is our home. Sergeant Rakestraw and Aunt Dolly are part of our family, too. Since he is going to live here, the sergeant has decided to invest some of his retirement funds in the ranch. While you're away, I'm going to build us a proper house and"—he grinned at Lily—"practice being a proper husband. I've been told that practice makes perfect."

"Will you go, Jim?" Lily asked, trying to erase Matt's plans from her mind. They weren't married yet.

"I don't know. . . ." he began.

"I really think Aunt Dolly would come back with you, if you asked her. She's never going to be happy living in the hotel when it belongs to somebody else. There's nothing left in Tennessee for any of us anymore."

Jim frowned as if he were studying his answer, then asked seriously, "Do you think Cook would come with her, too?"

Lily laughed. "What's the matter, don't you like my fried chicken?"

"I cannot tell a lie," Jim answered solemnly. "Frying chicken isn't your best feature, Lily."

"Oh, what would you say my best feature is?"

"Loving us, Lily," Matt answered for him. "Loving us all."

At the saloon, Matt helped Jim and the children from the wagon. Then he turned to Lily, opened his arms, and swung her to the ground. They started into the saloon, when Matt suddenly stopped and went back to the wagon.

"Where are you going, Matt?" Lily asked.

"I forgot something."

He reached beneath the wagon seat and pulled out Lily's shotgun.

"Why did you bring that?" she asked.

"I learned this from a very smart woman. Be prepared." He laid the shotgun on his shoulder, offered Lily his arm, and started inside, whispering, "Folks from Tennessee know how to go after what they want. I'm not about to let you change your mind."

Epilogue

The fort was closed in 1879, the reservation shortly thereafter. Reluctantly, Rides Fast, Allen, and Kianceta took the Comanche to Oklahoma but not before Matt's house was built, a house big enough for all the Logan family.

When the soldiers left, the land was returned to Texas. The governor reconsidered and approved the sale of the property between the Double L and the river to Matt Logan, who agreed to keep the range open to all. The Scotsman had accepted a new federal job in Oregon.

Few knew that he'd been highly recommended by Sergeant Rakestraw, who had convinced the governor of the danger of a range war if the sale of river land went through. Loss of a private water supply caused the foreign investors to pull out and the conglomerate to collapse.

Kitty and Little Hen stayed on the Double L to work with Matt and Lily. One-Eyed Jack did his job, and the herd grew. The first wedding held on the ranch was for Dolly Wilbanks and Sergeant Major Louis Rakestraw. A year later Kitty disappeared, only to return with Kianceta and Little Hen on the morning of the birth of Matthew Logan Junior.

Matt had practiced being a father very well, for some twelve minutes later, Lily Maria Logan came into the world, arms waving, lungs exercising the full extent of their capabilities.

The railroad eventually came to Blue Station, and the first herd of cattle shipped east were from the Double L Ranch.

Every year Lily and the children transplanted bluebonnets until the Double L was a sea of indigo in the spring. Happiness and good care kept Jim alive long enough to see Emily become a strong young Texas woman determined to make her own way in life and to see Will go back east to study medicine.

Throughout all the years that followed, a place of honor was maintained over the mantel for Lily's shotgun. Matt never failed to point it out to visitors as an example of the determination of the woman who came out west fully prepared to get what she wanted.

And did.

ABOUT THE AUTHOR

Bestselling and award-winning author Sandra Chastain has written thirty-eight novels since Bantam published her first romance in 1988. She lives just outside of Atlanta and considers herself blessed that her three daughters and her grandchildren live nearby.

Sandra enjoys receiving letters from her fans. You can write to her at P.O. Box 67, Smyrna, GA 30081.

"A master storyteller of stunning intensity."
—ROMANTIC TIMES

SANDRA CHASTAIN

Rebel in Silk

____56464-1 $5.50/$6.99 Canada

Shotgun Groom

____57583-x $5.99/$7.99

Raven and the Cowboy

____56864-7 $5.99/$7.99

Ask for these books at your local bookstore or use this page to order.

Please send me the books I have checked above. I am enclosing $____(add $2.50 to cover postage and handling). Send check or money order, no cash or C.O.D.'s, please.

Name _____

Address _____

City/State/Zip _____

Send order to: Bantam Books, Dept. FN 6, 2451 S. Wolf Rd., Des Plaines, IL 60018
Allow four to six weeks for delivery.
Prices and availability subject to change without notice.   FN 6 3/98